THE EDGE OF ANYTHING

The EDGE of ANYTHING

Nora Shalaway Carpenter

RP | TEENS
PHILADELPHIA

Running Press Teens
Hachette Book Group
1290 Avenue of the Americas, New York, NY 10104
www.runningpress.com/rpkids
@RP_Kids

Printed in the United States of America

First Edition: March 2020

Published by Running Press Teens, an imprint of Perseus Books, LLC, a subsidiary of Hachette Book Group, Inc. The Running Press Teens name and logo is a trademark of the Hachette Book Group.

The Hachette Speakers Bureau provides a wide range of authors for speaking events. To find out more, go to www.hachettespeakersbureau.com or call (866) 376-6591.

The publisher is not responsible for websites (or their content) that are not owned by the publisher.

Print book cover and interior design by Frances J. Soo Ping Chow

Library of Congress Control Number: 2019934247

ISBNs: 978-0-7624-6758-7 (hardcover), 978-0-7624-6757-0 (ebook)

LSC-C

10 9 8 7 6 5 4 3 2 1

FOR JOSH,

who always believed,

and for Garek, Zander, and Lyra,

who remind me daily that anything is possible

ONCE WE ACCEPT

OUR LIMITS,

WE GO BEYOND THEM.

—ALBERT EINSTEIN

CHAPTER ONE

LEN

THE FIRST THING LEN NOTICED WAS THE FLOOR. THAT WAS always the first thing these days, her eyes constantly scanning the places her boots had to touch. Unless she jumped about four feet, there wasn't a single clean tile to step on.

She didn't remember noticing them last year—all the streaks and brown bits littering the hallway—but that seemed impossible. Had she simply not cared?

"Move it, loser," someone muttered behind her. She didn't recognize the voice, but it didn't matter. Len was used to the insults. She didn't take her eyes off the floor.

"Weirdo," the kid said. "Seriously, hurry up. Varsity's already started."

Len's chest cramped as she tried to decide where to step.

"Come *on!*" someone else groaned, and Len forced herself to move up in line, one foot, then two. The sole of her boot tracked through a dark brown streak, and she told herself it wasn't dog shit. Someone else would have noticed if it was dog shit, right? And why didn't anyone else seem to care?

The slick squeaks of shoe soles on hardwood echoed from the gym. *It's just mud*, Len thought again, repeating the word like a mantra. *Mud, mud, mud.*

"Three dollars, please. Four if you want the raffle."

Len blinked at the librarian. When had he started taking ticket money? And what was Len even doing here? She didn't like volleyball, not really.

The librarian held out his hand. "You coming in, Len?"

"I—uh . . ." Heat speckled her face and neck. Had she always had such trouble making decisions? She turned to leave when the memory of why she'd come to the game jolted her. The phone, ringing, ringing. Seven p.m. on the dot. Fauna.

Len couldn't go back home. Not yet.

"Jesus, *Lemon*," said the first voice. "You in or out?"

Len shoved her cash onto the table and pushed her way into the gym.

CHAPTER TWO

SAGE

THWOPP!

Sage started forward, even though there was no way the ball would reach her. Probably wouldn't even make it over the net. That hollow thud meant a too-slack hand, a poor serve. Still, she crouched low, weight on the balls of her fire-orange Asics, in case she needed to sprawl.

The ball kissed the net, rolled a few feet sideways along the top, then dropped back on the opponent's side, sending Sage's bench into near-hysterics. Sage's Southview Rams hadn't defeated their hometown rival Asheville High in three seasons, and that missed serve kept her team alive.

Go time. Sage walked back to the server's box as the scoreboard ticked 13–14. Varsity matches went best of five, and this one had gone to the last game. Match point for Asheville. Again.

Kayla Davis ran up to her. "You got this, Sage," she said. "You *got* it."

Sage nodded. The line judge tossed her the ball.

Coach Craig held up four fingers beneath his clipboard, but Sage didn't need the signal. She knew Asheville's weak-side hitter was just that—*weak*. Even if she hadn't studied the game tape for the past three nights, a few plays into the match revealed who was most likely to shank her serve.

From the bench, her teammates shouted themselves hoarse.

"Pound it, Sage!"

"They can't touch you!"

"Come on, baby!"

Sage twirled the volleyball in her hands, then bounced it once—her ritual. She heard the cheers, but also didn't, like she knew she was breathing without thinking about it. She extended the ball onto her left palm.

If she mis-served, her rivals won.

The referee whistled, signaling her.

Sage stared down the opposing setter, making her think she was the target. Then she tossed the ball and hammered a topspin directly at position four. The girl barely had time to protect her face before the ball hit her elbow and ricocheted out of bounds.

The Rams' bench almost lost its mind. On the court, Sage performed the celebratory Ace ritual with her teammates—two stomps and a clap—but her face stayed stone flat. The ref tossed her the ball. Coach Craig held up another four.

This time Sage backed against the wall. She tossed the ball high, then leapt to meet it in a jump serve—more intimidating than her topspin, but not as fast. Asheville's receiver got a better handle on it, but the ball shot into the net and dropped to the ground before her setter could even touch it.

15–14, Rams advantage. Unlike the first four games that went to twenty-five points, the fifth game of a match only went to fifteen. But you had to win by two. This was it, then. Or could be. Sage walked back to the service line.

"Timeout!" Asheville's coach called. Kayla slung her arm around Sage as they joined Southview's huddle. "You got this," her best friend said, squeezing her shoulders. "I know you got it." Sage allowed a tight nod.

"One point and they're back in it!" Coach quieted the bench with a look. He pointed at Sage. "They're trying to ice you," he said, like she didn't know. "Hit six this time."

Sage made a face. "Four's shanked it twice. I'm in her head."

"She knows you're coming for her. She'll be ready."

"Doesn't matter," said Sage. "She can't hit it."

Coach raised his eyebrows, daring her to continue arguing. Last year Sage had ignored a call, and Coach had benched her, star player or no. It probably cost the team the game. "Six," he repeated. The whistle blew.

Sage held his gaze to let him know she disagreed, then cracked her neck and walked back to the server's box.

"Just one more, Sagey." Ella Cruz smacked her hip as she trotted past.

Only Ella could get away with calling her Sagey. But, then, nobody fed her sets like Ella.

Sage picked up the ball, the team's energy thrumming though her. Most of her teammates, good as they were, wouldn't trade positions with her for the world. She sensed this instinctively, the same way she intuited when a player was going to tip almost before the player did. With the game in the balance, her teammates didn't want the serve. Didn't want the risk of failure. That was the difference between Sage Zendasky and the rest: these were the moments she felt most alive.

Sage slapped the ball with her palm, her mouth twitching a faint smile just to mess with Asheville's players. This was why she showed up early to their three-hour practices and why she often stayed late. Why she played in an off-season travel league. Why she spent practically all of her free time with a volleyball in her hands.

The whistle shrilled. Sage tossed the ball . . .

and crushed it.

Asheville's back middle—position six—dug the serve perfectly. Sage had a heartbeat of indignation—*told you, Craig*—while she raced to position in the back row. She sunk down as Asheville's hitter connected with the ball.

"Me, ME!" Lyz Greer called, causing Sage and Nina Marto to scissor away from her.

"THREE!" Ella shouted, flipping a short set to the middle. Kayla drilled it, but position six made another perfect dig. Five times the ball exchanged sides, Asheville's hitters clearly avoiding Sage.

Come on, thought Sage. *One time.*

"Short!" screamed Ella as Asheville's middle flicked the ball over the blockers. Hannah Wainwright dove backward, managing to punch it up with her fist, but the ball rocketed toward the back wall.

Asheville's bench erupted as Sage took off. The ball was nearly a body length in front of her, but high, and she just might . . .

the wall . . .

She sprawled instinctually, hurling her fist upward. It connected, sending the ball sailing back to the court.

"MEEEE!" called Nina.

Sage heard Nina the moment before her momentum took her into the wall. Concrete met her cheek as her ankle turned awkwardly. She cursed, but pushed herself back to position in time to see Nina's free ball cross the net.

Asheville was disorganized, clearly thinking they'd won the point when Hannah shanked. They managed to get the ball back in three, but with an easy free pass right to Sage. Ella's eyes lit as she set Sage's perfect pass to Kayla.

Asheville formed a double block, but Sage saw the hole behind it.

"Q!" She shouted the code letter. "Kayla, Q!"

Kayla attacked the net like she hadn't heard, but at the last second pulled back her swing and tipped the ball into the gap behind the blockers.

The ball floated—movie-style-slow—and dropped to the floor.

"AHHHHHHHHH!" Sage screamed so her heart wouldn't burst. Her teammates echoed her, high-fiving and jumping on one another. Kayla thrust her chest out, nodding like a pro footballer while Ella punched the air.

"You!" Sage said, rushing Kayla. "That was perfect!"

"YOU!" Kayla said, shaking her. "I thought we were dead. Did you hit the wall?"

"Yeah, she did," said Ella, slapping her back. "She be crazy."

Sage smiled, light-headed from the high of victory. Hannah raced toward her, and forgetting her ankle, Sage leapt to meet her in a shoulder bump. As she peaked, she registered it all simultaneously: Kayla's whoops; her teammates' converging; Coach's wide and seldom-shown grin.

The thrill of it twitched her heart as she reconnected with the ground . . .

And fainted.

CHAPTER THREE

SAGE

"GIVE HER SOME ROOM!"

Sage blinked as blurred faces sharpened into focus above her. She tried to push herself up.

"No." A woman pressed her hand firmly against Sage's shoulder. "Don't move."

"Why?" Sage shielded her eyes. The lights seemed brighter from down here.

"You passed out for a few seconds," Kayla said. Sage found her face, upside down, in the mix. "You're okay," she added, and even though Sage knew she only said that to make her feel better, it worked.

"I'm going to elevate your feet," said the woman kneeling beside her. She was in her late forties maybe, with unruly red hair that had seen too much dye. Coach Craig appeared on her other side.

"What's your name?" the woman asked.

"Sage Zendasky." She turned, trying to avoid the glare of lights directly above her. "I'm fine, really."

"Excuse me!" a familiar voice called, then another.

"That's our kid!" Her parents' faces appeared above her, crinkled in worry.

"I'm okay," Sage said as Mom knelt beside her.

"Honey," Mom said, "what happened?"

Sage wished she knew. This was all so unnecessary. She hoped most of the crowd had left.

The red-haired woman cleared her throat. "What day is it, Sage?"

"Uh . . . Wednesday." She squinted at the woman. "Who are you?" If she'd really passed out, why wasn't the school's athletic trainer examining her?

"I'm an EMT," the woman said, "a mom from the Asheville team."

Sage reached behind her long dark ponytail. No bump. No pain. "Did I hit my head?"

The EMT exchanged a look with her parents. "You passed out when you jumped up with your friend," she said. "She caught you, but . . . you dove into the wall during the game."

Dad's thick eyebrows squished. "Don't you remember?"

"My head didn't hit the wall," Sage said. "It was more of my cheek area." She touched the spot. "And not that hard."

The EMT let out a sharp breath through her nose. "How many fingers am I holding up?"

"Three."

"How many now?"

"Four."

Mom squeezed her hand. "I *told you* you should have eaten more."

"Oh." The EMT sat back on her heels, the relief in her voice palpable. "You didn't eat?"

"I ate," said Sage.

Mom shook her head, flashing her a told-you-so look. "Cereal's hardly a meal."

"Mom—"

"That explains it, then," said Coach Craig. "Doesn't it?"

The EMT checked Sage's pulse, and then finally allowed her to sit up. "Do you feel light-headed at all?" she asked. "Nauseated?"

Sage shook her head.

"Doesn't she need a test or something?" Dad asked. "She could have a concussion."

Enough was enough. Sage pushed herself past the EMT's grip. "I can't have a concussion. My head didn't actually hit the wall."

"Honey, lie back down," Mom ordered.

"I don't think she has a concussion," the EMT said, as if Sage hadn't spoken. "But if she gets a headache or starts feeling queasy, take her to the emergency room right away."

Kayla put her arm on Sage's shoulder, edging her away from the swarm of concerned adults. Their teammates clustered at the bench a few yards away. Some of them had already slipped sweatpants over their spandex shorts, but most of them simply stood, arms crossed, watching Sage and Kayla approach.

"Everything all right?" Hannah asked as they joined the rest of the team.

Sage gave a short jerk of her chin, her no-big-deal nod. "Apparently, I didn't eat enough."

Kayla smirked. "There's a first time for everything."

Laughter rippled through the team; everyone knew Sage loved to eat. Even in front of guys, she'd eat till she was full, because how stupid was it not to eat what you normally would just because there was a boy around? She couldn't believe some girls actually did that.

Ella bumped her shoulder. "You can't scare us that way, Cap'n. Not if you're gonna lead us to states."

Sage smiled and sat down to unlace her Asics. At the start of summer conditioning, Coach had made them each write a goal. A lot of girls wrote, "regional champs." Some, like Ella, had dared to write, "going to states," a feat Southview had never accomplished. Sage hadn't told anyone yet, but her goal wasn't just getting to the state tournament. It was winning it.

Coach clapped his hands. "Party's over. And remember, practice starts at three tomorrow. None of this three-oh-two that's been happening. Three p.m. Sharp."

Sage turned to Kayla. "Did I really faint?"

"Your blood sugar must've dropped. It happens to my grandma sometimes."

"Because *that* makes me feel better."

"You know what I mean." Kayla zipped her duffle. "And anyway, no one will remember tomorrow."

The heat of her stiffening ankle kept Sage from responding. At least home was only ten minutes away, so she could avoid asking for ice. One hint of an injury and Dad would make her see every specialist in town. Worse—he might keep her from practice. She pulled on her sweats so no one would notice the swelling.

"Ready?" Mom appeared beside her. "Dad came straight from work, so we drove separately."

Sage nodded, eyeing her father. Why was he still talking to the EMT?

"You need a ride, Kayla?" Mom asked.

"Thanks, Mrs. Z, but I'm good." She nodded at an older woman on a cell phone. "Lyz's grandma's gonna drop me off."

Sage bumped the pinky side of Kayla's outstretched fist with her own, the goodbye action automatic for both of them, then followed Mom to the parking lot. Their silver Civic sat wedged between a Hummer and a minivan.

"I'm going to make you that chicken soup you love," Mom said, starting the car. "I just need to swing by the store."

Sage glanced at the dashboard. "It's almost ten."

"Honey, you *fainted* because you didn't eat enough." She inched the Civic backward. "God, why does anyone need a car the size of a boat?"

Sage's head fell back against the seat. Now that they were talking about it, she *was* hungry. "Don't you have a big meeting in the morning? I thought you wanted an early night?"

"What I *want* is to take care of my baby girl."

"Oh, Mom."

"I know, I know. But I don't care if you're seventeen. I wouldn't care if you were seventy-one." The car finally freed itself from the space, barely missing the Hummer's mirror.

"If I were seventy-one," said Sage, "that would make you . . ." She tapped her chin.

"Probably dead."

"Mom!"

"I'm kidding. My grammy lived to one hundred. You've got a long time to get tired of me."

Sage shook her head. "You're so weird."

"Seriously," Mom said, "do you want the soup or not?"

14

Sage rotated her ankle. She still could, which meant the swelling wasn't terrible. "Honestly?" She grinned. "Do you even have to ask?"

* * *

Dad sat at the kitchen table, thumb-typing on his iPhone. Mom kissed his cheek, then started pulling ingredients from the fridge and pantry. "I take it the district attorney filed that brief?" She ran the Keurig, filling the kitchen with the sweet scent of her favorite decaf coffee.

Dad sighed. "I was hoping he'd get an extension so I'd have longer for the response, but no such luck." He looked up as Sage tried to sneak by him to the freezer. "There she is," he said. "Southview's hero."

Sage rolled her eyes, but she couldn't hold back a grin. She filled a glass with ice, then found a ginger ale in the fridge. Once she got to her room she'd use the cold glass on her foot.

"Where's Ian?" she asked just as her younger brother emerged from the living room.

"Heard you beat Asheville!" he said. "Dad said you were epic, as usual." He took a bite of his sandwich—peanut butter and jelly from the stain on his white tee—and grinned. "Wish I coulda been there."

Sage smiled, silently thanking him for not mentioning the passing out. Dad had surely told him. "It was a pretty good night," she said. Well, minus the fainting.

"I hate Asheville High." Ian took another huge mouthful. "Can't wait to pummel them Friday."

Dad typed something else into his phone, not looking up. "How long you gonna wait to ice that foot, Sage?"

Mom stopped chopping carrots. "You hurt your foot?"

"How—" Sage started.

"I could tell by how you took your shoe off." Dad looked up, eyebrows raised. "It's stupid to waste time. Could cost you minutes."

Sage grabbed an ice pack from the freezer. That was better than ice cubes anyway. "It's just a tweak."

"Well, sit down!" Mom shooed her to the table. "How did it happen? And what kind of EMT doesn't notice a sprained ankle? Does that woman even have her license?"

Sage started to say something about how if everyone hadn't been so focused on her nonexistent head injury . . . but she thought better of it. Mom had veered off into what Sage and Ian called Grizzly Bear mode, which often happened when she was overly tired. They'd learned long ago that provoking the Grizzly was good for no one.

Sage slid onto the seat next to Dad, propping her iced ankle on the bench that sat beneath the oil painting Mom had recently purchased in the River Arts District. It was titled *Flowers in the Gully*, but Sage thought it looked more like a rainbow hurricane.

For two grand, she thought the subject should be more apparent. But then, she didn't really get art.

"Here." Ian handed her a throw pillow from the sofa.

"Thanks." She propped it under her ankle. "I think it's feeling better already."

Dad's smartphone pinged. "Ah, good," he said. "Nhu-Mai said to come by tomorrow at lunchtime. She'll squeeze you in."

Sage groaned. "You called her? That's the whole reason I didn't want you to know."

"Technically," Dad said, "I texted her. And what's the point of having a doctor as your best friend if you can't call in some favors?"

"She'll just tell me to ice it."

"Then that's what she'll say. Sectionals are only two weeks away. That means bigger scouts. You want to make sure you're in prime shape."

Sage looked at Ian, but he nodded agreement. She sighed.

Dad opened the stat book laying on the table. "You did great out there tonight, Sage. Ten for ten serves. That incredible save to win the game—"

"If we're being technical," Sage said, "it didn't actually win the game."

Dad waved her objection away. "It kept you guys alive. Speaking of which, I gotta get the game tape. That dive's

17

definitely making your recruitment profile. And that spike in the second game?" He smiled. "Your plyometrics are really working. We've got to measure your jump again." He made a note in the stat book.

Sage flexed her fingers, as if the motion could keep her excitement in check.

"The offer from App State is good," Dad said, "but you keep playing like this, you'll have your pick of schools. Penn State, even."

"Those girls are giants, Dad. Super talented giants." It was Sage's unspoken but well-known dream to go to Penn State, one of the best women's volleyball programs in the country.

"You've got talent," Dad said. "And five feet eleven is hardly little."

Ian licked a glob of peanut butter from his thumb. "You still like UNC?"

Sage shrugged. UNC hadn't officially offered yet, but they'd hinted they would soon. "They've got a solid program. Much better than the smaller schools who have offered, but it's not like all the superstars are gonna go there. I want to play, you know? Not sit on the bench."

Dad smiled. "How many MVP awards do you need to convince you?" he asked. "You *are* one of those superstars."

Sage adjusted her ice pack, eye-rolling away the praise. She'd never admit it out loud, not ever, but she loved the way Dad gushed about her skills. He worked almost every weekend and ate most meals while answering e-mails, but Dad never missed one of Sage's games. Sage tapped Ian's leg with her good foot. "What about you?" she asked. "You guys ready for Friday?"

He pursed his lips, in that way he did when teetering between nervous and excited. "We'll see, I guess." Although six feet two inches, Ian was only a sophomore. And while he was too skinny for most football positions, he was what people called a natural athlete and had beaten out a kid in Sage's class to earn the role of starting kicker.

"Coach pretty much tripled my drills this week," he said.

"I'd hope so," said Dad. "Asheville's defense is probably the best in the state. You should have a lot of field goal attempts."

Mom looked over from the stove. "Oh, that's exciting for you," she said.

"Not as good for the team, though." Ian popped open the ginger ale Sage had left on the kitchen island. "Those assholes at the paper don't think we have a chance."

"Please, Ian," Mom said. "Language."

"Sorry. Ass hats."

Sage snorted. Mom rolled her eyes.

"That new sports reporter doesn't know a football from a pom-pom," said Dad.

"It's true they're not a good match up for us." Ian took a seat beside Sage's propped foot. "But the game plan's solid.

I think it'll be good." He looked at Sage. "You're gonna be there, right?"

She swiped a swig of ginger ale. "Wouldn't miss it. Coach is even cutting practice short to give us time to eat first."

"Speaking of eating," said Mom, "who wants soup?"

CHAPTER FOUR

LEN

LEN PULLED THE FRONT DOOR SHUT HARDER THAN SHE'D intended, rattling the loose pane in the side window.

"Lennon?" her mom called. "Is that you, hon?"

Len cringed. "Yeah." She'd hoped to slip into her room unnoticed, but that door simply wouldn't close without a jerk. Dad said it added to the old house's character. Len thought it made them seem poor.

Her mom appeared around the corner, leaning next to the *Abbey Road* album poster thumbtacked into the beige wall. "Where'd you go?" she asked. "You missed Fauna's call again."

"Oh." Len tried to look like she hadn't planned to do precisely that. "She doing okay?"

Mom's smile slipped. "The same. It's just gonna take time, you know? For all of us."

Len shrugged out of her sweatshirt. "What about Nonni? Did you visit today?"

"Also the same." Mom wiped an eyelash from her cheek. "She recognized me for a few minutes, though, so that was nice."

Len couldn't imagine what it must feel like—your own mother not knowing who you were. It hurt Len that Nonni didn't recognize her anymore, but it must be a thousand times worse for her mom.

"She asked for you," Mom said.

Len's eyes snapped up. "Nonni?"

Mom shook her head. "Fauna. She said you haven't been emailing her like you used to." Her eyes cut into Len, searching. "I think she really misses you."

Len's breath caught, the words digging like rusted scissors in her chest. She wondered if this was how Brutus felt, in that play they'd studied last year, when Caesar uttered those famous last words.

Mom reached for Len. "I know it's been difficult."

Len skirted around her, into the kitchen. "There was a big volleyball match at school."

"Since when do you like volleyball?" Mom followed her. "Or sports at all for that matter?"

Len reached over the pile of pans she'd left drying on the counter and grabbed the shiny electric kettle. "Lots of people went," she said. "It was a big rival game." She nudged the faucet open with the top of her gloved hand and placed the kettle underneath. "I just . . . needed some time away."

"I understand," Mom said.

No, Len wanted to scream. Mom would never understand. No matter how much she missed her older sister, Len didn't deserve to speak to Fauna. Not now. Not ever again.

"Did you go with Hazel?" Mom asked.

Len switched off the faucet. "Huh?"

"To the game. Was Hazel with you, or who'd you go with?"

"Oh. Yeah. Yeah, Hazel." Len dug through the box of assorted teas—*Energizing, Total Relaxation, Peace Love Tea*—until she came to the one she was looking for: *Soul Clarifying.*

"She's a sweet girl, that Hazel," Mom said, plopping down at the three-person table shoved into the corner. Len nodded, like Hazel hadn't slowly stopped talking to her in the past couple months. Like she hadn't told people Len had gone all "abnormal" and that she only talked to her because their moms worked together at the food bank.

"Actually—" Len started.

"You're lucky to have such a nice friend." Mom said it with such relief, like at least there was one daughter she didn't have to worry about. She rubbed her face. "Were you going to say something?"

Len stared at the cracked green tile by her boot, sun-faded from the small window above the sink. "No," she said. "Nothing important."

There was a shuffle down the hall, and then Dad burst in to the kitchen. "Oh, you're back!" he told Len. "Wonderful!

I was just thinking we needed to have a Loving Kindness Circle."

Dread flooded Len, but Mom clapped her hands. "What a great idea! We haven't had one in a few days, and I could really use the boost."

Dad sniffed the air. "Is that *Soul Clarifying* tea? I'll take a cup." He squeezed by Len to grab a mug but accidentally clipped one of the pot handles on the counter, sending them all tumbling onto the linoleum.

"I'll rewash them," Len said, grabbing the sauce pan her dad was about to reshelf.

"They were only down for a sec—"

"We cook food in these, Dad." Len picked up the remaining pots and placed them in the sink. Carefully, she pulled off her gloves and put them on the window ledge behind the faucet. She ran the water again, warming it.

"Suit yourself," he said. "But let's do the circle before you start."

Len squeezed a capful of Dawn into the water, letting some drizzle through her fingers. "You guys go ahead. I'll clean up in here."

"Lennon." Her dad's bubbly voice flattened. "Your sister needs our support. And so does Diane." He turned off the water. "This can wait. Come on."

Len cringed, but dried her clean hands. Grabbing her gloves, she followed her parents through the living-room-turned-Dad's-artist-studio and into the small room at the back of the house. Most families would call it a sunroom, but to Len's parents it was the meditation room.

"Careful," Dad said as Len's elbow brushed a canvas of blue and green face-like blobs. "That one's not dry."

Mom tugged on one of the windows until it unstuck, letting in the quivers of the front porch wind chimes.

"Right, then." Dad sat cross-legged on the braided rug his grandmother had made and twisted his hair into a bun. Len and her mom sat across from him.

"We've talked about this," he said, as Len placed her gloved palm in his. "Gloves disrupt the energy flow."

"But—"

"Len . . ." her mom said softly. "Please. For Fauna." Len ignored the burning in her gut and yanked off her beloved knit gloves. She took her parents' outstretched hands.

Dad shifted on the floor, grounding himself. "Let's take a moment to settle in," he said, using his Reiki class voice. "Close our eyes and take a couple deep breaths: in through the nose"—he demonstrated—"and out through the mouth." Len's parents exhaled long and smooth, but Len's breath snagged in her throat. "Feel the floor beneath you," her dad continued. "The slant of the wooden boards. The tight fibers of the rug."

I shouldn't be doing this, Len thought. *It's not safe.*

"Notice the sounds," her dad said, as traffic noises battled the wind chimes. "If any thoughts arise, just notice and let them go. Let them float away like leaves on a river."

Len's face scrunched with determination. *Leaves falling, floating.*

"Imagine a white light," Dad said. "A healing light emanating from your heart."

Her mom exhaled a deep sigh. But the harder Len focused, the more her imagined light changed—Blue. Red. Blue again.

"On your next inhale, bring Fauna into focus."

Len's eyes shot open. Her parents looked so peaceful, their expressions smooth and full of purpose. *Why couldn't she do this?*

"As you hold Fauna in your mind's eye," Dad said, "imagine the white light from your heart surrounding her, protecting her." He squeezed Len's hand. "Send loving energy to her as your inner voice says, 'May you feel peace. May you feel peace.'"

A tear rolled down Mom's face, and Len slammed her eyes shut. *Get it together*, she demanded. *It's the least you can do.*

"Now, let the image of Fauna dissolve," Dad said, "and bring to mind Diane. You can envision a picture of her or imagine her doing something that makes her happy." Len visualized Fauna's pretty wife, standing in the kitchen of their adorable Atlanta townhouse, rolling dough for the pecan pie her grandmother taught her to make. The pie she'd promised to teach Len to make the next time she came to visit.

"May you feel peace," Dad murmured. Len zeroed in on the image with all her strength. *May you feel peace, Diane. May you feel—*

The image blurred with memory—*Diane, tearful but stoic, holding Fauna while Fauna cried in a way Len had never seen before, like the spark that kept her alive was giving out.*

Len pulled her hands free, gasping, and staggered to her feet.

"Lennon?" Mom's eyes had opened. She reached for Len.

"No!" Len backpedaled, bumping into a wicker loveseat. "I think, um, I might be sick."

Dad's eyes floated open. "It's okay, Lennon. It's normal for meditations to stir strong emotions."

Normal, Len thought wildly. *None of this is normal.* She tugged on her gloves, vaguely aware of her parents' whispers to each other.

"What can we do?"

"She needs some space, that's all."

"I'm okay. I—" What? What could she say to explain this? "I think I ate something bad." Len dashed to her room and crawled into bed, wriggling down until the comforter cocooned her, her breathing moist in the small space.

Safe, her brain said. *You're safe here.*

She never should have agreed to do the meditation, not with everything that was happening. But what *was* happening? Her thoughts spun to four years ago, when Nonni first started forgetting things—how she told Len she felt like she was going crazy. Did it feel like this?

She took a deep breath, in through her nose, out through her mouth, just like Dad had learned at the Reiki Training Center downtown, how he'd taught her. She was overreacting, of course. She was fine. Totally fine.

Somewhere in the house, the phone rang. Len took another breath, then another, counting as she waited. Mom or Dad would be in to check on her soon, and everything would feel right again.

She counted higher, slowly, all the way to fifty. The room outside her blanket remained empty.

Len pulled the comforter tighter and told herself that was okay. Besides, her parents were busy. The phone was probably Fauna again, so Mom would be consoling her. And then there was Nonni and the steady stream of medical bills. Dad hadn't sold a painting in forever, and a nonprofit salary bolstered by occasional commissions only went so far anyway. Her parents didn't have time to worry about her, and they didn't need to. She could at least give them that.

She rolled over, puffing the blanket away from her face with a deep exhale. What was it Dad always said? *Believe it and it will be.* She just needed to think positively. Len scrunched her eyes shut as thoughts whipped through her. None of them were good.

What were those positivity mantras Dad was always going on about? She thought she used to know—there were so many—but the space her memory reached into felt empty. *Blank.* She curled her body as tightly as she could, suddenly exhausted, and fell asleep without remembering a single one.

CHAPTER FIVE

SAGE

DAD LET SAGE DRIVE THE OLD SUBARU TO SCHOOL the next day, so at least the doctor's appointment had an upside.

A trio of sophomore girls passed the car as she and Ian climbed out. One of them gave Ian a smile that made Sage remember that to other people he wasn't just her little brother. Gross. She caught Ian's self-satisfied expression and knocked his elbow. "Good thing they don't know what a nerd you are."

"Me?" Ian snorted. "You like *Star Wars!*"

Sage feigned indignation. "It's totally back in pop culture. Everyone likes *Star Wars* now."

"Um, no. They don't." They stopped as a car pulled into the parking space in front of them. Sage took the opportunity to flex her sore ankle, which had swelled just enough overnight that she'd had to wear sandals.

"It's the Force, I think," Sage said, shifting weight back to her foot.

"What is?"

"The whole idea of it. It speaks to me."

"Because it gives power?" asked Ian.

She looked up at him. "It doesn't, though. The power is already there, good and bad, in everything. It's just that some people can control it more than others." They resumed walking. "It's not so different from sports, really, the body and mind control. Don't you think?"

Ian's eyebrows crinkled. He tousled his hair into perfect messiness and laughed. "I think it's good you play sports."

"Oh, shut it."

At the door, Ian gave her Spock's Vulcan salute.

"That's *Star Trek*, goober!"

"You would know!" He grinned. Then a tidal wave of sophomores overwhelmed them, and he was swept out to sea. Sage made her way to the first floor snack machine, where Kayla waited for her as usual.

"I can't believe they took away my beloved Reese's Pieces," she said. "Look at this stuff. Celery and tree bark. You got an extra quarter?"

Sage added the coin so the machine would release Kayla's animal crackers, then stuffed six more quarters into the slot. She chose the same granola bar she'd bought for the last two

31

weeks, when the new "healthy" vending machine replaced the candy dispenser. "I don't know," Sage said. "I kinda like it." She bent down to retrieve the bar.

"Ugh. You would." Kayla's phone pinged. She leaned against the plexiglass and pulled it out. "Oh no. Did you remember about the physics quiz?"

Sage stood up. "No!"

Kayla groaned. "I'm gonna *fail*, Sage. You're good at that stuff, but I haven't studied, like, at all."

"We have until after lunch," Sage said, but her head already pounded. She stuffed the uneaten bar into her bag as they took off for their lockers. Why did her dad have to make that stupid doctor appointment for the only time she might have studied? Why had she taken that extra elective instead of a study hall like a normal person? Why didn't she keep ibuprofen in her bag?

Two girls cut in front of them, both glued to their phones and completely oblivious that they'd almost been run over. Sage sidestepped them absently.

"One of these days," Kayla muttered, "I'm gonna bust someone." They turned a corner just as another girl rounded it, and Sage collided full force with her.

"Oh!" The girl's fistful of pens scattered to the floor.

"I'm so sorry," Sage said. "I didn't see you."

The girl froze, her gloved hands clenched stiffly by her sides. She watched two of the pens roll all the way to the opposite wall.

Sage dropped down to gather them. There must have been ten at least, maybe more. Brand new-looking, too. Sage appreciated the importance of being prepared—one of the gazillion things volleyball had taught her—but ten pens seemed excessive.

"Don't worry about it," the girl said, her voice slipping out like an accident.

"No, it was my fault." Sage stood up, both hands full of pens.

"You're that volleyball player." Gloved girl tilted her head.

"Oh. Uh, yeah. I'm Sage."

"Are you okay?"

It took Sage a moment to realize the girl must have seen her pass out. Or heard about it. "Yeah, I'm fine. Here are your pens." She nodded at the floor. "The last one's by your shoe."

Gloved girl stared at Sage's outstretched hand, expressionless. Behind Sage, Kayla gave an awkward cough.

"Right," said Sage. She hesitated a moment, then collected the final pen.

The girl inched backward. "You can keep them."

Sage frowned, suddenly uncomfortable. "Um, they're yours."

For just a moment, she held the girl's eyes. Gloved girl dropped her gaze, but not before Sage saw the panic that filled it. Sage glanced at Kayla, who was staring at them the way people watch a car crash.

"Please take these," Sage said. The warning bell rang above them. Slowly, the girl nodded and accepted the pens.

"Coming through!" A herd of sophomores, some of them Ian's friends, barreled around them. Gloved girl backed up, a move that seemed as instinctual as Sage's volleyball sprawl. Mumbling a quick thank-you, she hurried back the way she'd come.

Sage's eyes followed her. "That was . . . weird."

"You think?" said Kayla. "But it's Len Madder, so . . ."

"Her last name's Madder?"

"I know." Kayla made a face. "An unfortunate coincidence, since she's legit crazy."

Sage couldn't remember ever having seen the girl before. That wasn't out of the question, considering the size of their school, but it was more than that. Even now, she had trouble remembering what the girl had looked like: baggy sweatshirt . . . gray maybe? And was her hair brown? Or more blond? Sage frowned. It was like the girl—Len—had been a part of the background until the whole pen incident forced her into visibility. A person had to really try to be that unnoticeable, didn't she?

They'd reached their lockers. Sage turned back to Kayla. "So you know her?"

"She's in my study hall. She's a junior, though." Kayla spun her lock until it clicked. "She seemed normal enough at first, but trust me, she's not."

"Why?"

Kayla shrugged. "It's hard to explain. She just does weird things, you know? Like"—she flicked her hands—"whatever that was."

Sage looked back to where she'd collided with Len, realizing she'd seen the look in Len's face before. The first game of the season, Southview faced Weaverville. Not a bad opponent, but Weaverville was plagued with injuries. The third string sub had slunk onto the court during Sage's serve, and her stance, well, she knew she was out of her league. Way out. And the terrified, weakest-prey look she gave—right before Sage served a top spin line drive that bloodied her nose—was the same look Len had.

Sage bit her thumbnail.

"Hey." Kayla snapped her fingers in Sage's face. "You coming or what? We're gonna be late."

"Right. Yeah. I'll meet you there. I, uh, gotta check something." Sage left Kayla's protests and backtracked through the empty hallway, not even sure what she was looking for. Then a door clicked and Len exited the bathroom down the hall. She never made eye contact, but the way Len paused—a heartbeat too long—let Sage know she'd seen her. Len bolted down the Fine Arts Hall.

Sage couldn't help it. She pushed open the bathroom door. The trashcan sat in the far corner. Inside, atop a mountain of paper towels, lay a fistful of brand-new pens.

CHAPTER SIX

LEN

MS. SAFFRON WAS UPLOADING DOROTHEA LANGE IMAGES to the whiteboard when Len slipped into Photography. She couldn't believe she'd run into that Sage girl again, and what if she noticed the pens? The last thing Len needed was more whispers. More laughs. Another person thinking she was nuts.

She pinched the space between her tired eyes. *Please don't let her see the pens.*

"Len." Ms. Saffron's voice crumbled her thoughts. "How kind of you to join us."

A flush fanned Len's neck. "Sorry."

Ms. Saffron waved off the apology. "Notebooks out," she told the class. "We've got a lot to cover today." She opened a PowerPoint document beside the photographs.

"Um, Ms. Saffron?" Len moved closer to her teacher's desk. "Could I . . . borrow a pen? Please?"

Ms. Saffron shot her a you've-got-to-be-kidding look. "I believe you still have one of mine from yesterday," she said. "And two from last week, if I'm not mistaken."

The flush crept to Len's ears. She hated throwing away those pens, and she hated looking like an idiot. But at least now she was safe.

"I'm sorry. I keep losing them." Eyes peered up from notebooks, but she couldn't meet any of them. "I really don't have anything to write with."

Ms. Saffron sighed and dug out a thick, black pen from the eARTh cup on her desk. "Please," she said, holding it out, "return it after class."

Len's eyes ping-ponged between it and the un-touched writing utensils in the cup. Ms. Saffron shook the pen at her, clearly exasperated.

"Would it be okay if I picked another one?" Len asked. Someone behind her sniggered.

"Beggars really can't be—" Ms. Saffron met Len's brown eyes with her own fierce blue ones, then her voice trailed off. Len swallowed. What had her teacher seen that made her stop?

Ms. Saffron gestured to the cup. "Take your pick," she said, then turned to the rest of the room, business-as-usual. "Let's talk about documentary photography."

* * *

Len returned the pen as soon as class ended. Ms. Saffron put a hand on her sleeve.

"Is everything all right, Len?"

"What do you mean?"

A crease split Ms. Saffron's usually smooth forehead. "You don't have a quiz or anything next period, do you?"

Len shook her head. Her classmates filed into the hallway.

"Good. I'll write you a pass." Ms. Saffron walked to the file cabinet at the back of the room and returned holding a manila folder. *Madder, L* was written across the tab in small, tight script. "You know," Ms. Saffron said, "I was really excited to see your name on my roster again this term." She flipped through the file. "Last semester you demonstrated an immediate affinity for photography. A way of capturing images—of giving them a story, an *urgency*—that I haven't seen from a student in a long time." She held out a print. "This, for instance."

Len took hold of the image, a naturescape she'd submitted as part of last semester's final portfolio. Her beloved North Carolina mountains, slightly out of focus and bursting with juicy spring greens, colored the background. Several images of a wayward leaf—she'd been playing with shutter speed—were spliced together in the foreground. Len could almost see Fauna on the edge of the shot, grinning, just out of the camera's peripheral range.

"Was that taken on the Parkway somewhere?" Ms. Saffron asked.

Len nodded. "One of the trails, yeah. My sister and I used to explore them."

"And what were you thinking when you shot this?"

Len handed the photo back. "I don't know."

Ms. Saffron arched her plucked brows. "The assignment was to express your current mood with an image, so . . ." When Len didn't respond, she added, "This is clearly a joyful photograph. It's airy, light. *Free.* You were experiencing some kind of happiness, yes?"

Len's face tightened. Unwelcome memories split the cracks she'd tried to fill:

Fauna, whisper-shrieking the news. Len, her camera jamming against her chest bone as she bounced like an excited child. The stray leaf, swirling dance-like along the windswept trail. Fauna, arms outstretched and twirling, imitating it.

"I guess, yeah," Len said. "I was happy." She picked a gray fuzz off her sweatshirt. "I was sort of, I don't know, playing."

Ms. Saffron smiled. "Exactly. The shot's not perfect technically, but the viewer can *feel* that play—of you and the leaf—when we look at it. And that's what brings it to life."

Len tugged her backpack straps snugger as Ms. Saffron pulled out more images—Len's submissions from the start of the school year.

"And these." Ms. Saffron spread them on her desk. Another landscape. A black and white of her father painting the energy plant from the bank of the lake, right across from the high school and her house. A silhouette of her mom practicing yoga in Pack Square.

The bell rang for the next block period. Len's head jerked toward the door.

"It's my planning period," Ms. Saffron said. "We won't be disturbed." She tapped the photos. "Even though they're all different types of pictures, all of these exhibit the same kind of energy." Her hand waved, like it could pull the right words from the air. "Almost an *exuberance*."

Len's throat tightened.

"It strikes me," Ms. Saffron continued, "that most of the photos you turned in last month, just like the ones you took last semester, they're all outside." She spread more pictures—Len's most recent assignments on shadow and texture—on the desk.

"Your current work, however . . ." Ms. Saffron half-sat on the edge of her desk, her black slacks hitching up, revealing a silver anklet. "What were you thinking as you shot each of these? What made you take them all indoors?"

Anger caught Len off guard. "You tell us to vary our scenes," she said stiffly.

Ms. Saffron frowned. "You never got back to me. Are your plans the same as last semester? Do you still want to compete for the Melford Scholarship?"

Len focused on the image nearest her, a close-up of a battered, ornate mantel she'd found at her favorite thrift shop downtown. The Melford dream seemed so far away now. So ridiculously unattainable.

"I know it can be difficult to imagine," Ms. Saffron pressed, "being the first one in your family to attend college—"

"Fauna went to cooking school," Len blurted, though she didn't know why. It had been the perfect choice for her, pairing beautifully with Diane's finance degree to ensure their startup restaurant's success. But it wasn't technically a "college" college. Even Fauna said so.

Ms. Saffron crossed her legs. "That doesn't exactly answer my question. Do you—"

"Yes," said Len. For a tiny breath, she felt like old Len. Len from four months ago. Len from *before*. "I want the scholarship." Then she remembered the swollen front door. The pile of bills near the toaster. The house—once her refuge—that now squeezed her insufferably every time she stepped inside it.

There was only one way away from all that.

"I need it," she whispered.

Something else nudged the side of her mind, like the whispers of a dream wanting remembering. Len wasn't sure what it was, but she knew—she *knew*—she couldn't let it pierce her consciousness. Something terrible would happen. She put her hands to her temples.

Ms. Saffron's clipped, mango-colored nails clicked against the desktop. "Is there anything you want to tell me, Len? Because I know you could win one of those scholarships. You've got the talent. But it's extremely competitive, and the portfolio required is extensive. It can't be completed in one semester." She pursed her lips. "And, well, I hate to say this, but it's my job, if we're going to prepare you to have a shot. Lately"—she waved her hand over the photographs—"your works feels . . . quite honestly, it feels sterile."

Len had never been punched before, but she suspected it might feel a lot like the way Ms. Saffron's words tucked into her. She might be losing hold on the other aspects of her life, but her photography—she thought she'd managed to protect that part of herself. The best part.

"Len," Ms. Saffron said. "Is something going on?"

"No." Len stood as tall as her five-foot-six-inch frame allowed, determined not to let her last thread of dignity unravel. "I'll do better."

"You're very talented," Ms. Saffron repeated, but Len didn't need pity praise.

Len glanced at the clock. "I should get to class."

"Right." Ms. Saffron sighed. "I'll get your pass." She slid the photographs back into the file and handed Len a list of hand-written photo prompts. "Try these," she said. "See if they help unblock some of your creative energy." She scribbled out a hall pass, but before handing it over, added, "You know there's a counselor here."

Len thought she might be sick. She must have looked it, too, because Ms. Saffron added quickly, "Or I'm here, if there's anything I can do to help." She held out the pass. "I *want* to help you, Len. All you need to do is ask."

Len snatched the pass, forcing a tiny nod before darting out of the classroom. She squeezed the prompt list as she slipped through the empty halls, reading the words over and over without comprehending them. The thought of Ms. Saffron wanting to help spurred a bitter smile. Teachers always thought they could solve everything. Well, some things couldn't be solved. Some things just were.

CHAPTER SEVEN

SAGE

AS SOON AS THE LUNCH BELL RANG, SAGE SIGNED HERSELF out of school and drove the two miles to Dr. Surrage's office. Except for the receptionist sneaking bites of a sandwich behind her computer, the waiting room sat empty.

Sage hitched her backpack higher. The receptionist looked up.

"Sage Zendasky?"

"That's me."

"It'll be just a minute, okay?" Somewhere in the back, a little kid coughed. Then cried. The receptionist smiled weakly. "Flu season came early," she said. "We're running a little behind schedule."

Sage took a seat opposite a large fish tank and opened her physics notebook. If she got sick here, Dad would never hear the end of it. A black-and-white striped fish swam toward her, then darted away, and suddenly the incident with Len was in her head. She didn't quite know what to do with the discarded pens discovery. It was odd on the highest level, and Kayla would love the gossip. As a general rule, Sage told her best friend everything. But something—perhaps the same thing that compelled her to enter the bathroom in the first place—persuaded her to keep that particular bit of information to herself.

The door to the examination room opened. "Sage?" A nurse looked up from a clipboard. "You can come on back."

Sage dropped her bag and notebook on the room's single chair as the nurse opened a small laptop. "Let's see. You're here for your foot?"

"My dad insisted." Sage situated herself onto the exam table, crinkling the fresh sheet of butcher paper.

"You can go ahead and remove your shoe," the nurse said, then took Sage's vitals. "Dr. Surrage will be in shortly."

Sage glanced at the clock above the door. Even with a doctor's excuse, her physics teacher had a strict missed-test policy. Sage would have to stay after school, which meant being late for practice. Why had she let Dad talk her into this?

A knock rattled her thoughts. "Come in," she said.

Dr. Surrage's face appeared at the door, followed quickly by the rest of her. "Sorry to keep you waiting, Sage." She replaced the stethoscope around her neck. "Been one of those days."

"Thanks for squeezing me in. I told my dad it wasn't necessary, but, uh, he worries."

"Alek Zendasky worry?" Dr. Surrage set her laptop by the sink and washed her hands. "Surely not."

Sage smiled. Of all her parents' friends, Dr. Surrage was one of her favorites. She liked that she wore cute shoes but never heels. She liked that she'd tell hilarious stories about Dad in college, and how the memories themselves seemed to make her father grow younger and more carefree. Sometimes he even put down his smartphone.

Dr. Surrage sat on a stool, balancing her laptop on her knees. "Your dad said you ran into the wall?"

"Going after a ball, yeah. Everyone thought I hit my head, but it was actually my ankle."

Dr. Surrage typed something, then slid her stool closer. "Let's take a look."

"It's a lot better today," Sage said. "I'm sure it just needs ice."

"It's always better to check," Dr. Surrage said. "Tell me when it hurts, okay?" She rotated Sage's foot slowly, pressing her thumb in various spots along the ankle bone.

"There," said Sage. "That's sore."

Dr. Surrage nodded. "How about now?"

"That's okay."

She tested a few other spots on Sage's foot before nodding, satisfied. "You're lucky. It looks like a mild roll. If you ice and elevate regularly, I think you'll be full speed in a few days. Do you have a game tonight?"

"Not till Monday."

"Good. But take it easy at practice or you'll injure it worse and have to miss some games. No jumping. No running. Not for a couple days."

Sage nodded at the expected diagnosis. What a waste. The clock read 12:41 p.m.

Dr. Surrage pulled out a roll of medical tape and bound Sage's ankle with the quick, sure movements of someone who'd done it a thousand times. Sage admired the precision, the confidence. Maybe she should be a doctor. She liked the idea of helping people. Only, she wasn't a big fan of blood, and okayness-with-bodily-fluids seemed like a major part of the job requirement. Also, medical school wouldn't allow time for volleyball, and she was going pro anyway. She felt it as clear as her heartbeat. It wasn't lucrative by any means, but Sage didn't need much money. She only needed to play.

Dr. Surrage broke off the tape near Sage's heel. "I'm wondering about what you mentioned earlier." She wound a new piece of tape around the first one. "About not hitting your head. You said you didn't hit it against the wall?"

"Right. Well, my cheek kind of grazed it, I guess, but definitely not my head."

Dr. Surrage frowned, her face an unasked question.

"Dad told you I fainted," Sage said.

"Yes. He said it's never happened before."

"Never!"

"And it happened when you were in motion? You were jumping?"

Sage nodded. "I jumped up to bump shoulders with Hannah, and then . . ." She shrugged. "I was on the ground. It was so stupid. And I had plenty to eat. I mean, cereal's not a lot. But I'd had two cheese sticks and a sandwich after school. I usually eat a ton, but I keep telling Mom I can't stuff myself before a big game. It makes me sick."

Dr. Surrage nodded. "Do you have a history of low blood pressure?"

"Uh, I don't think so."

She finished the wrap. "A fluke, then. It happens sometimes." She pushed back her stool. "All set."

"Thanks again," Sage said, "for seeing me on your lunch break." She slid off the table, careful to avoid too much pressure on her taped foot, and grabbed her bag from the floor.

Dr. Surrage made no motion to leave. "Sage," she said, "I think I want to give you an EKG—an electrocardiogram."

Sage froze. "Why?"

"Precautionary." Dr. Surrage typed something into her laptop. "Just a quick check of your heart activity. It's not an uncommon test when someone loses consciousness." Her tone was nonchalant, but Sage recognized the subtle tells, the same ones weaker opponents gave, trying to project a confidence too stiff to be real. "The body does strange things from time to time," she continued. "But I'm a doctor, and doctors like to know for certain."

"But . . ." *Didn't people used to faint a lot, like, hundreds of years ago? And Mom said her grandmother had fainting spells and she lived to be a hundred!*

"My grandmother fainted sometimes," Sage said. Then, "I have a quiz at one."

Dr. Surrage's face softened, her manner relaxed again. "It's a five-minute test. Easy." Sage looked for the crack in confidence she'd seen before. Had she imagined it?

"I suspect," Dr. Surrage added, like a secret, "this is the only way we'll truly get your dad to stop worrying."

And then the pieces dropped neatly into place. This was about her dad; of course it was. Alek Zendasky was one of North Carolina's most successful federal public defense attorneys because he relentlessly pursued a line of inquiry. He'd never been concerned about her foot. He was worried about her head. That's what Dr. Surrage was hiding. And if she could give him 100 percent certainty, there wouldn't be more squeezed-in lunch visits.

Sage's fingers released her backpack. "Okay."

Dr. Surrage stood. "Great. And we'll have you out in time for that quiz."

CHAPTER EIGHT

SAGE

DR. SURRAGE KEPT HER WORD. TECHNICALLY, SAGE HAD TO run an almost-red light and cut off a pickup, but she made it back just as her teacher was passing out the quiz. Sage ticked off the formulas easily, feeling immensely productive. Easing Dad's fears and acing a quiz all in a few hours.

The rest of the day was, as usual, just time to pass until Sage could hit the gym. When the last bell rang, she rode the wave of exiting students to her locker and grabbed her duffle bag. Like clockwork, Ella and Kayla came down the hall as she shut her locker door. She fell in step with them on the way to the gym.

"Hey," Ella said to her, then tipped half a box of Tic Tacs into her mouth.

"You eat more of those than anyone I've ever seen," Kayla said. "You want some real food?" She held out a bag of Doritos.

"I just like clean breath."

"Because you plan on kissing someone in the next twenty minutes?"

Ella cracked one of the candies between her teeth and shrugged. "You never know." Sage opened her mouth to laugh when a dark, baggy sweatshirt caught her eye. At the far end of the hallway, just past the gym entrance, Len Madder was walking with erratic, stop-and-go movements.

"What the—" said Ella.

"Watch it!" a boy yelled at Len, swinging his trombone case wide as she hopped in front of him.

Kayla grabbed Sage's arm. "What'd I tell you?"

Sage tried not to stare, but it was no good. Len seemed headed for the door, but kept stepping sideways, then forward again, then pausing, irritating everyone trying to get by.

Just walk, Sage willed her. *Walk normally out the door.*

"Are you seeing this?" Ella said. She and Kayla exchanged baffled smiles. And yeah, Len did look ridiculous. But Sage couldn't help thinking that she also looked like she didn't *want* to be walking that way. Like her body was somehow out of her control.

"Total weirdo," Kayla muttered. She reached for the gym door just as Lyz Greer burst through.

"Greer!" Kayla said, jumping. "You trying to give us a heart attack?"

"You guys!" Lyz shook like she'd downed three Pepsis. "A scout's here!"

"What?" Ella raced into the gym, pulling Kayla after her. She was only a sophomore, but her ambition was immense. Sage admired her for it. She threw a last glance toward the exit, but Len—and the chaos she'd caused—was gone.

"Sage!" Kayla popped back through the gym entrance. "What's wrong?"

"I . . ." She frowned. Len was fine. She'd probably been practicing some kind of weird dance or something.

"The scout, Sage! We've been dreaming about this since we were twelve years old!" Kayla held out her fist. "Offers from the same school!"

Sage's heartbeat surged. She pushed away everything but volleyball and met Kayla's fist with her own. "Let's show 'em how we do."

* * *

A woman sat at the top of the bleachers talking to their assistant coach. Her khakis and white polo gave no hint of school affiliation.

A few girls already dressed for practice kept glancing toward the bleachers, whispering. Sage tried not to limp as she crossed the court to the locker room, the reality of her injury pulling her back from the high of learning about the scout. If only the scout had come next week.

Coach's eyes snagged on her wrapped foot when she reentered the gym. "What happened?" he asked.

"From last night. A light sprain. The doctor said I'll be fine in a couple days."

"A couple days till you can practice or a couple days till you can play full on?"

"I can practice now, just no jumping."

Coach rubbed his chin. "We can work with that. Schools want to know how players handle themselves in situations that are less than ideal." He glanced to the bleachers. "I'll tell her it's not a big injury. She might want to come back, but today we'll have you showcase back row attacks and peppering, stuff that you don't have to jump for." He clasped Sage's shoulder, his voice low. "And I don't want to put too much pressure on, but she's from a D1, PAC 12 school. And she's *really* excited about you."

Sage allowed one glance at the bleachers and the passive-faced woman scribbling at a clipboard. Her dream was so close. All she had to do was grab it.

Coach raised his eyes as Kayla joined them. "Same for you," he added, though Kayla hadn't heard the earlier conversation. "She's interested in both of you."

Sage's pulse surged to her throat as she and Kayla exchanged glances.

"D1," Sage told her. Kayla's eyes widened hungrily.

"Showtime, ladies," Coach said, and the girls slid on their game faces as easily as they pulled up their kneepads.

Sage and Kayla grabbed balls from the rack the freshmen had just loaded. Dad had been right. If she hadn't gone to Dr. Surrage, the scout might think she was injured worse than she was. Word might get out, her stock could drop, and in the few days it took for her injury to heal, scouts might have set their sights on someone else. Days were precious things in the business of sports.

Sage brought her own ball behind her head before rocketing it—and all thoughts of ankles or scouts—off the wall.

"Three o'clock!" Coach called. "Outside!"

Kayla cracked her neck, then led the rest of the team out the gym doors, as the captains always did. On a normal day, Sage would be beside her.

Coach handed her a stopwatch. "I think some of the JVers are slacking," he said. "Can you clock times while I set up?"

Sage nodded. Coach clapped her on the back.

As she moved to the outside door, Sage realized she was walking right where Len had looked like she was playing a demented form of hopscotch. Sage looked around for whatever could have made Len act like such a freak in the middle of a crowded hallway. But there was nothing. Just the tile floor, streaked and speckled with skid marks from the nonstop tread of shoes.

Outside, the late September sun blazed, burning off some of her nervous energy about the scout. Sage shaded her eyes, her brain tugging back to Len. It was a welcome distraction from the scout. She couldn't help feeling bad for her. High school could be rough enough when people acted normally. Len seemed to go out of her way to make it worse.

Before long, her teammates rounded the school. She clocked their times absently, reminding herself not to overthink the drills she'd soon perform for the scout. *Your greatest opponent,* Coach liked to tell them, *is your own head.*

"Ugh!" Kayla shouted, coming to a stop beside Sage and breaking her reverie. "That felt worse than usual."

"Maybe if you ate more tree bark?" Sage teased, and Kayla punched her arm.

"Serves!" Coach yelled after Sage and Kayla led the team through stretches and conditioning. "You know the drill," he said. "Ten in a row. You miss—"

"You start over," the girls finished.

The gym echoed with pounding volleyballs, a beat that synchronized with Sage's heart. She caught Hannah's floater and stepped back to the service line, nerves about the scout evaporating as muscle memory took over. When colleges first started reaching out to her, Mom had hounded her about meditation, about how good it was for the brain and for managing stress. What Mom didn't realize—and what Sage didn't quite know how to articulate—was that *volleyball* was her meditation. Scouts and homework, gossip and grades—it all smudged into a fuzzy backdrop once she got on the court.

Sage flexed her right fingers, then served a fierce topspin. It sailed to the back line, just in bounds.

"Nice!" Kayla said. From the corner of her eye, Sage saw the scout scribble something on her clipboard.

"Seniors," Coach called, "go around the clock." Sage and Kayla served to positions one to six, in order. Kayla had two errors to Sage's one.

"Time to pepper!" Coach called. Next to Sage and Kayla, Coach tutored a JV pair. "Try to keep the flow," he told them. "Pass, set, attack. Pass, set, attack. Like your captains."

Sage allowed a small smile. *There's nothing like it*, she thought. To make something they'd worked so hard on look effortless.

"Let's do two hundred," Kayla told her.

"Two fifty."

"Done."

Except for Kayla's occasional counting, they didn't speak. There was no need. It quenched both of them—their easy silence, the concentration on the ball—almost as much as water. Sage drank it in.

Pass. Set. Attack. Pass. Set. Attack.

Her meditation.

"Sixty-two," Kayla said, as she set the ball. "Hey, what's your mom doing here?"

Sage's spike veered left as she looked to the door. Mom strode purposefully to Coach, her heels clicking sharply against the wooden floor.

Mom talked. Coach rubbed the back of his head. Neither of them smiled.

Sage caught the ball.

"That was only seventy-one!" said Kayla.

"Something's wrong." Sage marched across the floor.

"Hey, honey," Mom said. Her smile was too wide.

Sage turned to Coach. "What's going on?"

"Nothing," Mom answered. "Well, I'll tell you in the car."

Someone had died. Sage knew it. Her heartbeat fumbled and tripped over itself. "Is it Grandpa?"

"What? Oh. No, sweetie. Nothing like that."

"Then, what?" Sage hugged the volleyball to her chest. "There's a scout here, Mom." Her eyes flicked involuntarily to the bleachers. "From a big-time school. I can't just leave."

Coach touched her shoulder. "It's fine. I'll explain and make sure she comes back. Really, Sage, it won't impact anything. I'll make sure of it."

"Grab your stuff," Mom said in a way that told Sage to hurry. "We can't be late."

Kayla followed Sage to the bleachers. "What's happening?"

"I don't know." She nabbed her duffle and backpack, conscious of the team watching, and let her game face still her features. "I'll text you."

* * *

As soon as the gym doors banged behind them, Sage whirled on Mom. "Tell me what's going on!"

Mom's face tightened. "It's just precautionary."

That word again. "*What's* precautionary?"

They were outside now, both of them squinting. "Dr. Surrage called." Mom shaded her eyes. "She told me she gave you an EKG and she thinks, well, she wants you to get an echo. Just to be safe."

"An echo?"

"Yes. It's an ultrasound of your heart."

Sage stopped. "But, why?"

Mom tugged Sage's wrist lightly, forcing her to keep walking. "All she said was that it was better to be overcautious, so she wanted a more conclusive test. Which is good because nothing less will satisfy your father." A tired breath escaped her. "Come on. Dr. Surrage knows the cardiologist and he added you to today's schedule as a favor."

Sage frowned, trying to make sense of Mom's broken bits of information. "Dad's the one insisting I get the echo?"

"No. It was Dr. Surrage's idea. But I'm sure it's mainly to placate your father."

Sage climbed into the car, keenly aware of the quick pounding in her chest. *Nerves*, she told herself. *Just nerves.*

"What was on my EKG, then?"

Mom released the parking brake and flipped on the engine. "I don't know exactly. Maybe nothing. She said it wasn't conclusive. Hence the echo." She pulled onto the road.

Sage thought of the scout. The perfect, but missed, opportunity.

Mom blew a loose length of dark hair off her face. "Try to think of it as a good thing. You'll get cleared and then everyone can breathe easy." She gripped the steering wheel tighter. "And Dad won't be able to hound you about any more tests."

Sage nodded. "I guess." The storefronts zipped by and her gaze settled on BAKED, the dangerously delicious pie shop that had opened when she was a freshman. It had been a long time since she'd let herself go there, or have sweets of any kind. It'd be worth it, though, keeping her body in prime condition. Just a couple more months, maybe less, and she'd have a signed contract.

Only...

She shifted, wishing she'd brought a volleyball to steady her hands. She wouldn't get the kind of offers she wanted if she wasn't around when Division 1 scouts showed up. "I should be back there, Mom," she said. "I have to prove myself to get an offer."

"You're going to get an offer," Mom said quickly. "More than one if Coach knows what he's talking about."

"But only if I'm on the court!"

Mom reached over and squeezed her hand. "I know how much you want this, honey. And it's going to happen, okay? I know you. I know how you work. You're going to make it happen."

Sage squeezed back. Mom might think she knew how badly Sage wanted a full ride to a big-time program, how it would set her up for a professional career overseas and maybe even—when she really let her dreams run wild—a bid on an Olympic team.

But the truth was, no one truly understood how much Sage wanted those things. How volleyball felt as much a part of her as her brain or lungs or any other organ necessary for life. Sometimes Sage thought she might ignite from the sheer force of wanting.

Mom pulled into a medical park. Sage had passed it umpteen times on the way downtown but had never been inside.

"This is it," Mom said.

Sage took in the three-story building with the humongous blue heart on the side, annoyed by how the sight of it made her pulse pound a bit harder. Elite athletes controlled their bodies, not the other way around. What was she even worried about anyway? She was in great shape. She took a few deep breaths, slowing her heart rate, then slipped on her game face and followed her mom inside.

Dad sat alone in the waiting room. A patient clipboard balanced on his lap while he typed on his phone. "Sage." He stood up. "How are you feeling?"

"I'm fine, Dad. Really."

He nodded. To Mom, he asked, "You okay, Rena?"

Sage glanced between them. "Why wouldn't she be?"

"He means my meeting," Mom said quickly and gave Dad a sharp look. "It was fine. Tiring. I'm fine."

The waiting space was small but pristine, with warm colors on the wall and chairs softening the hospital feel of the place. A children's nook complete with chalkboard wall and a basket of toys took up one corner.

"I've filled out most of your paperwork." Dad handed Sage the clipboard. "You just have to sign a few places."

"I'm missing a scouting session right now," she said.

Dad frowned. "From where?"

"A PAC 12 school!"

Dad's mouth fell open. Mom shot him another look.

"There'll be plenty of those," he said. "Let's just get this over with."

A woman in scrubs stepped into the room. "Sage Zendasky?"

"Yes."

"Right this way." She nodded at Sage's clipboard. "You can sign that back here and then we'll get you all set up, okay? Mom, you're welcome to come back now, if that makes Sage comfortable. Dad, I can get you when Dr. Friedman's ready with the results?"

Dad nodded and resumed his seat.

"We so appreciate you fitting us in," Mom said as they followed the sonographer.

The woman gave a tired smile. "Dr. Friedman bends over backward to make sure people get proper care." She led them into a darkened room where a large machine sat next to the patient table.

"How long is this going to take?" Sage asked, studying the mass of wires.

"Forty-five minutes or so." The sonographer stepped around the examination table. "And I know it looks scary, but it doesn't hurt. We'll get these leads on you, use the scope"—she held up a wand-like tool—"to take some pictures of your heart, and that will be that." She handed Sage a hospital gown. "Go ahead and put this on, opening in the front. I'll come back when you're ready."

The woman was right. Nothing about the echo hurt, although all the electrodes on her chest did make Sage feel a bit like an experiment in a sci-fi movie. Despite her annoyance at missing the scouting practice, she found her eyes glued to the monitor. She *felt* her heart beat every day, but she'd never actually *seen* it.

She pointed to a largish, gray area on the black-and-white screen. "What is that?"

"That," the sonographer said, "is one of your ventricles. The right one. Could you turn toward me just a little?" She adjusted the probe higher on Sage's chest. "See that pulsing there? That's a valve, opening and closing. Cool, huh?"

She typed something into the machine, then pointed out the different chambers of Sage's heart, and how the blood moved through them. It was clearly against office policy, however, for her to offer any opinions about a diagnosis. Sage tried multiple times.

"Don't worry," the sonographer said as she unplugged Sage's leads. "Dr. Friedman knows what to look for and he'll be in to discuss the results as soon as possible." She handed Sage paper towels to wipe the excess ultrasound gel off her chest and turned on the lights.

As soon as Sage was back in her normal clothes, Dad knocked.

"How'd it go?" he asked as Sage opened the door.

"Fine." Sage hopped back on the exam table to keep her injured ankle elevated.

"They were very professional," Mom added.

"Good, good." Dad pulled out his phone, eyes gleaming. "I just saw some photos of last night's game. Check this one out." He leaned against the table, turning the screen so Sage could see. Mom squeezed in on her other side, clasping her hands when she saw the image—a close-up of Sage spiking, her head just under the top of the net.

"Oh, Sage," Mom said, "you look like you're soaring!" She squeezed Dad's arm. "Send it to me! I've got to order some for the grandparents. And my desk at work."

Dad pushed back from the exam table, grinning like a little kid. "I already put it on Instagram. And made it my Facebook profile."

"Oh, my God, Dad," Sage said. "That's kind of embarrassing."

"What?" said Dad. "It's the perfect photo. My daughter—volleyball warrior."

Sage's face split into a huge smile. She couldn't help it.

"I'll upload it to your recruitment profile when we get home," he added.

A light knock made them all look up. In the excitement surrounding the photo, Sage had almost forgotten where they were. "Come in," she said.

A curly-haired man stepped into the room, a stack of papers in his hand. He looked younger than her parents, but not by much.

"Hey, everyone," he said. "I'm Dr. Friedman." He shook Sage's hand first.

"Good news, I hope?" asked Dad.

Dr. Friedman glanced at him, then turned his full focus to Sage. "I understand from Dr. Surrage that you're a fantastic athlete—"

"A Division One prospect," Dad cut in. "Guaranteed, actually." His face beamed, radiant.

Dr. Friedman nodded. "Which is why this is going to be really hard, and I feel horrible having to talk to you about it."

The air rushed from Sage's body, like she'd taken a ball to the chest. Mom wrapped a protective arm around her shoulders.

"Your EKG revealed a thickening of your left ventricle," Dr. Friedman continued. "That means the left side of the heart. Your echo results are very consistent with that, so I'm afraid there's no doubt that you have a condition called hypertrophic cardiomyopathy."

Sage took in his folded hands, the sad tilt of his head.

"Just say it!" she blurted, startling the room. Her mom tightened her grip, and Sage realized she was shaking. "What does that mean? For me, as a volleyball player?"

"It means," said Dr. Friedman, "you have a thickening of the heart muscle that's very dangerous. It's the number one cause of sudden death among athletes—"

"I could die?" Sage asked as Mom gasped.

"Yes," Dr. Friedman said. "Absolutely."

"How do we fix it?" Dad asked. It was his lawyer, take-action voice. Sage sat straighter. Whatever it took—surgeries, physical therapy, special diets—she'd do anything.

Dr. Friedman glanced at his papers, then back to Sage. "I know this is terrible for you to hear, Sage, but I'm afraid there's nothing medicine knows how to do right now that can make it safe for you to play volleyball."

Mom's hand went to her mouth. For a moment, no one breathed. Then Sage's cold bark of a laugh pierced the room. "No," she said. "You're wrong." She was fine. She felt fine. No, she felt *excellent*.

Dr. Friedman held out two pieces of paper to her, seemingly unfazed. "These are some images so you can see what I'm talking about." Sage just stared at him. Mom and Dad took the papers together.

"This is a normal heart," Dr. Friedman said. He pointed to the first sheet. "And this," he indicated the next image, "is what a heart with hypertrophic cardiomyopathy looks like. What Sage's heart looks like." He handed over more papers. "We'll go over everything and I will answer any and all questions, but I wanted to go ahead and give you some additional information—"

"No." Sage slid off the exam table, her eyes level with Dr. Friedman's. "You don't understand. I *have* to play. Volleyball is everything to me. My whole life!"

Again, Dr. Friedman didn't break eye contact. "I know this is difficult—"

"Difficult!" Sage's voice turned shrill. "You're trying to ruin my life!" She whirled on her parents. "I'm not stopping," she said. "You can't make me stop!"

Mom was full-on crying. She turned to Dr. Friedman. "There was a kid, um, in the newspaper last year . . ." Her voice had a fragility Sage wasn't used to hearing. "From Hendersonville. He died playing basketball. Is this hyper . . . whatever-it's-called? Is this what he had?"

"Hypertrophic cardiomyopathy." Dr. Friedman nodded. "Yes, I remember that. And yes, it is. Whenever you hear those stories, about sudden death in teen athletes, that's almost always the case."

Dad put his hand against the wall and slumped into the orange plastic chair by the exam table.

"So, Sage could have—" Mom covered her face. "Oh, God."

"Truthfully, she's fortunate she passed out," Dr. Friedman said. "For a lot of people, there are no warnings."

Sage shook her head so hard her brain hurt. "You're *wrong.* You have to be wrong. Dad, tell him!"

But Dad only stared at her. Sage had never seen her father look that way, the olive complexion she'd inherited from him so pale and faded. He looked like someone had opened a valve and drained away his spirit.

"Dad!"

He stood, regaining himself, and faced Dr. Friedman. "You're really telling me there's no other option? In this day and age, with all the medical advancements we have, there's *nothing* we can do to make it safe for her to play?"

Dr. Friedman's pained expression said everything. "Please try to understand," he told Sage. "It would be like playing Russian roulette with your life. Every practice. Every game." He kept his voice calm and even. Sage hated him for it.

"I want a second opinion," she spat.

"Of course." Dr. Friedman nodded. "That's a lot of information and it's not what you want to hear. You can see one of my partners here in the office, or I can send you to a practice in Charlotte. If there's someone else you have in mind, I can facilitate that as well."

Sage didn't know what she'd expected, but the fact that Dr. Friedman wasn't the tiniest bit bothered by her demand somehow made it worse. *Because he's that sure*, she thought. She covered her face.

"Is this the kind of thing that's not always clear?" Mom asked. "Can there be false positives?"

Dr. Friedman shook his head. "EKGs can sometimes give false positives, which is why we order the echocardiogram," he said. "The echo, however, is quite clear."

Sage heard her parents ask more questions and press for more specifics—*Is it genetic? Has she always had it? What's the next step?*—but everything sounded muffled and far away. Dr. Friedman answered it all evenly, occasionally pointing to the papers, like he had nothing else to do but talk about her defective heart. He mentioned more tests and the possibility of something called a defibrillator, but her brain wouldn't focus enough to understand it. Her mom still hadn't stopped crying.

If this was real—if she truly couldn't play volleyball again— none of the tests or next steps even mattered.

"But she can still go into games?" Dad asked. "For a few plays at least, maybe in the back row? As long as she doesn't jump or increase her heart rate?"

"I'm sorry," Dr. Friedman said. "She can't participate in any kind of competitive play at all."

"But practice is okay, right?" Mom asked, making a sad attempt to salvage her smeared mascara.

Dr. Friedman clasped his hands. "I understand this is hard to fathom, especially for someone as talented as Sage. But no. A person with this diagnosis cannot participate in sports at all, not even in a practice setting."

There was a terrible, heart-splitting sound, so raw it convulsed Sage's body, and dear God, why wasn't someone stopping it? She looked up, taking in her parents' wide eyes,

Dr. Friedman's worried frown, and it hit her like a serve to the face: the sound came from her.

"Sage." Mom tried to hug her.

"No." Sage pulled away, gulping air. This wasn't real. It couldn't be. She'd figure it out. She couldn't think was all. None of them could think straight in this awful, suffocating room. "I need to go," she said. "There's a scout at practice. I have to get back."

"Sage," Dad said. Why did he sound that way? What was wrong with him?

"Come on, baby." Mom wiped her face and took Sage gently by the arm. "Dad can finish here and set up your next appointment. I'll take you home."

CHAPTER NINE

LEN

LEN DIDN'T EVEN BOTHER TRYING TO CLOSE THE FRONT door gently. The glass panes bounced as she tugged the rusted knob and snapped the door into its jamb.

"I know, I know," she called out, waiting for Dad to chastise her from the next room, but the house stayed quiet. The thin scent of acrylics pricked her nose. Len peeked into the living room. One of Dad's easels was missing. A note hung from another: *Painting at the lake. Back by dinner.*

Unexpected good luck. She could be alone while she did this.

Len slipped into her room and dropped her bag on the bed before heading to the narrow desk in front of her closet. Her gaze, as usual, avoided the empty cobwebbed area below the single window, as if the space didn't exist. She added a recharged battery to the Canon that Fauna and Diane had given her two birthdays ago, and pulled the photography prompt list from her pocket, flattening it against the desk with her palm.

1. Vertical
2. Gravity
3. Reflection
4. Part of whole

The list went on—twenty-four prompts in total. Len slipped the camera strap over her neck, eyes glazing. The only word she could focus on was the one Ms. Saffron had used to describe her recent submissions: *sterile*.

She crumpled the list and, before she could lose her nerve, took off, letting the door slam as she jumped the stone steps that led to her thickly-treed front yard.

A horn blared from the four-lane highway that sat below the small cluster of homes opposite hers, followed by the loud belch of an 18-wheeler. Len ignored the tightening of her throat and snapped a few test shots, measuring the light.

Then she froze. She'd forgotten the first prompt.

Her gloved hands fumbled to uncrumple the paper. *Vertical.*

Len shielded her eyes, discomfort stretching over her like shadows from the large oaks. She needed more sleep. That's why she'd forgotten the word. Her eyes followed the tree trunks upward.

Vertical.

She could do something with that, something interesting, if she found the right subject.

A jet of sun spliced the leaves and fell across her nose, warming it. Why *had* she stopped shooting outside? Outside was wonderful. Outside, she felt like herself.

A tug gripped her insides, calling her to lie on the grass. She used to do that as a kid, letting the sun evaporate all her second-grade worries. And from the ground she could surely find an awesome shot, right? The perfect angle for *vertical*.

She squatted down, but couldn't quite bring herself to sprawl out. Some mushroom clusters caught her eye—they grew in the more heavily shaded areas. And some kind of beetle tiptoed along a particularly high dandelion weed. Disgusting. She remembered the stray cats that wandered the neighborhood, encouraged by the widowed man who left out food for them.

Len's neck tensed. The cats probably peed all over this grass. They probably had diseases, too. Maybe even parasites had dropped off them and lay in wait in the weeds. She imagined the diseases lurking, invisible to the human eye, biding time until an unsuspecting human sat on them.

Len crouched as far as she could without toppling over, then snapped a couple photos of the treetops. She checked the camera screen. The pictures were blurry.

Somewhere in the dense leaves above, a nuthatch twittered. Then a chickadee trilled its name. Len looked up, trying to discern their shapes in the branches. Nonni had taught her dozens of birdsongs, and chickadee was one of her favorites. "*Chick-a-dee-dee-dee,*" she mouthed along with the bird.

Before she realized it, she was scanning the branches for a blue jay. They weren't common guests in the yard, but they'd always been Nonni's favorite and were the first bird she'd searched for with the binoculars Nonni had given her on her seventh birthday.

Len still had those binoculars, somewhere.

"For our nature walks," her grandmother had said when she gifted them, and Len had grinned conspiratorially. Their walks were about much more than nature. They were Len's free space, her safe space to let her ideas tumble out unfiltered. The place she reported her grade school dilemmas. Nonni had always helped her work things out.

It was Nonni who first told Len that photography could be more than a hobby; Nonni who got her into a real photography class—a summer session offered through Root and Wings, the private art school downtown. Len's family never could have afforded it, but the instructor was in Nonni's book club and said Len could come for free.

"Where there's a will, there's a way." Nonni had winked at her. "Remember that, Len."

Len pushed aside her overgrown bangs and the memory with them.

The chickadee called again, and this time she saw it, the black cap of its white head a stark contrast to the leaf that half-concealed its fragile body. She zoomed in and snapped several close-ups before it flew off. When she checked to see if she'd gotten anything decent, Len's head went light. The last photo was slightly blurry from movement, but there was no mistaking the large bird that photobombed it: a blue jay.

Len scanned the trees for minutes, but it was no good. The bird was gone. She looked back at the photo.

Dad talked about signs sometimes. Being so in tune with what he and Mom called the Life Force that he felt the universe sent him messages sometimes—answers to questions about his path. Mom had had fewer signs than Dad, but she'd definitely received some, and Fauna used to talk endlessly about the sign that led her to the bakery where she'd met Diane.

She felt guilty about it, but privately Len had wondered if they all weren't mixing up signs with coincidences.

She replaced the lens cap and switched off the camera, the guilty feeling blooming wider. Those thoughts were probably *why* she'd never had a sign before. They were probably also why her brain was messing up so much lately, because it *was* messing up, wasn't it? She hadn't always been afraid of mushrooms and the possibility of cat pee on the grass. Had she? The fear jabbed her, so visceral that it was hard to remember. She rubbed her head, wondering if she was slowly losing her mind.

Above her, the chickadee called again, and Len looked up. "I'm just tired," she muttered, and she maybe kind of believed it. Anyway, she couldn't think about herself anymore, because she'd had a sign, finally. And she was going to act on it.

* * *

Fifteen minutes later, Len pulled Nonni's old Chevy C/K pickup into the parking lot of North Carolina Assisted Living in Hendersonville. She should not have driven it; Mom and Dad had let the insurance lapse last month, since Mom was the only one who really needed a car for work, and they needed the extra money. The C/K was strictly "for emergencies only."

Len eased into a shaded parking spot. This was an emergency of sorts, though, wasn't it? A *sign*. She thought Dad would think so, though she hadn't walked to the park to check. Besides, it still needed to be driven occasionally. Wouldn't cars die if they sat too long? She thought she'd heard that somewhere.

She grabbed her camera bag from the passenger seat and hopped out. The gardens surrounding North Carolina Assisted Living were magazine beautiful. *They should be*, Len thought, given what they had to pay, but then she felt guilty immediately. She didn't begrudge Nonni—only the fact that anyone should have to end up in a place like this, however lovely the landscape or skilled the nurses. Life wasn't just unfair. Sometimes it was downright malicious.

"She's in the atrium," the woman at the front desk said when Len signed in. "Do you know where that is?"

Len nodded. "Is Jamie with her?"

The woman checked a chart. "That's right."

"Thanks." Len followed the floral carpet to the east wing of the building. She couldn't remember the last time she'd visited Nonni without Mom. In the beginning, she'd come often, bringing flowers and photographs she'd taken, trying to recreate things how they used to be despite the new living arrangements. Nonni had recognized her then and could participate in a lot of the conversation. But her memory declined quickly and once—the last time Len had come by herself—Nonni had even been afraid of her. The head nurse, Jamie, said it wasn't personal, that it happened with dementia patients sometimes. But Len hadn't been able to shake the image: Nonni, who'd held her hand and kept her secrets, curling away from her in fear.

She'd only visited with Mom after that.

Len pushed the memory to her mind's back burner before her unease boiled over. The hall uncurled to reveal a spacious, window-filled room overlooking the gardens. Fresh gardenias in slim white vases scented the air. A few elderly patients peppered the room. One of them played cards with a younger man, probably his son.

Nonni sat near a pair of double doors, spools of cherry red and lilac blue yarn in her lap. Her fingers worked with expert speed. Jamie sat near her, reading from Nonni's favorite Mary Oliver book. A pang of longing shot through Len. How many times had Nonni read to her from that same book—had used its poems to quiet Len's fears?

When you're creative, Nonni told her once, pulling the book from the shelf, *your heart is more open. Your body's more sensitive and alive. We feel everything deeper, Lennie, even the bad things.*

She'd give anything for Nonni to read to her again. Her fingers ached to touch the pages once more, the paper worn to velvety smoothness by Nonni's raisined fingertips. Instead, Len's hands clenched in her gloves and she remembered a favorite phrase of Mom's: *Impossible dreams waste time and the soul.*

Nonni grinned, and Len followed her gaze outside.

Of course. The bird feeder.

Another sign? Len took a quick breath and plastered on a smile, steeling herself. "Nonni!" She nodded a hello to Jamie, and then walked close enough to her grandmother to let her know she was talking to her, but—she hoped—not too close to startle her. "Hey, Nonni," she said again. "How are you?"

Nonni's eyes flitted upward, her face open and childlike. "Hello there. What's your name?"

Len wasn't sure why her chest clenched; she'd known what was coming. She sat on a tufted plaid chair next to Nonni. "I'm Len," she said, squeezing the edge of the cushion. She stopped herself from saying "remember," like Jamie had taught her. Instead she added, "Your granddaughter."

"That's a nice name, Len. Unusual, but I like it." Nonni blinked. "Are you a new nurse?"

Jamie gave Len an encouraging smile, then laid the book aside and went to check on another resident.

"No, I'm not a nurse. I'm here to visit you." Len scooted her chair closer. "How are you, Nonni?"

Her grandmother stopped knitting. "Who's Nonni?"

Len closed her eyes. Opened them. She regained her smile. "I have something to show you. A photograph of a bird. Would you like to see it?"

Recognition lit Nonni's face. "I love birds."

"Yes, I know. Look here." Len held out her camera, a close-up of the blue jay on the screen. "The tail's a little blurry, but can you tell what it is?"

Nonni's fingers reached for the image. "A blue jay."

Tiny flakes of hope rose inside Len, warm and buttery as the rolls she used to help Nonni bake. "Do you remember we used to look for them together?" she asked. "I didn't even know there was one in our yard until I saw it in the photo. It made me think of you and, I don't know, I thought it might mean something?" She paused, embarrassed slightly. She and Nonni had always been the more skeptical ones in the family, although after everything that happened, they'd clearly been wrong.

Len tried again. "It seemed like a sign that I should visit today—that maybe you'd remember." She swallowed. "That you could help."

Nonni took Len's gloved hand in her own, patting it. "You remind me of someone."

Len's eyes widened. Nonni's memory did return sometimes, or at least pieces and flickers of it. Maybe today was one of those times. Wasn't that why the blue jay had sent her?

"Yes," Len encouraged. "I'm your granddaughter, Lennie. We used to be together, like, all the time."

"Lennie," Nonni repeated, nodding, and Len's hope sparked hot and white. Nonni blinked. "Do you work here?"

Len sat back, disappointment crashing through her. What had she expected? Did she really think a blue jay sent her here? A dull ache crept up her temples. But what were the odds? Plus, she and Nonni hadn't bought into the signs idea, and now they were suffering. Was that a coincidence, too, or a punishment? Some kind of cosmic karma?

Len pressed her hands together, bringing them in front of her face. She needed to get a grip. She needed to breathe. Her eyes closed, Dad's voice echoing through her. She needed a positivity mantra.

"Why are you sad?" asked Nonni.

Len's eyes blinked open, but her mind went as blurry as the blue jay's tail. No, not just her mind. *She* felt blurry, her whole self. She sat straighter, trying to remember a useful mantra, when her eyes snagged on a dark splotch on the carpet. Too large for ink. The wrong consistency for paint. Her pulse quickened. Probably a drink stain, that's all. But this was a care facility, so what if it was blood? Or urine? Or, dear God, remnants of feces? So many of the residents needed bathroom help. Had she stepped in it? What if they hadn't cleaned it correctly?

Her heartbeat dropped to her wrists, its pulsing wild enough to scare her. This wasn't right. She wasn't right.

Nonni patted Len's gloves again, yanking her from the dizzying thoughts. "Is it cold out there?" Nonni asked. "It looks nice."

Len stared at her amber-flecked brown eyes, the same eyes Len recognized from the mirror. Some part of her was still in there, wasn't it? The Nonni she'd grown up with, to whom she'd told all her secrets? Maybe she could still help, somehow. "Nonni," Len said. "You told me once, um, before we knew you were sick, you told me that sometimes you felt like you were going crazy." She licked her lips, not quite sure how to ask what she needed. "Did you worry about"—she swallowed—"things you never worried about before? Things that now really scare you?"

Nonni's head bobbed thoughtfully. "Mmhmm." She squeezed Len's hand.

"Nonni?" Len leaned in, so close that she breathed in the lavender essential oil Nonni had worn as long as she could remember. The scent of it cracked her voice. "I think I might be going crazy."

Nonni tilted her head sharply, her eyes boring into Len as they'd done when she was problem solving, and for a moment Len thought that this must all be a mistake. Nonni wasn't sick. She remembered Len perfectly and she'd say so and they'd leave here together and Len would take her home where Nonni could fix everything.

"My daughter!" Nonni said, so decisively that Len pulled away, startled. Nonni pointed at her. "That's who it is." She chuckled, pleased with herself. "You remind me of my daughter."

Len wasn't sure what to say. "Yes, well, I'm *her* daughter."

"She's about your age."

"No—" Len began.

"I wish she visited me," Nonni said. "My own daughter never visits me."

Len's vision darkened. "Oh, Nonni." Thank God Mom wasn't here. "She *does* visit you. Every day, nearly. She loves you so much."

Nonni looked back to the bird feeder, sadness pulling down her mouth.

"Please don't ever say that to Mom," Len begged. "Okay?" Reasoning with a late-stage dementia patient was nonsensical, Len knew, but she couldn't *not* say it. Had Mom already heard it? She never gave Len exact details from her visits, other than that Nonni was declining fast, but Len hadn't realized it was like this. What else was Mom not telling her?

When she looked back, Nonni was smiling again, eyes as wide as the deer's that sometimes passed through their yard. They were vivid eyes. Eyes still so full of life and stories. Len forced a small smile back.

"Hello," Nonni said. "What's your name?"

* * *

"Try not to take it personally," Jamie told her, walking Len to the edge of the atrium. "The disease, it's terrible."

"It's just happening so fast."

"Yes."

Len rubbed her arms, trying to shake a chill billowing from her insides, and took a look around the room. Another attendant was talking to the young man playing cards, helping him with something. "Wait," Len said. "Is that guy *a resident*?"

Jamie glanced back, confused. "They're all residents."

"But that one," Len said. "That man. He's so young, isn't he?"

Jamie let out a long sigh. "Relatively." She bit her lip. "Unfortunately, not the youngest I've ever seen, not by far."

The words jolted Len. "How old was the youngest?"

"You don't want to know."

"Tell me," Len said. "Please."

Jamie glanced back at Nonni, who had returned to her knitting. "When I worked in DC," Jamie said quietly, "I had a patient who was ten years old." She swallowed. "Hardest time of my professional life."

Len almost dropped her camera. "A *child* with dementia?"

"It's incredibly rare, of course. So rare. But it does happen. Oh, are you all right?"

But Len was already booking it down the hall.

CHAPTER TEN

SAGE

"YOU SURE YOU DON'T WANT TO COME?" ELLA ASKED SAGE after practice. "Since when do you turn down a chocolate cherry shake from Cookout?"

Sage gripped the bleachers, where she'd been camped out all practice, and managed a half-smile, her knuckles white from the effort. "Since I'm benched."

Ella gave her a sympathetic grin. "I'm sure you'll be cleared soon."

Sage couldn't make her mouth work. She'd told Kayla—and by extension, the team—that she was waiting on test results, which was technically true, since Dr. Friedman had agreed to send her echo to a hypertrophic cardiomyopathy specialist in Charlotte for a second opinion. She'd neglected, however, to let them know the most important part—that that specialist might confirm Dr. Friedman's diagnosis, and what that confirmation would mean— that Sage would never play another point of volleyball again.

Honestly, Sage wasn't sure her mouth could form the words.

Ella's look turned questioning, like she was waiting for Sage to respond. Sage thought she might throw up.

Kayla moved beside her. "Y'all go on ahead," she told Ella. "We'll meet up with you at the game."

For a second, Sage thought Kayla had guessed her secret. But then Kayla smiled at her, and Sage was sure she had no idea. "You should go with them," Sage said, hating to keep her friend from their team dinner ritual before football games. Cookout was Kayla's favorite when it came to fast food. "It's fine."

"Nah, I'm not feeling Cookout today." Kayla slung her gym bag across her chest. "Come on," she said. "Let's go to the bridge."

Relief gushed over Sage. "Yeah. Okay."

Fifteen minutes later, they were driving along the Blue Ridge Parkway, winding higher and higher through the mountains. Kayla sat at the wheel of the Subaru, since Sage hadn't felt like driving. Sage stuck a steaming curly fry in her mouth, the first real piece of food she'd eaten since yesterday afternoon. She still wasn't hungry so she hadn't protested when Kayla suggested Arby's, but she could never resist the fries. "There!" she said suddenly, tiny fry bits flying from her mouth. She pointed to the unmarked trail just before the curve.

Kayla slammed on the brakes and jerked the car into the tiny, just-wide-enough pull off. Sage grabbed onto the roof handle as gravel flew up and clunked the underside of the car.

"Sorry," Kayla said as the car lurched to a stop. "I don't know why I always think it's one turn up."

Sage grabbed the Arby's bag and led the way to the overgrown trail, which looked more like a deer path than an actual hiking trail. Kayla fell in step with her, pushing aside weeds and snapping fallen twigs with almost every step. They couldn't see the ravine yet, and wouldn't if they stayed on the path, but they never stayed on the path. Instead, they made their way to the root side of a massive fallen oak tree that formed a natural bridge to the other side of the ravine, almost twenty feet away.

Sage climbed up first, testing her footing. Although the trunk was thick—more than three feet in diameter—it was ancient, too, and covered in green lichen. The bark in a few places looked more like mulch.

Kayla let out a sigh. "We need to come here more often. There's something about this place, you know?"

Sage did know, and she knew that's why Kayla had brought her here. They'd discovered it by taking a wrong turn on a family hike a few years before, and as soon as they'd earned their licenses, it became their secret shared sanctuary: the place they came to when one of them needed to get away. She wasn't sure how to explain why they kept returning, except that the place had an energizing *feel* about it, a way of reminding a person there was more than the small orb of existence they dwelled in. A way of helping them just *be*.

Sage glanced down. The ravine wasn't extreme—maybe twenty-five or thirty feet—but the mossy boulders at the bottom would make a fall treacherous. Probably deadly. She suspected that's part of why she and Kayla liked it—the risk entwined with beauty. It was a little twisted, now that she thought about it.

"Careful." Kayla tapped a darkened piece of the trunk with her sneaker, and it broke away, revealing a stream of scurrying beetles. "Looks like it's rotted some since we've been here. There might be other places."

Sage nodded, bizarrely thankful for the possible threat, something else to focus on besides her heart. Stepping carefully, she found her way to her favorite perch, a nook between the main trunk and an offshoot that formed a surprisingly cozy seat. As soon as she took it, the tension around her heart released. Some of it, anyway. Out here, with the damp, earthy scents and the soothing swish of wind-blown leaves, she could almost pretend she'd entered another world—a world where her heart was normal and she'd play volleyball for as long as her legs would hold her.

Kayla sunk onto the trunk beside her, the crackling Arby's bag dissolving Sage's fantasy. "So."

Sage couldn't look at her. She was thankful Kayla had known to take her here, known she couldn't possibly have fun at a restaurant with the team today, but she wasn't sure she could answer Kayla's unasked question.

"Thanks," she said instead. "For this. I needed to get away."

Kayla's shoe nudged her leg. "What really happened yesterday," she asked, "with those tests?"

Sage dug her nails into the tree bark. "They think"—*game face*, she told herself, *game face*—"that maybe my passing out has to do with my heart." She hoped Kayla couldn't hear the strain in her voice.

"What does that mean, exactly?" Kayla took a huge bite of her crispy chicken sandwich.

Somewhere, a woodpecker's knocks echoed. Sage glanced up, pretending to try to locate the bird, but all she saw was a flash of blue. "I don't really know. That's why they're doing the tests."

Bullshit, she called on herself.

"Yeah, but, like, you're gonna be okay, right?" Kayla took another bite of chicken. "It's not, like, super serious or anything?"

Sage kept her eyes on the trees. "I mean, it's my heart."

"Right, but they would have told you if—"

"I'm fine," Sage blurted, meeting Kayla's eyes, because she couldn't say otherwise. Her mouth literally could not form the words. Speaking it might somehow make it real, and she was still waiting for the second opinion. In this moment, there was still hope.

"Okay, good." A small drop of dressing had caught in the corner of Kayla's mouth. "You've just been, I don't know, weird today. I thought it was something worse."

Sage stared at her. Part of her wanted Kayla to guess it. Maybe more than part of her. She couldn't say the words, but she could nod her head if Kayla said them for her. And why couldn't she? They communicated with eyebrow jerks and the subtlest of body tells. They finished each other's sentences. She'd noticed something was wrong enough to bring her here. Surely she'd figure it out. That was a best friend's job, wasn't it?

Kayla unwrapped the rest of her sandwich.

Sage turned toward her slightly. *Notice!* she willed Kayla. *I need you to notice.* If Kayla just prompted her a little, maybe she could force the words out.

"I have some news," Kayla said.

Everything Sage hadn't said gushed out of her. She pieced her game face back together. "Oh?"

Kayla nodded, radiant. "You had a rough day yesterday, and I didn't want to tell you until I found out more about your test." Her eyes narrowed, a question.

"I told you I'm okay," Sage snapped. "What is it?"

Kayla's smile cracked her face wide open. "Coach called me last night." She clapped her hands together, little-kid excited. "UNC called about me. *Chapel Hill!*"

Sage's hand reached out, faltering as she felt for the tree trunk.

"Whoa!" Kayla grabbed her other arm. "Careful, girl."

Sage righted herself, blinking. "That's . . . wow." Her mouth closed. Opened again. "Kayla, that's . . ." She went light-headed and for a moment couldn't think of a word that applied. Then it came to her. "Wonderful." She forced the edges of her mouth upward. This was her best friend. She *would* smile for her. "It's really wonderful."

Kayla put her hands up, trying to temper the celebration. "I know you might go someplace better, but if you decide not to and my offer comes through . . . I mean, it's no guarantee, just because they're interested, but Coach says they'll be scouting me pretty heavy. And I'm sure you'll get one, since they've been talking to you since last spring." The cords in her neck tightened. "Sage, we could play for the same school! Maybe start together one day!"

She doesn't know, Sage told herself, *because you didn't tell her.* But another part of her whispered, *She should have known anyway.*

"I couldn't tell anyone else, because jealousy and stuff, you know? It sucks."

Sage's forehead went sticky with sweat. *You can't tell her now. You can't make this moment about you.* "Yeah," she whispered. "Sucks."

"And I still have to get the offer, of course, but the fact that they called Coach—"

"It's awesome," Sage said, wondering how it had gotten so hot in the shade. "Really. And you just keep doing what you do. I'm sure you'll get an offer." Her fingers clenched, breaking off bits of bark. "I know it."

I hope you don't. Sage jolted at the thought, repulsed by it. But it was true, she realized. She put her hands to her head.

"What's wrong?" Kayla asked.

"Nothing." Sage forced a laugh, but it sounded semi-hysterical. She shut it down instantly and reached for her phone. "What time is it? Ian's game."

"Oh, right!" Kayla crinkled the empty sandwich wrapper and stuffed it into the paper bag. "We should go." She stood up, offering her hand to Sage.

"Kayla? I—"

"Yeah?" She pulled Sage up so they were face-to-face. *Look at me,* Sage thought. *How can you not see it?*

Kayla raised her eyebrows.

"I'm really proud of you," Sage said. And she was. She *was*. Just because she might never play again, that didn't mean she couldn't—*shouldn't*—be proud of Kayla. "Congratulations."

The branches quivered above them, sending a ray that brightened Kayla's smile even more. It was odd, Sage thought, how Kayla's news ripped her heart, but the condition that could potentially kill her—she couldn't feel that at all.

CHAPTER ELEVEN

LEN

LEN DIDN'T REMEMBER DRIVING HOME. SHE SORT OF remembered unlocking the truck and unsticking the brake, but then she was parking Nonni's pickup in the carport behind her house. The not remembering might have been concerning if she hadn't been struggling to breathe.

She unclipped her seatbelt and tried to fill her lungs, which weren't cooperating. Her fingers tingled, like she'd submerged them deep into icy water. Her heart slammed at an unnatural rate.

I'm dying.

Len jammed her eyes shut and shoved her foot against the brake, like that might slow the terror and give back control of her body. But it was pointless. Her hands shook, and she was sweating everywhere. She was coming undone.

This is it, Len thought. Mom and Dad would come home and find her slumped over the steering wheel, her mouth hanging open, wide and ungainly, because she was probably about to have a seizure.

A high-pitched moan scraped her throat, because what if they *didn't* find her? Why would they think to look in Nonni's pickup, after all? She might stay slumped in there for days, bleary eyed and steeped in her own vomit, before the smell caught someone's attention.

Her eyes flew open. Why would she think that, something so grotesque? That wasn't like her; it had never been like her. Not before. Her fingers dug into the wheel, desperate to hold something. Because it was true, her worst fear, the one she kept pushing to the deepest part of herself. She couldn't deny it any longer: she was losing her goddamned mind.

Her body convulsed, cold suddenly, and she curled against the seat, aching to temper the bitterness in her stomach. It was fitting, though, wasn't it? She would suffer while dying—painfully and alone—because poetic justice was a bitch. She deserved this. Maybe some part of her even wanted it. We call our destinies to ourselves, Dad always said.

"No!" Len screamed, arching suddenly and slamming her head back against the headrest. She did *not* want to die—was terrified of dying, actually. Whatever was happening, whatever was trying to take over her, she would battle it. She would tear out its heart and throat.

She clamped her gloved hands over her ears and screamed again. It was a horrible sound, horrible to know it came from her. But it seemed to break something, too—something she couldn't name but knew instinctively needed to be shattered.

And then, as fast as it had descended, the terror abated. Her heart still thudded, but there was feeling in her hands again. Her brain cleared, her jumbled thoughts burning up like the last shreds of fog at sunrise. She took a long gasp, air finally sinking deep into her grateful lungs.

When she could think again, when she was sure she could stand, Len scrambled out of the truck, slipping on the long grass as she made her way to the house and her room. She flipped open her school-issued laptop and threw a few search words into Google.

It took about three seconds to discover she'd had a panic attack. There were all the symptoms, lined up on the screen.

Shortness of breath. Sweating. Chills. Overwhelming feelings of doom and despair. Certainty that life will end.

Her eyes scanned more hits. *Possible causes: severe stress, health conditions.*

She cleared the search bar and forced herself, hands shaking, to type three more words: dementia in teenagers.

There it was, in stark black letters on the white screen: *Frontotemporal dementia. Frequent causes of childhood dementia.*

She skimmed the rest of the hits, the words slamming into her like punches, again and again. Her eyes kept losing focus.

It was real. Of course it was—why would Jamie lie?

Len widened her eyes, forcing them to refocus and concentrate. She read just enough to learn that it was incurable and often genetic, then snapped the laptop shut.

But Jamie had said it was rare. *So rare.*

Doesn't matter, her brain spat back. This explained everything, and she knew it was true. The blue jay *had* been a sign, leading her to the interaction with Jamie. She clenched her hands into fists, thudded them against her forehead.

She'd kept asking what was wrong with her. The universe had given her an answer.

The landline rang in the kitchen. Mom, probably. A new wave of nausea struck her. How would she tell Mom?

Len thought about Mom's expression when she'd returned from Nonni's the night before, tired and hollow, but how she'd talked to Fauna for a whole hour anyway. And last week, how Len had woken at 4 a.m. to discover Mom making Nonni's favorite molasses candy because that was the only time she could find to do it.

She never visits me, Nonni had said.

The phone rang again. Len steadied herself against the desk, trying to lasso her mind under control. Her thoughts seemed outside of her somehow, descending into a spiral that was spinning faster than she could understand. A tiny part of her wondered if maybe her thinking wasn't completely adding up, but that didn't matter. Probably her uncertainty was just a symptom of the disease.

She pushed herself to standing. The phone had stopped. The emptiness of the house clawed into her, pricked the back of her neck, and for a fuzzy second, she forgot. She looked at the space beneath the window.

"No," Len said, but she was too weak; she'd let her guard slip. The memories spilled into her consciousness, dragged her down to their depths.

Blue lights whirling, reflecting in her bedroom window. Another reflection, blue. Everything so very, very blue.

Len bent over, dry heaving. She reached for her camera, the weight of it bringing a small drop of calm to her center, then bolted for the kitchen and scribbled a quick note. It was Friday, wasn't it? Maybe there was a home game. She had to get out of here, lose herself in a crowd of people. She had to escape all the blue.

CHAPTER TWELVE

SAGE

SAGE SAT WITH KAYLA IN THE STUDENT SECTION OF THE concrete bleachers, crammed between friends of the varsity volleyball team and the screams of fanatical parents. Everyone was so focused on the rivalry game that no one noticed how little she spoke or how she only clapped when Southview intercepted the ball, instead of yelling her heart out every play like she usually did.

Southview came up short on third down, so the field-goal kicking team took the field, led by Ian. Sage's chest twinged as she remembered his knock on her door last night. How he'd told her, in his endearingly awkward sophomore-boy way, that he was sorry and that it was okay if she didn't want to come to his game; he understood.

Of course she would come, she'd said. Why wouldn't she?

Ian had fidgeted and shrugged, his pity obvious and horrible as a real-life monster. And Sage had known in that moment that once her secret spilled out nothing could ever be right again. People would treat her as weak, would think she couldn't handle the most ordinary things. That her *own brother* had already started.

"I'll be there," she'd said, and slammed the door.

It could still be okay, Sage told herself. The second opinion doctor hadn't called yet. They'd thought they'd hear today, but maybe it was a good thing they hadn't.

A kid from Sage's class spun the football laces out, and Ian nailed it through the uprights.

"Thatta boy!" Dad yelled, calling Sage's attention to where he stood with other team parents, above and to the left of the students. Mom was standing there, too, clasping another mom's hand and jumping along with the rest of the crowd.

"Damn," Kayla said, elbowing Sage. "Ian's a powerhouse. We might actually pull it off."

Sage glanced at the scoreboard. Southview was down 12–14, but there were still three minutes on the clock. Everyone around her was jumping and pointing, screaming about defense. Southview hadn't defeated Asheville in six seasons, which made this much more than a game for her school. It was a matter of pride. Of identity and worth.

Sage loved that about sports. How games were always about so much more than the actual physical process of scoring more points than the other team.

"Asheville's fumbled!" the announcer boomed. "The ball is out!"

Whistles trilled as bodies piled on the ball. Dad yelled louder, his voice scraping hoarse, like he could make the ball Southview's by sheer force of will. Sage turned again, ready to smile at him, when she noticed: Mom was gone.

She strained her neck, squinting up the long rows and then down to the people milling and crowding along the sidelines. Mom would never leave at the apex of a game like this, *never*. Not when Ian could be up any minute. Unless . . .

"Go Rams!" Ella screamed. "Go Blue!"

A steady chant of "Asheville sucks!" grew louder and louder as the band played a short riff. Noise squeezed itself into every corner.

"Southview has it!" the announcer roared, just as Sage spotted her mom behind the far end zone, close to the entrance gate, her white sweatshirt bright against the graveled entrance. Both her hands pressed against her ears.

She's on the phone.

Sage almost leapt from the bleacher. "Excuse me!" she said, sliding between the press of bodies and down the steps. "Coming through. Sorry."

"Where are you going?" Kayla called after her. "There's only fifty more seconds!"

Sage waved her hand, almost tripping over an empty soda cup. She didn't slow until she reached the entrance.

Mom stood with her back to the field, hugging herself. One of her hands still clutched her phone.

Sage walked up behind her. "That was them, wasn't it?" Sage asked. "The Charlotte office?" Her throat tightened. "The results?"

Cheers went up from the bleachers as the announcer reported a long pass, a Southview first down. Mom looked at her, and Sage knew what the specialist had said. "Tell me," she whispered anyway.

Mom's face was red and streaked, but Sage needed her to say it. It was her life about to be ruined, and Sage needed to know it was real. Mom could at least say the words.

"Sage, baby." Mom's head gave the tiniest shake. "I'm so sorry."

Sage hadn't known how much hope she'd harbored until that instant. She'd thought she'd prepared herself, but no. Deep down, in her heart of hearts, she'd really thought she'd be cleared.

Noise swelled around them, and Sage had the feeling she should cry or do something. Mom looked like she was waiting for it, bracing herself for the break. Sage waited, too, searching inside herself.

There was nothing. She was empty.

"Sage," her mom said, and the spell was broken. Sage's feet pounded the pavement toward the exit gate. Faster. Faster.

"You can't run!" Mom screamed after her, the fear in her voice a living, writhing thing. It hooked itself into Sage, forcing her to slow down. *Fine,* Sage seethed. She would slow down. She would walk. But she would not break down here. She *would not.*

"The pass comes up short, and it's fourth down," said the announcer. "Now the field goal squad is out for the fifth time. Zendasky has been four for four, but his longest field goal is forty-one yards. Can he push it another five tonight?"

Sage stopped. She was so close to the exit gate, mere feet, but Ian . . . She turned, forced herself back past Mom and to the chain link fence that kept spectators off the field and the track that surrounded it. She spotted Ian at the far end, counting off his paces as he lined up to kick.

"I'm sorry," he'd said earlier, when he'd cleared the echo he'd had that morning because apparently her heart condition was genetic. "I'm sorry I asked you to be here." And she'd called him an idiot and hugged him, and it felt good that he'd wanted her there, that even at sixteen he'd needed his older sister in case his news echoed hers. But his heart had checked out, and of course she was happy for him. It wasn't his fault she'd lost the genetic roll of the dice.

Her face twisted as she recalled the way Mom had hugged Dad, how her tears spilled as much as they had after Sage's results. How they'd meant something completely different.

Sage grabbed on to the fence, thankful Mom hadn't followed her back to the field. Her eyes locked onto her brother's back. She visualized the ball piercing the goal posts dead center, the same way she envisioned her own serves before she took them. "Drill it, Ian," she whispered.

Ian shook out his hands and tapped his right foot behind him, his pre-kick ritual. Sage closed her eyes, her skin tingling with the energy of the stadium's collectively held breath.

"And it's GOOOOOD!" the announcer cried. "Ian Zendasky has kicked five for five field goals and the Rams have won! The Rams have won! For the first time in six years, Southview has defeated Asheville High!"

Sage opened her eyes to watch Ian joyously tackled, then hoisted by his teammates. Students rushed the field and a low hum grew into a buzz, a chant. "I-AN. I-AN."

At midfield, Ian threw off his helmet, his sweaty face aglow beneath the stadium lights. Sage knew that look, the ecstasy that accompanied a triumph earned from years of hard work and dedication. The fence dug into her palms. She lived for that feeling. She would never have it again.

Without warning, her gut revolted. She was going to vomit. The bathrooms were too far, and already the exit was backed up with Asheville's defeated fans trying to beat the mess of traffic.

Another belly lurch and she was moving, away from the exit and Mom's pity for her, desperate to find somewhere she could stay unnoticed. She couldn't bring attention to herself. This was Ian's moment, and she would not destroy it.

She dodged the crush of people descending the visiting stands, then realized she could go beneath them, where they stored the hurdles. Yes, that was perfect.

She barely made it. As soon as she slipped between the fencing under the metal stands, her knees gave out, her stomach contents splashing to the stale, powdery dirt. She was pretty sure some got in her hair.

Someone made a gagging noise. "Oh, my God," a voice said. "Are you okay?"

Sage's head shot up. She recognized that voice. Her eyes adjusted to the dark, assembling a figure deeper inside the bleacher's underbelly.

"Len?" Sage pushed herself up, wiping her mouth. "What are you—" Her eyes took in what Len held, a camera. "You're taking pictures?" she said, recoiling slightly. "Here?"

"I needed a vertical," Len said, whatever that meant. She pointed to the aluminum beams around them. "The bleachers have interesting lines," she added, and slipped the camera around her neck. It was a *nice* camera, the kind that professionals use. Len still had on her gloves and the too-big sweatshirt, her hair loose and straggled. As she looked Sage over, something in her face changed.

"Oh." Len's voice was soft. "I'm so sorry."

Sage wiped her hands on her shorts. "What?"

"I hadn't noticed before," Len said. "But now . . ." She nodded. "I see it on you."

"What are you talking about?" Sage said, because she was pretty sure Len didn't mean vomit. She ran a hand through her hair, just in case.

Len stepped closer, a tiny crease in her forehead. "It's all over you."

"*What?*"

Len's eyes narrowed, like it should be obvious. "Loss."

Above them, footsteps clanked and banged. Bands of light cut through the darkness as fans exited, letting the stadium light slip through the emptying bleachers. A long, bright strip fell across Len's face. Sage clenched her fists. Kayla had been right. Len was the definition of bizarre. Maybe even downright freaky.

"Okay," Sage said shakily. "That's a super weird thing to say."

Len stared at her, her expression unchanged, and Sage wondered if she'd even heard.

"I'm gonna go now," Sage said, backing out and almost tripping on a hurdle. Len remained in the darkness.

As she resurfaced, Sage's phone pinged with texts—Kayla probably, wondering where she was—but she left it in her pocket and kept her head down, blending into the exiting crowd. She wouldn't be joining the celebratory bonfires tonight.

Mom stood waiting right where she'd left her, hands wringing. But at least she'd stopped crying. At least Sage had a ride home. The team hadn't returned from the locker room, which was good, because Sage couldn't face Ian, not yet. She was proud of him and she'd tell him so, but not right now.

"I know," Mom said before she had to say anything. "Ian will understand." As Mom put an arm around her, Sage had the distinct feeling someone was watching. She whirled back to the bleachers.

People filed out in a steady stream. Behind them, under the stands, there was only darkness. Len Madder was nowhere to be seen.

CHAPTER THIRTEEN

LEN

LEN WOKE IN A COLD SWEAT, HER DREAM REMNANTS CLAW-
ing to remain in her consciousness. *She'd been with Nonni.
They'd sat together on the football bleachers, and Len showed
her how to use the Canon. The field was empty and still, but the
air swirled with color; blue jays circled and dove in an elaborate air dance. Len had summoned them somehow, and Nonni
had giggled and clapped like a young girl, snapping photo
after photo.*

Murky morning light leaked from the window, and Len
swung her socked feet to the side of her bed, the heaviness of
her legs jarring. Dream Len had been weightless, she realized,
and flying—somehow a blue jay but still a girl, too. She tried to
recall the exact feeling—it had been perfect, she was sure of it,
daring and free. But her body couldn't quite recall it, the dream
dimming with every moment. *She'd landed next to Nonni—that*

she remembered—*and her grandmother's long, pianist fingers moved deftly between the focus ring and shutter-release. "Look,"* Nonni *said as Len fluttered back and forth, laughing and playful.* "Look, *Lennie."*

Len turned, took in Nonni's body, Nonni's hands, Nonni's short, storm-white hair. Then her grandmother lowered the camera, and Len locked eyes on her own face.

Outside, the wind chimes tinkled faintly, the sounds dissolving the last of the dream images. Not the feeling, though. That clung to her, dark and sticky, like a warning.

Len made herself stand, made herself slip on the sweatshirt that hung over the wooden desk chair. She grabbed the chair as the weight of yesterday, of Jamie's revelation, crashed back over her. Was the dream another sign? Further proof she was going the way of Nonni, her brain slowly dissolving?

Sounds crept under her door. Then the warm scent of tea. Len pulled on her gloves. Maybe she should tell her parents after all.

She found them in the living room, Mom draped along the sofa, Dad rubbing her bare feet. Both of them spoke softly. It was a tender moment. A private moment. And Len was an intruder. She tried to back up, but the floor creaked, giving her away.

"Lennie!" Dad said. "How's our girl?"

Mom wiped her face quickly, a too-wide smile pulling her cheeks tight. It couldn't hide the evidence: she'd been crying.

"What's wrong?" Len asked.

"Oh, nothing." Mom waved her over to them. "I'm just tired is all. How are you?"

Len gave a small shrug, stepping around several canvases to reach the sofa. She perched herself on the edge, next to Mom. "Do you guys think dreams mean anything?"

"Definitely," said Dad.

"Carl Jung certainly thought so," said Mom. "And Freud, although that man had major issues, so I tend to ignore him."

Len raised her eyebrows.

"Sorry," Mom said. "Never mind. What was your dream?"

Len tried to pull back the wispy fragments. "Well, it was about Nonni," she said. "We were together, taking pictures, and there were blue jays, and—Mom?"

Tears spilled down Mom's cheeks. She covered her mouth.

"Are you okay?" Len asked.

"Sorry," Mom said again. "I just—" She tried to laugh, which only made her look more pitiful. "Dad and I were just talking about her before you came in."

Dad nodded. "I bet you picked up on that energy."

Len took a deep breath, her nerve starting to give out. If she was going to tell them what she learned, about childhood dementia and her own symptoms, she had to do it now.

"I need to tell you something," Len and Mom said at the exact same time.

"Whoa," said Dad. Mom rubbed Len's gloved hand, her smile shaking.

"It's okay," Len said. "You can go."

Mom slipped her palm beneath Len's and squeezed her hand. "I know you know that things have been a little tight lately." She winced, like the words physically hurt. "And I don't want you to worry, because we've got things under control, but, ugh, I'm sorry. I'm such a crier!" She pinched the bridge of her nose. Dad moved closer and rubbed her shoulder. She moved her hand from Len's and placed it on top of his. "We found out last week that Nonni needs to switch medications, and the new one, it's, well, it's more than the last." She pulled out a crinkled tissue and wiped her nose. "Dad's taken a part-time job with a painting company, which will help offset things a little, but we just need to be a bit more careful with money for a while, okay?"

Len wasn't sure how they could be any more careful, but she nodded anyway. Things must be much worse that she imagined. Dad had had a lot of random jobs to boost his cobbled income from commissions, but they were always in line with his artistic sensibilities—local theater set designs, visiting art professor summer workshop leader, that kind of thing. He would never have taken a job with a house painting company—a job that's not only *not* creative but that would take time away from his own projects—unless things had gotten dire.

"Maybe," Len said, "what if I got a job?"

"No." Mom's voice was the end of a sentence. A solid wall. "Your job is school, to get good grades, to get yourself into a good college."

"But if I can't pay for it . . ." Len didn't know why she was arguing. How could she get a job when her brain was falling apart?

Mom sat up, pulling her legs off Dad's lap. "There are scholarships. What about that one your teacher wrote home about last semester? The Melvin?"

"The Melford."

"Yes, that one."

"It's really hard to get, Mom. It's not—"

"Your teacher told us you can do it. Len, I know you can do it. Dad does too. You just have to believe."

Even tucked in gloves, Len's hands went cold. There was no use arguing with her parents when it came to college. They just didn't get it. Sometimes she thought they didn't want to, like they were happier believing it was some kind of supernatural thing that made wishes come true. That if you worked hard enough, if you tried your best, you could go and somehow magically not have to pay for it.

She wished Ms. Saffron had never told them about the Melford Scholarship, had never implied that Len had a chance. Ever since, both of them had assumed it was a given, not a very, very slim longshot.

Len stood up, suddenly conscious of all the flecks on the sofa. What were those?

"Wait," Mom said. "What was it you wanted to tell me?"

Len looked down at her, curled up like something fragile. The skin of her face lacked its usual color and hung looser than it should on her cheekbones. Deep half-moons sunk below her eyes, mirroring—she just realized—the ones on Dad's face. Had either of them slept in days? Weeks?

How could Len drop this on them? That their daughter's mind was slowly unraveling, that she probably had childhood dementia, and, sorry, there was nothing they could do, but by the way, the medical care would surely bankrupt them? They didn't even have healthcare.

Her legs—the parts that had touched the sofa—went tight and twitchy. It wasn't like telling them could change anything. There was nothing anyone could do.

"Len?"

"Nothing," she said. "Never mind. I'm gonna get a shower."

Her parents' eyebrows bent, confused, but she left the room before they could speak. As she passed through the kitchen, the phone on the wall rang.

"Grab that for me, Len?" Dad asked. "I'm expecting a call."

Len slipped off the receiver. "Hello?"

"Lennie?"

Len's chest convulsed. The voice was Fauna's. And she was crying.

"Len," her sister said, "is that you? Hello?"

Len's mouth opened. But then there was blue everywhere, bleeding across her memories and blurring her vision. Sirens. Wall. Lips. Terrible, terrible blue.

She couldn't do this. Her whole body went hot. Slimy. She needed a shower. The word snagged in her brain, banging again and again. *Shower. Shower. Shower.* She couldn't do anything until she took a shower. That would make things okay again. That would help her breathe.

"Lennie?" Fauna said. "*Please*, talk to me."

The phone fell from her fingers, hit the floor with a sickening crack.

"Everything okay?" Dad called from the sofa, but she was no longer around to hear.

CHAPTER FOURTEEN

SAGE

FOR THE FIRST TIME IN HER RECENT MEMORY, SAGE DID not join Ian for their regular Saturday morning run. Sage, who wasn't sure if she'd slept at all, heard the familiar sounds of Ian exiting his room, the water from the sink as he brushed his teeth. He paused at her door, which made Sage both happy (because he hadn't forgotten her) and then so dejected that she'd rolled over and let herself sink into the depths of her sadness until it resembled something like sleep.

Now, three hours later, Sage sat on her bed, motionless. Her parents stood in her room, saying something about it not being healthy to stay in bed, but Sage's attention faded in and out, like XM radio on the Parkway.

"There are still plenty of options," Mom was saying, pacing between the two windows. She threw open the blinds as high as possible. "Coach and I have talked at length."

"Nhu-Mai's been in touch with some friends from med school, too," said Dad. "They've got connections to some of the top heart specialists in the country and, oh, I wonder—" His fingers typed furiously at his phone.

"There's absolutely no reason you couldn't be a college coach," Mom said. "Coach said so himself. With your talent, no reason at all."

"I know I met someone involved in this clinic," Dad said. "I must be looking in the wrong file." He poured back over the screen.

Sage stared at them. They were fixers, both of them, real get-it-done-ers. It was something she'd always admired, a quality she supposed they'd passed on to her. *Don't take no for an answer. Hard work solves everything. Do something over and over until you are the absolute best, until you get exactly what you want.*

"Yes," Dad said. "Found it."

The problem with fixers, Sage realized, is that their whole system is inherently flawed. They can only function if a solution to a problem actually exists.

"Is this person gonna give me a way to play?"

Mom stopped pacing. Dad met Sage's eyes. "Well—"

"Unless they have a way for me to play again, there's no point calling any clinic."

Dad's brow crinkled. "They might be close to a solution," he said. "Maybe a cure in the works."

"Close enough it could help me?" Sage asked. "You're telling me that, even though Dr. Friedman didn't say anything about it, you think someone else is so close to a cure for this that it could save my volleyball career?"

Dad's face twitched. He prepared for every question, which made him a phenomenal attorney. But he wasn't prepared for this. "Probably not," he admitted. "But we could—"

Sage zoned out again, cocooning herself with the numb static of her mind. None of this felt real, so maybe it wasn't. Maybe if she just pretended it was a terrible dream, a supremely real nightmare, it would disintegrate the same way vampires were supposed to crumble in the sun.

Her eyes caught on the long rectangles of sunlight that poured from her windows, falling just short of where she sat on the bed. If only what stood in her way was an actual vampire. She'd have absolutely no qualms about stabbing it through the heart. She'd do it twice, maybe three times, for good measure.

Mom was talking. Slowly, her voice chipped a crack in the static, and Sage could make out her words again.

"I think that's a good option," Mom said. "Don't you?"

Sage blinked. "Huh?"

Mom frowned, registering that Sage hadn't heard most of what she'd said. "Coach said you can get on as a manager with a college team," she explained, "and transition to a coaching position from there. Probably even a big-time program. He's got lots of strings he can pull."

Something ugly wedged itself in Sage's throat. What Mom suggested, being so close to people living out *her* dream, watching them every single day, while she had to sit there? Her body shook with loathing.

"Sage?" Dad started for her, but Sage waved him off. She curled tight against her pillow.

"She might not want to be a manager," another voice said.

Sage startled. Ian watched her from the beanbag chair beneath a shelf overflowing with MVP plaques and trophies. His long body hunched forward, elbows on his knees. Had he been there the whole time?

"Why?" Mom looked genuinely confused.

"It sounds like a fresh form of hell," Ian said. "To me, anyway. Being so close to other people doing what you can't do anymore."

Sage gave him a tiny, grateful nod.

"Right," Mom said. "Okay, we won't decide anything now." She rubbed her forehead. "Ian, honey, what time do I need to drop you at the field today?" Her eyes cut to Sage. "I mean, I'm sorry. I shouldn't have—" Her face buckled, close to tears.

"You can still talk about sports in front of me," Sage snapped, fire blooming inside her. "I'm not fragile. I can handle it."

"I know you're not—" Mom covered her eyes, but tears slipped around her fingers. "I'm sorry, Sage. I don't—" Her voice cracked. "I don't know what to do."

Dad slipped his arm around her, like she was the one needing comfort. Sage didn't want to feel pissed at them. They were trying to help, she knew that. Nothing prepares you for this kind of shit. Still, sparks of rage flicked inside her. Just the smallest breath, she knew, could ignite them. "I wanna be alone now," she managed.

Dad nodded. Mom kissed Sage's forehead and said she'd be back to check on her, that they'd get through this together.

"Would you like to go to the school later, to the gym?" Dad asked. "I could pass for you, if you wanted."

"Alek, no." Mom looked like he'd suggested that Sage set herself on fire. "It's too risky."

"It's not like she can't *touch* a volleyball," Dad said. "Dr. Friedman said she can bump and set, minor things like that, as long as her heart rate doesn't increase." He glanced at Sage, expression pained. "As long as it's on her own."

Sage curled back into her pillow. It was one of the most unfair things about the whole treacherous business. She didn't have to never move, but she'd been ordered to "listen to her body." To pay acute attention to any changes in her breath or heart rhythm. To slow activity immediately if she felt in any way stressed.

Dr. Friedman had called Sage personally as soon as she and Mom got home from last night's game. Sage suspected that Mom had called him after getting the second opinion, but he'd apparently requested to speak to Sage. Sage had asked, in every way possible, why she couldn't listen to her body while playing on her team, but for as concerned as he was, Dr. Friedman was just as firm as he'd been in his office. Ethically, she could not be cleared to play. There was no changing that. No loopholes, no way around it, nothing at all he could do. Sage simply could not participate in any kind of practice or game setting.

"What do you think, honey?" Dad nudged. "The gym?"

"Not today," Sage said, facing the wall. Her body, already thrown off by her missed run, ached to sweat. To sprint, to scream, to punch something until her hands bled. To fly on the high of her endorphins. But none of that fell under the "relatively safe" forms of exercise Dr. Friedman had listed.

"This isn't the answer, Sage. Staying in bed—"

"Leave her be, Alek," Mom said. Sage heard her approach again, felt the coolness of her palm stroking her forehead. "I'll be back in a little while," Mom whispered. "You just rest."

She heard the two of them leave together, their footsteps not quite in sync as they moved down the hall. Sage kept silent. She hadn't heard Ian leave and was almost certain he was still in the room. She thought she heard him breathe.

"Sage?" he asked after a minute.

Her fingers clenched the pillow.

"I just wanted to say—"

"Don't. Please."

"I'm sorry." He said it anyway.

She wished she could look at him, to give him permission not to feel guilty, like she knew he wanted. The pillowcase zipper dug into her chin, but she didn't turn. No part of her body would move.

"I guess," Ian said to the back of her, "I'll leave you alone, but—" His voice was deeper than usual, scratchy and hoarse from last night's victory. Sage squeezed her eyes shut. "I'm around," he said. "Okay? Like, if you need anything." The floorboards creaked beneath him. "You just let me know."

Sage realized she was holding her breath. She forced herself to take in air, to nod. To acknowledge him. She could give him that much.

Her ears followed his footsteps down the hall, down the stairs. The front door opened, as she expected, then shut. Like she did—or, rather, like she'd done until now—Ian dealt with things by movement. By pushing his body to the max to clear his brain.

She imagined she could hear his steps still, his trainers thudding against the cracked sidewalk, gradually picking up speed. She opened her eyes.

Ian was a good brother, miles beyond most teenage boys she knew. She was surrounded by good people, in fact. By people who cared for and loved her, all of whom wanted to help. She figured that would have made a difference.

It didn't, though. Good intentions were worthless when no one knew what to do with them. When no one had an inkling of what to do or say. When no one could even begin to imagine how she felt.

She rolled over, wrapping herself in the comforter, exhaustion consuming her for no reason at all. She gave in to it, her last thought the recognition of dreaming of a small, empty boat. There was no way to steer it, she noticed. No motor, no sail or oars. She didn't care, climbed in anyway, and let herself float off, adrift.

CHAPTER FIFTEEN

LEN

LEN WAS USED TO BEING THE LAST TO KNOW THINGS. BUT as eyebrows raised and questions rippled through the crowd at Monday's volleyball match, she knew she wasn't the only one confused about why the team's star sat the bench.

Sage glanced at the scoreboard. Southview was losing spectacularly.

Sage's replacement, a junior with spiky, orange-dyed hair, seemed decent enough; it wasn't like she was embarrassing herself, but even Len could tell she wasn't in the same universe as Sage talent-wise. It wasn't just that, though. The absence of Sage changed something much deeper about the team than the makeup of the roster.

She watched a girl in the back row pass the ball, straight up, causing confusion about who should pass next. When Sage was on the court, they all moved together, almost like one organism. This match, though, the Southview players were subdued, their reaction times slower. Sage's absence roared in the silence, her energy—now that it was gone—clearly vital to the team's life force. Len wondered why Sage wasn't calling out support from the bench.

"This is gonna be three and done," a man near her said. "I can't believe it. That hasn't happened all season."

"Don't think that way," said a woman. "They might rally."

The man snorted.

Len tucked forward, elbows on knees. She was far from an expert, but she had to agree with the man on this one. If the team was an organism, Sage must be its heart. Without her, nothing worked right.

"They're going to drop three places in the standings at least," the man continued. "I don't get it. Hannah said Sage just had a sprain."

"Has anyone talked to Alek?" asked the woman. Together they turned to the top row of the bleachers. Len followed their gaze. A man sat there, alone, his high cheekbones a mirror of Sage's. He hunched over a smartphone, typing madly.

Coach's sharp voice brought her attention back to the court. "Substitution." His voice was loud, but stale. He'd screamed his head off the first two games, as if he could replace Sage's missed energy; but now, as the third game wound down, he'd gone cold and quiet.

Not for the first time, Len's eyes trailed to Sage, who sat stiffly beside the assistant coach. As far as Len could tell, Sage hadn't opened her mouth the entire match. Once, the girl from her study hall—Kayla—had put a hand on Sage's shoulder, but not in the usual, shoulder-slap way. Her expression reminded Len of a funeral home. Len's memory ping ponged back to Sage under the bleachers, how an almost-palpable despair had clung to her. Maybe something even darker. Len tried to shut the word from her thoughts, just in case, but it only slammed into her harder—*death*.

The word burned her nose and behind her eyes, so Len pinched the inside of her thigh. The last thing she needed was to cry right now in front of everyone. She could already hear the taunts: *crazy, crying Len,* or *Crybaby Lemon.*

She pinched harder, until the sting in her nose faded. Her eyes stayed clear. She'd probably have a bruise on her thigh, but it was totally worth it.

"Excuse me." The man from the top bleacher bench—Sage's dad, Len assumed—moved down the aisle steps. He gripped a briefcase in one hand, phone in the other.

Len leaned forward, watching him descend behind the team. He spoke, and Sage turned, her lips tight and thin. Whatever he said, she nodded, and he left, her eyes glued to the exit long after he'd walked through.

The whistle sounded, and the team trotted to the sidelines. Sage stood up to join the outskirts of the huddle, and that's when Len noticed: Sage was shaking.

Len pulled her camera from its bag, zooming in to be sure, but yes, there was no doubt. Sage even grabbed one hand with the other, trying to get them to stop. She stepped away from her team and fanned herself. Len lowered the camera.

No one else seemed to notice, and the game resumed. Southview rallied a bit, and for a moment Len thought they might force a fourth game, but no. The match was over. Sage stood, but instead of joining the handshake line, grabbed her bag from the bleachers and shot out of the gym.

Len's indecision lasted only a heartbeat. Then she was fumbling down the bleachers and out the door. She picked her way through the parking lot, keeping to the asphalt directly under the lights in order to see her footing.

Just when she started to think her intuition had been wrong, she heard it. Stifled breaths. Gasping.

She found Sage between two compact cars, doubled over and sucking air that her body didn't seem to know what to do with. Len bent next to her, speaking before she lost her nerve.

"I think you're having a panic attack."

Sage's eyes rolled up at her, pupils wide and dilated, just before she stumbled and dropped to one knee on the asphalt. Len wanted to touch her but couldn't quite bring herself to do it.

"You're okay," Len said instead, parroting the advice she'd read, about how to come down from an attack. "It doesn't feel like it, I know, but you're okay." It was unnerving, seeing someone this way. Part of her wanted to flee, to give Sage privacy, because this was personal, and maybe she shouldn't be seeing it. But a bigger part of her knew she couldn't leave.

Sage grabbed on to Len's arm, making her flinch.

"I can't—" Sage gasped.

"Can't breathe," Len said. "I know it feels that way." She wished Sage would move her hand. "Just keep trying. The choking feeling will go away."

The hard crack of the gymnasium door banging open announced the crowd's exit from the gym. Voices drifted nearer. Sage's breathing got worse and she ducked lower, trying to hide from view. Len understood that feeling, too, though only now, seeing it on someone else, did she recognize it for what it was: *shame.*

"Is one of these yours?" Len asked, nodding at the cars that flanked them.

Sage shook her head, her eyes widening even further as she registered what that meant. People were coming. Lots of people. Someone was going to see her this way. "My dad," she managed between breaths. "He . . . had to run . . . to his office." She sucked in another gulp of air. "He thought we'd go to a fourth game."

Len made another split-second decision. "You think you can walk?"

Sage nodded, her face ashen.

"Okay." She helped Sage up. "My house isn't far, just across the road behind the trees. You can stay there, if you want, until the attack clears."

Sage choked down another breath and nodded. Then Len started walking, Sage shuffling as fast as she could beside her.

CHAPTER SIXTEEN

SAGE

SAGE WASN'T SURE WHAT SHE WAS DOING, LETTING LEN lead her away from the school. But Dad had left—an urgent call, apparently—and she had to get as far from everything as possible. Her brain felt like a bruise, and she tried to shove out the thought that refused to leave her head. Never—not since Sage first picked up a volleyball—had Dad left one of her games early. Not until today.

She stumbled on a piece of broken macadam, and Len steadied her, leading her across the parking lot to the crosswalk. Sage's breathing became more regular, her terror dulling to an aching discomfort. Still, her nerves were taut, her entire body on edge.

"Right up here," Len said, as they crossed into an unkempt neighborhood. Even though it was dark, she'd driven by this area enough to know exactly what it held: a cluster of trailers and cheap ranches built decades ago, before the area had become desirable. She'd always wondered who lived back here—she and Kayla had even talked about it once—in this place she'd only heard referred to as "the trash triangle." A rush of shame ached her bones, and she lowered her head more, as if Len had heard her thoughts.

They passed the first house, whose porch still had Christmas lights on the banister and a deflated Santa crumpled in its front yard. Sage hadn't noticed the tiny, curvy side road before, but that's what they followed to an even smaller house. The siding's color, illuminated by a flickering light above the front porch, reminded her of what she'd expelled last night under the bleachers.

Len turned the knob, then threw her shoulder against the door, which shuddered as it unstuck. She could leave, Sage thought. She wasn't herself, but she wasn't terrified anymore. She no longer felt like she was dying. But when she looked back toward the school, the gym lights just visible through the trees, the out-of-control feeling swelled again. The gym wouldn't be vacant yet. Teammates and fans always loitered.

Sage followed Len inside the house.

Spaghetti smells tinged the air, mingling with something else, something industrial. Sage sniffed. *Paint?*

"Hey, Dad," Len said into the room on their left. A man sat on a tired couch, his hand flicking intense strokes over the canvas set up before him. If he heard them, he gave no indication. Len shrugged at Sage and kept walking. Somewhere, a woman's muffled voice came through the walls—a one-sided conversation, like she was on the phone.

Len opened a door. "Here." She smoothed her comforter, a bright orange sunburst that caught Sage off guard. She'd expected lots of black.

"You, uh, should probably lie down," Len said. "I'll get you some water."

As soon as Sage was alone, the tremor returned. She sat on the bed, wrapping her arms around herself to try to get a grip. She'd done so well, she thought, sitting the bench without cracking. Letting her teammates' and the fans' confusion roll off her without letting it in. She hadn't been able to cheer, though. She'd have to work on that.

Only yesterday had she told Kayla that she couldn't play, and she'd only been able to text, not speak the words aloud. Even when her phone exploded afterward with Kayla's calls and texts—dozens of them—Sage had managed only the barest of responses:

Kayla: OMG OMG. Should I tell the team?

Sage: No

Kayla: Ella? Hannah?

Sage: No one. Not yet.

Kayla: OK let me know what to do.

Kayla: Im so sorry

Kayla: We'll figure it out.

Kayla: How can I help? What do you need?

She remembered the answer she'd wanted to type: *a new heart*. What she wrote instead: *Idk*.

Kayla had kept texting after that, but Sage had turned off her phone.

Part of her knew that keeping her condition secret wouldn't solve anything. But she reasoned that her sudden ineligibility would be such a blow to her team's confidence, and such a boon to their opponents', that they might not even make the tournament. She wanted to delay a public announcement as long as possible.

At least, that's what she told Coach, and he'd reluctantly agreed to go along with her idea. For a little while, he'd said, and she'd pretended not to hear the concern in his voice.

Sage pulled a loose thread from Len's comforter. She really wanted to sleep, but she couldn't lie down on a stranger's bed. That was too uncomfortable.

Len appeared at the doorway, a plastic cup in her hands.

"I'm sorry," Sage said, fresh mortification washing over her. "I don't know what came over me."

Len handed her the cup. "You should drink this."

"Have you had one before?" Sage asked. "A panic attack?" She took a sip. "Is that how you knew what was happening?"

Len rocked back on her heels, avoiding Sage's eyes. It was a pretty personal question, Sage realized, so she added, "It was terrifying."

Finally, Len gave a tight nod. "It's like a wave, you know?"

Sage frowned. "What is?"

"The panic." Her eyes found the laptop on the Ikea desk beside her. "I read about it. The panic rolls over you, so you have to keep breathing even when it gets worse, when it feels like you're drowning. That's the top of the wave." She looked back at Sage. "It gets better after, before it comes back."

"It comes back?"

Len glanced to the window, then away. She nodded. "You didn't play today."

It was more question than statement. Sage tipped back the cup, debating her answer. Her eyes snagged on the wall behind Len, the photographs covering every space of it. "Whoa," she said, standing, and moved beside Len for a better look. Vivid 8x10s, smaller black and whites, even a long panorama, all of them depicting art studio–worthy landscapes. "These are beautiful."

"Oh," Len said. "Um, thank you."

"You took them?"

Len nodded.

Sage's gaze fell to a 5x7 on the desk. A framed photo of two girls in shorts and tank tops. They were related; Sage could tell by their noses, the width of their smiles. The blond one's face felt familiar.

"Oh, my gosh!" She picked up the frame. "Is this *you*?"

Len's face tightened. "With my sister, Fauna. Yeah."

Sage's eyes darted between real Len—baggy gray sweatshirt, jeans, and gloves—and photo Len—bright red tank, white shorts, freshly washed and curled hair.

"When was this?" she asked, failing miserably to keep the shock from her voice. Photo Len seemed so happy, a girl who had fun. A girl who was normal.

Len pulled her sleeve down over her hand. "Last year."

What happened? Sage thought. The question must have been all over her face, because Len snatched the frame from her hands and placed it back on the desk.

"Don't touch, okay?" she said.

"Sorry." Sage turned as she stepped back and noticed more pictures, thumbtacked row by row on the wall above the bed. "Did you take these, too?" In two steps she was across the room, her hands raised to the images.

"Please!"

There was a strangled quality to Len's voice that made Sage's insides freeze. "Right," she said, remembering. "No touching." She clasped her hands behind her back, then followed the photos around the room. Some of the places she recognized. Graveyard Fields. Pack Square. The smoke stacks on Lake Julian. "Is this up on Craggy Mountain?" Sage asked.

Len nodded.

Other photos were more general—a forest. Birds on a wire. Headlights blurring the dark.

Sage's mouth caught in a half-smile. "Len, these are incredible. I mean, really—"

"Don't walk there!"

Sage's foot froze midstride. She looked at the carpet where she'd been about to step. Nothing. Just a dead fly by the floorboard and a cobweb under the windowsill. "What is it?"

"Just, please." Len motioned her back, like it was a matter of life and death. "You just can't be over there, okay? Come back."

Sage narrowed her eyes but did as Len asked. Len couldn't seem to keep still, wringing her gloved hands and moving them in and out of her pockets, her feet shuffling like she was nervous in her own room. She was very obviously not looking at the window.

Sage watched her for a moment, then studied the layout of the room. It was strange, really, a clear waste of space. The room felt colder suddenly. "Why can't we go over there, in that empty area?"

"It's not empty." Len's voice was hollow.

"It looks pretty empty," Sage said, taking one step toward it. "You could fit a whole—"

"I said you can't go there, okay?" A small sound escaped Len, and she jammed herself onto her bed, nails clawing into the edge of the mattress. Her eyes stayed glued to the tan carpet.

The shadow over Len's mood poisoned the air, curdling Sage's curiosity. She reached for her bag, for her phone. Something was really off, clearly, and Sage needed to leave.

Her phone buzzed once, and then again a few seconds later. *Thank God.* She didn't even have to lie. "Dad's on his way back," she said, checking the screen. "And Kayla's looking for me, too."

Len nodded, slowly prying her hands from the mattress. "That's nice."

Sage paused. She was pretty sure Len wasn't being sarcastic. "What is?"

Len looked up. "Oh, I don't know." She hugged herself tight. "You said your friend is looking for you. I just think that's nice, you know?" She shrugged. "People checking on you."

A discomfort she couldn't name slipped over Sage. "I mean, people check on you, right?"

"Oh, yeah," Len said too quickly. "I didn't mean it like that. I mean, totally. My mom and dad." She gave a small, strange laugh. "Totally."

"Okaaay." Whatever this feeling was, Sage hated it. Hated that she couldn't name it, that it had sneaked up without her control. "Well, see you later." And then she was away from the room, away from the house, away from the serious weirdness of Len Madder.

CHAPTER SEVENTEEN

LEN

LEN CURLED UNDER HER COMFORTER. WHAT HAD SHE been thinking, bringing Sage to her house? To her room? Len had held it in as best she could, but her freakness had slipped through the cracks anyway. Sage would probably tell all her cool friends how crazy Len was, and they'd tell the whole school, and—

Stop, Len. Just. Stop.

She flattened herself on her back, eyes closed beneath the blanket, and pictured the worry as one of Dad's thought leaves floating away on a river. But the leaf kept swirling instead of moving ahead.

Whatever. Bad visualizations were the least of her problems. Did she really have dementia? A sharp stab of intuition gutted her in the ribs. *You know you do.* And if she was losing her mind, why even bother with the Melford? With anything at all?

You can't just give up. Intuition again. *It might take years.* Nonni had held on for so long, alternating stretches of confusion with equally long stretches of clarity before the confusion finally won out.

The air beneath the comforter grew hot and stifling. Len threw the blanket back and sat up. Maybe she should Google *childhood dementia* again. She'd only read a few lines in one online entry, enough to tell that her symptoms were the same. Maybe there was something else, though, some kind of home remedy?

Don't! Her brain screamed. *What if you read something worse?*

Her body, half-poised to get out of bed and open her laptop, froze. Of course she would find something worse—another worry for her brain's riptide, another thing to drag her under. No, she couldn't look. She didn't want to know.

Across the room, the emptiness near the window beckoned her, pulled at her like a magnetic force. She strained so hard to *not* look that her neck muscles twitched.

She turned on the bed, away from the window. Without the Melford Scholarship, she'd never get out of here, and she *had* to get out of here. And if she lost it before then, well, at least she'd have something to focus on. Something to drown out the horrible shrieks of everything else in her head.

Len pulled her camera onto the bed and flipped through the digital images she'd taken Friday night under the bleachers. A couple of them had potential—odd angles and bizarre shadow patterns. Several of them might even be usable. Not by themselves, probably, but perhaps as part of a larger project.

She found the final ones, the ones she'd shot right before Sage staggered under the stands, right before she vomited everywhere. "I wonder," Len muttered. She zoomed in, searching for any hint about where Sage had been, a clue Len maybe unknowingly captured. Because something had happened to Sage, Len felt sure of it.

Len's head cleared a little. She flipped to the next photo and zoomed again, forcing all of her concentration to the image.

Nothing.

Still, it comforted her, knowing that even superstar athlete Sage Zendasky had pretty bad moments—that nobody's world was perfect all the time. Len could barely believe the Sage from her room was the same person who, last week, had made her opponents look like they were about to cry.

Len set the camera next to her. What was stranger, though, was the way she'd felt when Sage had been here. For the first time in months, she'd felt close to normal. Or closer, at least. Too bad she hadn't been able to hold it together for the ten minutes Sage had stayed.

Footsteps padded down the hall, and Mom appeared at the door. "Hey, sweetie." She took in Len's bed, the comforter twisted and sprawled like a shattered cocoon. Her eyes moved to Len and she must have seen something she didn't like, because her face changed, saddened. She stepped into the room. "What are you up to?"

Len picked up the camera. "Just going through images." She shrugged. "For the Melford."

It was impossible to miss the glint of pride in Mom's face. Len looked away.

"How're you doing?" Mom sat down, and Len scooted a few inches, making room for her on the twin mattress. Her mouth stayed shut.

Mom pulled Len's hair away from her neck, combing it with her fingers. "You're still sad," she said, softly, "about what happened."

Len's head snapped up. "Aren't you?"

"Of course I am." Hurt bloomed in Mom's voice. The circles beneath her eyes looked darker. "It's just that it's been several months now." She stroked Len's hair again, kneaded the pressure point at the base of her skull. "I miss your laugh."

The cords of Len's throat tightened as Mom glanced across the room to the window. "You know, that extra bookcase by our bed would fit perfectly there. Should I—"

"No." Len's eyes slammed shut, her teeth clamping her tongue until she felt blood mingle with saliva.

"What about moving the desk there, then, like it used to be? You'd have better access to the closet."

Len's eyes shot open. "I like my room the way it is, okay? Is this why you came in? To talk about decorating?"

Mom's shoulders slumped. "It was just an idea, Lennie. A random thought."

They both knew that wasn't true. They both pretended that it was.

"Actually, I came to ask you a favor." Mom smoothed the blanket beside Len's knees.

"What kind of favor?"

Mom sighed, long and tired. "I just remembered I promised to bake that pear and apple crisp for the birthday at work tomorrow. Everyone's bringing something, and people specifically requested the crisp. Even gave me money for the ingredients—" Her voice wavered, and Len knew how it must have pained Mom to take money for such a small thing. It pained Len just to hear about it.

Mom rubbed her forehead. "Anyway, I completely forgot, and I've got some food on the stove for Nonni, and some things I'm taking tomorrow. Would you mind terribly running to the grocery?"

Len nodded, glad for the excuse to leave. "Yeah, sure." She stood and found her boots, slipping her socked feet inside.

Mom frowned. "Won't you be hot in those?"

She might be, actually. But that was a small price. "I like them," she said stiffly. "Are the keys by the door?"

Mom's brow stayed scrunched, but she didn't press. "Yes." She handed Len a five-dollar bill, six ones, and a coupon for 50 cents off a produce purchase. "If there's any left, maybe grab a milk, but only if it's on sale."

* * *

Len stood between the two sets of automatic doors at Ingle's Grocery, staring at the rows of carts. She'd already let three people go around her because she couldn't decide. Why did all the carts have rust spots? Or a previous patron's garbage littered inside? Who'd want their food touching that stuff? She watched an elderly man unhook one of the smaller carts from the line and push it into the store, oblivious to the plastic deli bag caught in the cart's base.

It wasn't until one of the cart collectors asked if she needed help that she finally forced herself to choose one that looked fairly new, muttering a "No, thanks" that came out so softly she was certain nobody else heard.

She found the apples first. It didn't make sense to choose four single ones when a whole bag of Galas cost about the same.

Plus, some of the single apples looked grimy. She found a decent looking bundle and grabbed the gathered plastic above the tie to lift it into the cart.

The pears were a bit trickier, spanning colors from greenish yellow to light brown. What were ripe pears even supposed to look like?

"You have to feel them," a voice said.

Len looked up. A sharply dressed woman, probably close to Nonni's age, smiled down at her.

"The pears," the woman said. "You're trying to choose, aren't you?"

Len nodded.

"Like this," said the woman. She reached out and squeezed the tops of different pears. "You're looking for one that's not quite firm, but not too soft, either. You need just the right combination. A balance."

Len's insides twisted. The woman was touching all of them. Who knew what else her hands had touched, what she was transferring to the fruit. Len sneaked a glance at the woman's cart. Rust spots speckled the handle bar.

Len's heart jumped. Rust caused tetanus. Could you get it by eating traces? Had her parents had tetanus shots? Had she? How long did those last? Was there tetanus on all those pears? What if she bought some and Mom used them and people died, all because of her?

Thoughts, mountains of them, piled on top of her.

"Honey?" The woman's voice brought her back. Len managed to nod.

"This one." The woman held out a pear, mottled green and yellow. A dark spot marred its side.

Len's hands didn't move. "It looks, uh, damaged."

The woman *tssked*. "They've all got a few marks, but that's just their nature. Trust me. This one will be perfect." She placed it into the top of Len's cart. "How many more do you need?"

Len shrank away from her. Didn't this woman have her own shopping to do? "That's it, thanks." She pushed the cart away quickly, like she had someplace she needed to be. The pear bounced along, nearly slipping out the leg hole in the child's seat.

Child.

The word spun through her. *Child. Child. Child.* It twisted and reformed. *Nadia.*

Nadia would never sit in a shopping cart. She'd never shop for groceries or help Fauna and Diane cook. She'd never do *anything.* Because of Len. Because Len hadn't been careful.

Len whirled the cart into the bread aisle, away from the stares of customers meandering the produce section. The pear bumped and tumbled, this time tipping out the hole. It hit the ground with a dull thud and rolled to the edge of the bottom shelf. Len knelt down, her hands still clinging to the cart handle, and waited for the panic to pass.

When she could finally breathe again, her body felt weightless, her head airy. When was the last time she'd eaten? What time was it? How long had she been here? She stood up.

"Hey," said a guy in a *Save the Bees* T-shirt. He scooped up the battered pear. "This yours?"

Len considered the fruit, then the cart beside her, holding the solo bag of apples. There was rust on the side, a bit near the back, too. How had she missed it?

Heat poured into her. She needed to get out of here. She needed to take a shower.

"Hello?" the guy said again.

"Not mine," she said, and turned, leaving the pear and the cart behind her.

CHAPTER EIGHTEEN

SAGE

SAGE FELT LIKE A JERK ALL NIGHT. LEN WAS THE ONLY reason the entire school hadn't witnessed her mortifying breakdown, and she was pretty sure she'd left without even saying thank you. Yeah, Len was odd and it had gotten kind of uncomfortable at her house. But that was no excuse for leaving like she did.

Tuesday morning she lingered in the Fine Arts Hall, where she'd seen Len disappear the first day they'd met. The warning bell rang, then the late bell, but Len never showed.

"That's your second tardy, Sage," her teacher said as she slipped into Calculus. "Don't let it happen again."

Sage nodded and slid into her seat in the second row. Maybe Len had come early, before Sage arrived? Or maybe she had a dentist appointment or something? Sage tapped her pencil against the side of her notebook, trying to focus, but Len's words echoed in her head: *I just think that's nice, you know. People checking on you.*

145

"Does anyone have questions about last night's assignments?"

Sage looked down at her work. It wasn't just Len's words that bothered her, but the way she'd said them. The longing in her voice.

As she copied down equations from the board, discomfort vined around her, the same something's-not-right feeling that had made her leave so abruptly the night before.

* * *

As soon as Calc ended, Sage raced upstairs to Kayla's study hall.

"What are you doing here?" Kayla asked.

"I need to talk to Len." Sage craned her neck to look behind Kayla. "She has this block with you, right?"

"Right, but..." She crinkled her nose. "Len Madder? Why?"

Sage scooted by her into the classroom.

"She usually sits over there." Kayla pointed to the far back corner. "I don't see her stuff, though."

"Does she often miss class?"

"I don't know, Sage. She sits back there and doesn't talk to anyone. Half the time I don't even see her. What is going on?"

Sage raked her hands across her face. "Nothing. Forget it."

"Hey," Kayla said as Sage headed out. "We still haven't talked." She widened her eyes knowingly. "About...everything."

Sage had been so focused on Len that for a few blissful moments she'd almost forgotten her own misery. "There's nothing to talk about," she said. "We texted anyway."

"Barely," said Kayla. "And that's not the same." Her face turned soft. "How are you?"

"Fine," Sage snapped, looking anywhere but Kayla's eyes. "I'm dealing with it."

"Are you?" Kayla whispered, and Sage's whole body burned. "When are you going to tell the rest of the team?"

"I will tell them," Sage said. "I just—"

Kayla raised her eyebrows.

"There're some more tests," Sage blurted. "They take longer. I'm waiting until then."

"Really?" Kayla asked. "There's a chance you could still play?" The hope in her voice was unbearable.

Sage wrapped her arms around herself. "A small one, but yeah." What was she doing? "I just"—she shrugged—"I wanna wait until then, okay? Until it's for sure, for sure."

Kayla looked at her for a long moment, but finally nodded. "I guess I get that."

"I'll see you." Sage ducked back into the hallway. She felt bad for lying, but it was hard enough having to face pity from her family. Once the team found out, the whole school would know. The pity would pile on, mountains and mountains of it. It would bury her alive.

She grimaced. She was stronger than futile worrying, and she didn't have time for that anyway. The late bell sounded and Len still hadn't showed up to the study hall room. Sage took off at a walk-run, switch-backing several times to avoid hall monitors.

Part of her felt stupid. She was probably completely over-reacting, and she barely knew Len anyway. But Len *had* helped her yesterday, and Sage had heard enough schoolwide lectures to know that sometimes people couldn't ask for help directly. What if Len was one of those people? What if yesterday was a plea and Sage ignored it? If something happened, she'd never forgive herself.

She burst through the double doors and fast-walked to the edge of the parking lot, stepping into the road just as a navy Camry rounded the corner.

"Sorry, sorry," she said, as its horn blared. The driver flipped her off.

She cut through a backyard to save time. The house, more of a tangerine color than it appeared at night, was still easy enough to find. A pickup truck stood under a carport, but the house looked dark.

"Len?" Sage rapped on the front door.

Somewhere above her, birds trilled and answered. Sage knocked harder.

"Len! Are you there?" She put her face to the glass and the door gave a little. Before she could think better of it, Sage leaned into it, like she remembered Len doing, and pushed her way inside.

CHAPTER NINETEEN

LEN

LEN SAT ON THE EDGE OF THE TUB, HER SNOOPY PAJAMA pants rolled up thigh high. She couldn't remember the last time she'd shaved. She spread a thin layer of green body wash onto her legs and pulled the razor from ankle to pajama fabric, erasing a smooth line of hair. Again and again she pulled it, like a mantra.

It felt good, shaving. Like starting over. Or becoming new.

She turned on the tap and splashed a couple drops on her face, still groggy with sleep. The morning was half over, but if the construction sounds of the new condos going in behind her neighborhood hadn't worn through her subconscious, she'd probably still be in bed. Not that she'd done anything taxing yesterday. Not really.

She glanced at the digital clock perched on the sink, still surprised she'd slept through her alarm. Dad had left a note— *painting at the lake again*—but she wished he'd nudged her before leaving. Wasn't it kind of his job to make sure she got to school?

Her arm grazed the shower curtain, which was gathered on her left side, and she noticed the cloth had a dark stain. Mildew, maybe, or mold. Wasn't black mold deadly? She should take it down. Throw it in the washer. But what if the spot accidentally touched her? She squeezed a drop of body wash onto her arm and bent forward, holding it under the faucet.

The water pounded against her skin, hot and brutal. It echoed the pounding of her heart when she'd arrived home last night, empty-handed.

"I don't understand," Mom had said when Len thrust the money back at her. "You were gone almost an hour. Why don't you have the groceries?"

Len hadn't known how to explain the confusion that had sent everything spinning. The certainty that she couldn't buy any of the things in her cart, that they were dirty and might hurt someone. That she was trying to keep everyone safe.

"What's going on?" Dad had asked, appearing in the kitchen with paint brush in hand. "What's wrong?"

"I just wanted a little help," Mom had said. "I have to make that crisp for the morning, and now I've lost an entire hour." She'd covered her face, shoulders trembling. "I'm just so tired."

"The fruit wasn't good," Len had said, but Mom stopped her.

"That doesn't make any sense! All of it was bad? In the entire store?"

Dad had pulled Mom into a hug, shooting Len an "unbelievable!" look over her shoulder. "It's okay, hon. I'll go."

"You've got to finish that commission," she'd said to his chest. "We need that money! That's why I asked Len in the first place."

"It's fine. You go to bed and get up early to do this, okay? Tell me what you need."

Mom did then, zombie-like, and left the kitchen without another word. She'd looked truly terrible. Dad snatched the car keys from Len's hands. "Are you doing drugs?"

"What? No!"

"What were you doing, then? For the last hour?"

"I told you. The fruit was bad." She'd looked down, away from the disappointment radiating off of him, and wrapped her arms around herself. "I'm sorry."

"Your mother was counting on you," he'd said, opening the front door. "We'll talk about this later."

Len had cried herself to sleep, but not before the first drips of daylight invaded her room.

The pounding against her arm intensified, and with a jolt, Len snapped back from the memory, jerking her arm away from the gushing water. Her skin was red and raw.

"Len!" a voice cried, and Len screamed, almost falling backward off the tub. She jumped up, razor high to defend herself, and found herself face-to-face with Sage Zendasky.

Her brain struggled to compute what it saw. "Sage?"

"You're okay!" Sage said, hand flying to her chest. "Wait." Her eyes zeroed in on Len's razor. "Were you gonna do something stupid?"

It took Len a moment to realize what she meant. When she did, humiliation swelled and crashed over her, usurped quickly by anger.

"Was I going to kill myself?" she said. "No, I was shaving." She stepped out of the tub, dripping water onto the plastic tiles. "I might have problems, but they're not that kind."

Sage's forehead wrinkled, and Len immediately regretted using the word *problems*. How dare Sage make her feel small in her own house. "What are you doing here?" Len demanded.

For the first time, Sage looked like she might realize how strange this was. "Looking for you," she said. "You weren't at school."

"Yeah, I slept in." Len was growing more pissed by the second. Who did this girl think she was that she could just barge into her house? She was lucky Len's family wasn't gun crazy. A few houses down and she might have had her head blown off. "What do you care, anyway?"

"I—" Sage shifted uncomfortably. Len snorted and grabbed a towel for her legs. Thank God she hadn't been naked.

"I'm sorry," Sage said. "And thank you."

Len looked up. "What? Why?"

"For helping me yesterday," Sage said. "It was really nice of you, and I'm sorry I left like I did, without thanking you. It was shitty."

Len frowned. It was a good apology. It seemed real. But she was too used to snark and mockery to be certain. She bent down to dry her feet.

Sage leaned against the small vanity. "You seemed so upset yesterday, so when you didn't show up at school . . ." She shrugged. "I got worried, I guess."

Len tried to fathom it. Sage—popular super athlete—worried about her? She rolled her pajama pants back down. "I know I freaked you out yesterday," she said quietly. "I freak everyone out." *Myself most of all*, she thought. She stood up. "It was nice of you, though, to check on me. A little weird, but nice."

Sage gave her a small smile. "Anyway," she said, "do you want to go somewhere, maybe? Because honestly, I don't feel like going back to school."

Len didn't even try to keep the shock from her voice. "You mean, like, hang out? You and me?"

Sage's confidence flickered. "I was just offering," she said, and if Len hadn't known better, she'd have thought Sage was embarrassed. She tried to envision how this might be a setup—how she might be the punch line of some cruel joke.

"Can I pick the place?" Len asked.

"Sure."

"And I can drive?"

Sage shrugged. "Okay."

Len bit the inside of her cheek. This was not an emergency. She should not drive Nonni's uninsured pickup. But she also realized—suddenly and surprisingly—how much she really, really wanted to go. And if she went, she needed to be in control.

"Meet me by the front door in five."

CHAPTER TWENTY

SAGE

"THANKS FOR THE HOOKUP." SAGE TOOK ANOTHER SIP OF
her espresso drink. The small remaining chunk of vanilla ice
cream bobbed against her top lip. "What's it called again?"

"An affogato." Len smiled. "I can't believe you've never had
one." She wrapped her gloved hands around her own hand-
crafted mug. "And that you've never been here."

They sat at the back of Espresso Yourself on either end of a
three-seater sofa with the kitschiest fabric Sage had ever seen:
dogs and roosters frolicked along an ideal country landscape,
complete with apple trees and fish in ponds. Oddly, the sofa and
the two chairs opposite it sat on a platform about eight inches
above the rest of the floor. If it hadn't been for the furniture,
Sage would have guessed it was a stage.

"We don't ever come to Hendersonville," Sage said. "I like
the vibe of this place, though." She stared back at the long line
by the bar, every table in the place full. They'd been lucky to

grab the sofa, although apparently it wasn't the most coveted seating. "Honestly, I can't believe how packed it is. It's a week-day morning."

"Apple season brings the tourists," Len said. "It gets almost as bad as some of the Asheville shops. My Nonni and I used to come here all the time. The owner loved her, hence the free drinks." Her voice faded, and her focus narrowed on a large canvas on the wall. "The art is good, though. All local. And they bring some fun bands."

"So this *is* a stage?"

Len nodded. "All the sound equipment is behind those curtains." She pulled her drink close to her. "I mean, I haven't gotten to go in a while. But it's what they used to do."

Sage bristled, because something in Len's tone recalled that night under the bleachers. She'd shocked Sage first by her mere presence, then by her words: *It's all over you . . . loss.*

Anyone else would have seen a senior vomiting beneath the stands and thought one thing: alcohol. Or, if they were more naïve, maybe food poisoning. But one look at Sage, and Len had known it was so much more.

No, Sage realized. She didn't just know it. She *recognized* it. Because she'd lost something, too. She thought of the picture in Len's room, showing the sleeveless, smiling girl she used to be. What had happened to her?

Sage's iPhone buzzed. Len didn't look up, but Sage angled it away from her just in case.

Kayla: Where are you?

Sage ran her thumb across the screen as Len sunk deeper into her chair, her hair falling forward to partly conceal her face.

Sage: Home. Didn't feel great. Talk later.

As she switched her phone to silent, the reality of her situation slammed into her—skipping school to sip ice cream coffee with Len Madder. In Hendersonville. It was not how she imagined her day. It wasn't the worst time she'd ever had, though.

She let out a tiny, bemused laugh.

Len's head snapped up. "Are you making fun of me?"

"What?"

"Because if you are," Len said, "let's cut the bullshit and leave right now." She stood up.

"Whoa," Sage said, glancing at the table nearest them, which was crowded with three college-age people. None of them looked up from their laptops. "I'm not making fun of you," she said. "Why would you even think that?"

Len's eyes narrowed. "You were laughing," she said. "Looking at me and laughing, right after you texted." She pulled her mug closer, shrinking into herself. "Your friend thinks I'm a loser. I can tell. Why else would you be here? This"—she gestured to herself and then to Sage—"doesn't make sense. I don't know what I was thinking." She turned to leave.

"Wait!" Sage jumped up. She had no idea what to say, only that they couldn't leave, not like this. "You're right," she said. "You and me, together, here. It's random. Sure. But *that's* what I was laughing about, honestly. And look." She handed over her phone. "That text was Kayla asking where I was. I just left, remember?"

Len stared at the screen. Sage wanted to tell her she had the wrong idea about Kayla, that she wouldn't have purposefully made Len feel bad. Something stopped her, though. Because what if she had?

She looked at the floor before meeting Len's eyes. "I'm sorry Kayla was shitty to you. But I'm not her, and I swear, all I wanted to do was get away from school. From everything. And honestly, you looked terrible when I found you, so, I don't know, I thought maybe you'd want to come, too."

Len handed back the phone. "You didn't want her to know you were with me."

"What?"

"Kayla." Len crossed her arms. "You told her you were at home."

Sage rubbed her eyes. "I couldn't say where I was without answering a million questions, and honestly, I'm kind of having a good time just sitting here."

That was true. But maybe, possibly, what Len said was true, too. Sage shoved the thought away. "Look," Sage said, "what are we doing? Do you want to leave or not?"

Len huddled further into herself and shrugged. "Whatever."

Sage sunk back into the sofa. "Cool, because I want to finish this deliciousness." She picked up her mug and took a huge gulp. "Honestly, this might be the best thing I've ever tasted."

Len sat back down, her head tilted. "You say *honestly* a lot."

Sage blinked at her, then lifted a shoulder. "I guess I need to work on my vocabulary."

That made Len laugh—a genuine, honest-to-God, I'm-okay laugh. She'd been so miserable a moment before, and now she was laughing. Sage smiled back at her. It was such a little thing, but for some reason she felt like she'd just scored an ace. Now she could capitalize on it.

"Since we're being *honest*," Sage said, nodding toward Len's hands, "what's the deal with your gloves?"

Len's smile evaporated. "What do you mean?"

"Come on. It's seventy-something degrees outside and you're wearing long sleeves, jeans, and knit gloves. You wear them to school, too. Why?"

"I just like them." Len's whole body had gone rigid, like it might break if she moved the tiniest fraction. "Artistic flair and all."

Sage stared at her over her mug. Len was lying, and she was pretty sure Len knew that Sage knew she was lying. "Okaay," Sage said slowly.

The espresso machine whirred behind them. Soft jazz cooed over the speakers. Sage wondered if maybe they should have left before, when Len wanted to.

"I get cold," Len said suddenly. "It doesn't matter how hot it is. Sometimes"—her eyes fixated on the refurnished hutch by the wall, faux flowers spilling from the vases atop it—"I get really, really cold."

It wasn't a full answer, Sage could tell. But the way Len's voice strained, the tight way she held herself, like it took all her energy to keep still, Sage knew those words had cost her something.

Sage thought again of that night under the bleachers and later how Len had recognized Sage's panic, had helped her without ever asking what was wrong. She remembered her first interaction with Len, when she'd sized her up as weak and fearful.

She had miscalculated, Sage realized. There *was* fear, definitely. Probably pain, too. But underneath all of that, there was something else. Something terribly strong.

"I can't play volleyball anymore." Sage snapped her mouth shut, shocked that the words had tumbled out. She kept her eyes on the hutch, but felt Len's gaze swivel toward her.

"You mean, for the rest of the season?" Len asked.

"No." Sage met her eyes. "I mean for the rest of my life."

Len's eyes widened the tiniest bit, but she didn't twist her face into pity. She didn't mention that surely coaching opportunities were available and she could still be part of the team even from the bench. She didn't tell her it was going to be okay.

"I have this heart condition," Sage said. "It's why I fainted." She flexed her palm, like she did—used to do—before serving. "I can't play because they say I could die."

Len put her mug down on the table. "I'm sorry."

Sage nodded, and her heart unclenched in what felt terribly similar to relief. She wasn't sure what it was from precisely, but her body vibrated with the force of it.

Something vibrated from Len, too. Sage could feel it. Not pity, though. Then the word came to her, and for the first time in her life she thought she really understood what it was: *empathy*. Len could give it because something in her life was terribly wrong as well—something she didn't want to talk about. Sage could almost feel Len's sadness, a heaviness thrumming in her bones. And yet there she sat, holding the weight of Sage's grief without cracking an inch.

She took a deep breath, Len's strength making her braver. "You're the first person I've actually told that to," Sage said, forcing back the hot pricks behind her eyes. "My family knows, obviously, and they told my coach." Her voice cracked. "And Kayla."

Len nodded. "Why did you tell me?"

"I don't know." Sage felt stupid suddenly. "I guess I thought you'd get it."

Len nodded. "I won't say anything," she said. "You'll have to tell them, though, won't you? The rest of the team?"

"Yeah." Sage's voice made a flat, deflated volleyball sound. "I need to wrap my head around it first, you know? Prepare myself. Because the team, when they find out . . ." She didn't know how to finish.

"You're afraid they can't handle it," Len said. "And then you'll have to hold their disappointment, too."

Sage hadn't thought of it in those terms, but that was it, exactly. It was simultaneously comforting and unsettling, the way Len nailed down her own thoughts.

She couldn't talk about this anymore. "Have you ever shown anything here?" she asked.

Len looked confused.

"You're an artist, right? A photographer? Have you ever had your work displayed here?"

Len laughed like that was the most ridiculous thing she'd ever heard.

"Your photographs are good, Len. I bet you could make a killing from the tourists."

But Len didn't seem to be listening anymore. Her eyes were stuck on the couch, on a spot next to her knee. "What is that?"

"I don't see anything." Sage bent close to the cushion. "Oh, this?"

"Don't!" Len cried, but Sage had already brushed her hand over the streak. "It looks like pen, maybe? What's wrong?"

"Are you sure?" Len's eyes were closed, her breathing fast. It reminded Sage of the old cartoons she watched with Ian, when Bruce Banner turned into the Hulk. "One hundred percent sure?" Len asked again. "It's just pen?"

Sage wasn't, actually. It could have been from a marker or maybe just a defect in the fabric. She stared hard at Len, who looked like she was in physical pain.

"I'm sure," Sage said. "One hundred percent."

Slowly, Len's breathing returned to normal. A flush filled her cheeks as she opened her eyes. "I'm sorry," she said, covering her face. "I'm sorry."

"No, it's okay," Sage said, pretending she wasn't even a tiny bit weirded out. "It's fine."

Len stood up. "I have to go the bathroom," she said. "And then I want to go home."

"Oh," Sage said, taken aback by Len's abruptness. "Um, okay. Sure. I guess I'll meet you by the door, then."

Len nodded and squeezed through the tables at the end of the platform, leaving her mug half full.

It was like something switched inside her, Sage thought. *So bizarre.* She collected Len's mug and took it along with hers to the bussing station by the exit. Colorful want ads and notices created a paper mosaic in the window. One flyer—a neon yellow paper right at eye level—had a picture of a volleyball.

REPLACEMENT PLAYER NEEDED ASAP FOR LEVEL A VBALL YMCA TEAM. HITTER PREFERRED.

Sage peeled the paper from the window. She was already a Y member, so her parents wouldn't have to sign anything. She stared at the handwritten phone number at the bottom. She should hang the paper back up. She wasn't allowed to play anymore. She couldn't.

Her hand grasped the edge, crinkling the corner below the number. This team wouldn't know that.

Behind her, she heard Len say something to the barista who'd served them. She pocketed the paper just before Len came up beside her.

"Anything good up there?" Len asked.

Sage made a show of looking at the remaining ads, like she'd been studying all of them. "Nothing," she said, pushing open the door. "Nothing at all."

CHAPTER TWENTY-ONE

LEN

"I THINK IT'S TIME FOR SOME GRATITUDE SHARING." DAD dished a salmon patty onto Len's plate.

Len wrinkled her nose, but not at the salmon patty. Even Mom didn't seem particularly enthusiastic about the idea.

"Come on," Dad said. "Gratitude has been proven to increase happiness levels and, well, that's something we could use a bit more of around here, I'd say."

"Wouldn't that be nice?" Mom squeezed the ketchup bottle, which exhaled a red blob onto her plate. "Len, would you like to start?"

"No," she said. *"Thank you."*

Dad pointed his fork at her. "I see what you did there. Clever."

"It is a hard time to be thankful," Mom admitted, "but I think that's Dad's point, isn't it? There's always something to be grateful for. Please?"

Len sliced her patty into tiny pieces. She wasn't homeless. She had food to eat. She knew how to read. Those felt like cop-out answers, though, and she'd used them before. Why did Dad make them do these stupid things? She started to refuse, but the way Mom looked at her, so expectantly, so desperate for even the smallest piece of happiness, she had to say something. Especially after her spectacular failure the previous night. She wracked her brain, but she had nothing. Unless—

"Sage," she blurted.

Mom sat back, puzzled.

"I mean, coffee," Len amended. "Coffee, with sage. You know, the herb?" She speared a salmon piece and shoved it into her mouth.

"What an odd combination," said Mom, eyebrows raised. "I'll have to try it sometime."

Dad cleared his throat. "Okay. It's good to appreciate the little things, after all. Debra?"

Mom added another scoop of mashed potatoes to her plate. "Momma told me that her daughter visited her a few days ago."

Len's knife slipped, cutting an ear-splitting scrape into the plate. Dad grimaced.

"I'm grateful that she knows I'm there," Mom said. She wiped her mouth with a napkin. "Even if she doesn't know it's me."

Dad put his hand over hers. "You're a good daughter, Debra." Their fingers interlocked and Dad squeezed her hand tightly. "She knows you love her."

Mom nodded, unable to speak. Guilt lit up Len's body.

"What about you, Dad?" she asked, desperate to change the conversation.

"Me?" Dad sat up straighter. "I'm thankful for knowledge in unexpected places."

Mom blotted her eyes. "Oh?"

"After painting today, I went to Reiki, and I met the most amazing person, a new student. We got to talking and he's a recovering alcoholic—clean four years—but his body has taken a beating. Apparently, he had liver cancer, and the doctors gave him only a few months to live."

"How awful," Mom said.

"But get this. Instead of giving up, he started meditation." Dad's eyes practically glowed with excitement. "He took up a daily practice of imagining healing energy going into his liver, combined with positivity mantras about how good he felt. And how he was healing." Dad leaned over his plate. "That was *two years* ago!"

Mom's eyes widened. "Incredible."

"Isn't it?" Dad tapped his head. "*That* is the power of the mind."

"Wait," said Len. "You're saying that this guy healed *himself*? With his mind?"

"With positive energy," Dad said. "By tapping into the Life Force."

"He probably also had some medicine," Mom added.

Dad shrugged. "He didn't mention it. Even so, you're not convincing me it's a coincidence that he started recovering at the exact same time he began energy work."

Len sat back in her chair. Her brain felt like one of Nonni's yarn spools that had come undone and been rewound haphazardly. An idea tugged on the end, trying to unravel it again.

"Len, honey." Mom touched Len's back, making her flinch. "Are you all right?"

Len realized she was cradling her head and forced her hands down to the table. "Yeah." She started to grab her fork, but there was no way she could eat any more. "Ms. Saffron gave me these prompts," she said, standing. "For the Melford. I don't wanna miss the light."

Len walked to her room, eyes fixated only on her camera until she got back into the hall. She wasn't actually itching to go outside by any means, but she couldn't stay in any longer, not after what Mom had said about Nonni.

She was outside before she realized she didn't have her prompt list. Whatever. She held the camera to her eye and started snapping, everything and anything. She loved how the world looked this way, manageable and confined through a lens that she controlled. Like nothing outside the edges existed. She walked slowly, keeping to the mushroom-free section of the yard, her finger glued to the shutter release.

Dad's story poked into her mind. The power of the brain. Of thoughts. If positive thoughts could heal, that meant—

Don't think it.

She swung the camera up, then increased its aperture to blur the background. Tiny pieces of dust drifted slowly through the last traces of sun, perhaps debris from the trees over-head. The *chut-chut-chut-chut-chut* of the camera steadied her, gave her something else to focus on—something to keep other thoughts out.

Motion appeared on the lens's edges, and she turned, adjusting the zoom. Fireflies. Their dark bodies traced patterns through the deepening shadows until they blinked—beautiful—like magic.

Len followed them. Fireflies were lovely when illuminated, but Len liked them best the moment before the spark, when they were dark and small and nearly invisible—tiny gems of overlooked potential.

She snapped an image of two of them, unlit, circling each other, just before they glowed at the same moment, their light echoed by others behind them. Then, as suddenly as the sparks flickered, came a rush of memory:

Len was six. Laughing. Fauna, sixteen, held her up, and Len reached for the moon. As she cupped her hands together, fireflies flashed above them: two simultaneously, followed by three more.

The memory burnt out, but it left Len doubled over.

It's your fault, her mind said, and she cursed herself, because she'd stopped focusing. And now the thought was in, burrowing into her brain. *Your fault.*

Len's foot snagged on something, and she almost fell face first. "No," she whispered, even though she knew it was true. She lowered the camera and suddenly the world was huge. Disorienting. She couldn't move or step anywhere. There were tons of diseases in dirt—some life-threatening. She'd made the mistake of Googling it once. What if she stepped in one and carried it back into the house? And what if Mom touched it when she was picking a book off the floor, or Dad did when he was sweeping, and they got sick, and one of them died?

She bit her wrist, hard, because she couldn't scream, not without people hearing. The last thing she needed was someone calling the cops. Her mind yarn was loosening by the second, everything coming more and more undone.

The dementia, she thought, and remembered another Google search—how fast it could consume young victims. Cicadas called loudly, swallowing every other sound. She looked toward the house. Were Mom and Dad still at the table? Had Fauna called? Had they even thought about following her?

It's okay, she thought. This was the whole idea behind karma, wasn't it? It wasn't anything more than she deserved.

The left tail light of Nonni's pickup reflected the street lamp, and Len forced herself toward it. Mosquitoes had come out, and she couldn't just stand there. She convinced herself she could Lysol her boots, and the idea gave her enough calm to will herself to the truck.

Locking herself inside the cab, she watched the last drips of sun leak into shadows. She'd always hated dusk. Nonni had told her once that she found it the most peaceful time of day, but Len couldn't imagine feeling that way. She didn't mind darkness, which Nonni thought was somehow a paradox, but it wasn't the night that bothered Len. It was the shifting and how it happened. Dad said it was a magical time—the in-between— but Len thought there was something profoundly sad about the way sunlight lost its grip, overcome, and was swallowed up by the dark.

Alone, as the final light died outside, she couldn't suppress the truth any longer. If positive thoughts can heal, then the inverse also had to be true: negative thoughts could damage. Could destroy.

Your fault.

She closed her eyes, squeezing the steering wheel so tightly she thought the skin across her knuckles might split open. "Nonni," she whispered.

"Len!"

For a brief, miraculous moment, Len thought her grand-mother had answered her. Then light spilled into the yard, and Len heard her name again. Mom looked out of the house.

Len squeezed the wheel harder. She didn't want to get out, but she couldn't let them find her here. They might notice the truck had been moved.

"*Len!* Where are you?"

Softly, she opened the door and jumped out, timing her response—"Coming!"—with the click of the door to mask the sound. It was simple, slipping from the truck unseen. Len had always fit in with the dark.

CHAPTER TWENTY-TWO

SAGE

THE NEXT DAY COULDN'T MOVE FAST ENOUGH. AS SOON AS
Len had dropped her off the day before, Sage had called the
phone number on the flier. A college student answered, and
while he was pleasant enough, Sage could tell he was skeptical
when she explained that her grades had kept her off the high
school team this year—no doubt he thought she just wasn't good
enough to make the cut. Still, he'd invited her to meet the team
the next evening at the Hendersonville Y.

"You're jumpy," Lyz told her at lunch. "What's going on?"

Sage did her best to look surprised and forced her knee to
stop its twitch beneath the table. "Nothing."

"Probably just pent-up energy," Ella said, taking a huge bite
of green beans. "When are you gonna be able to practice again,
anyway?"

Kayla's wide eyes shot Sage a look.

"Those tests, you know?" Sage plastered a fractured smile on her face and shrugged. "The results take a while." She ignored Kayla's frown.

"I can't wait till you're back," Hannah said. Nina nodded.

"Gotta follow doctor's orders," said Sage. Her knee resumed its twitch, because that was precisely what she wasn't going to do. Tonight would be her first time on a court since her diagnosis. A normal person might be terrified—there was, technically, a chance her heart might give out. But Sage had never been normal when it came to volleyball. Besides, Dr. Friedman had said it was theoretically possible she could go into sudden cardiac arrest at any moment, even when not working out. Of course that was unlikely—so unlikely, in fact, that he'd determined Sage didn't need a defibrillator. But it was nonetheless theoretically possible.

It was also theoretically possible that she could continue playing and never have a heart attack. A lot less likely. But again, *theoretically possible.*

Kayla's frown seared into her, but Sage was suddenly very busy with her mashed potatoes.

"Do you guys know that chick?" Hannah bumped Sage's elbow. "She keeps staring at us."

"That's the girl from the other day," Ella whispered. "Isn't it?"

Sage looked up just as Len dropped her eyes back to her sandwich. She sat on the far end of a long table, four seats between her and a cluster of theater students. Sage's chest twinged. Did Len seriously not have any friends at school?

Kayla made a face. "That's just Len Madder."

"Don't do that," Sage said.

"Do what?"

"Why'd you say *just* Len Madder?"

"I don't know. Hannah asked why she was staring, plus she's weird. I was only saying—"

"Yeah, well," said Sage, "I think maybe she's dealing with some stuff, so edge off."

Kayla's face turned hard, but before she could answer, Nina asked, "What kind of stuff?"

Sage shook her head. "I don't know exactly. But . . . something."

Kayla snorted. Len lifted her eyes again, and Sage gave a small wave. Len glanced over her shoulders, apparently to check that Sage was, in fact, waving at her and not someone else. It hurt Sage's soul, and before she knew it, she was calling Len to their table.

"What are you doing?" Kayla whispered.

"Give her a chance," Sage said between her teeth as Len hesitatingly gathered her things and approached them. Ella slid over to make a space between her and Hannah, but Len didn't take it. Her eyes skidded between their faces, and Sage saw her register that, should she join, she'd be the only non-volleyball starter at the table.

"Come on," Sage encouraged. "Sit." Ella patted the open space beside her.

Len stared at the seat. "Actually," she said, glancing at Hannah, "would you mind . . ." She swallowed, and Sage had the distinct impression Len was struggling with herself. "Could I maybe sit on the end instead?"

"Oh." Hannah shot a quick look to Kayla. "Um, okay." She slid down toward Ella, allowing Len to have the end seat.

"Here we go," Kayla said, just loud enough for Sage to hear.

"Thanks." Len perched on the very edge of the bench, her gloved hands still gripped on her tray, like it might fly away at any moment.

"So," Sage said, thinking maybe this had not been her best idea after all. "Everyone, this is Len."

Ella, bless her, didn't let the awkward start bother her. "Hi," she said at once, and introduced herself.

"Hi." Len's voice squeaked in a rusty chair kind of way. "I think we have Biology together?"

Ella's smile slipped. "Really? Third block? I thought I knew everyone . . ."

Len nodded. "It's okay. It's a big class. I sit in the back."

"Oh," Ella said, confidence faltering. "Well, great. Um, this is Hannah and Nina."

"I'm Lyz," Lyz added. Everyone looked at Kayla.

"We've met." Kayla crossed her arms.

"Len's a photographer," Sage said quickly.

"Oh!" Nina perked up. "My brother studies photography at UNC."

"Really?" Len finally loosened the grip on her tray. "I'd love to go there."

"Their facilities are amazing," Nina added. "It's pretty competitive, though. And expensive."

Len picked up her straw, pushing it against the table to break the paper.

"Ugh," said Ella, pulling her roll in half. "*Everywhere* is expensive, even in-state prices. My parents started a fund when I was little, and I'll still have to work full-time if I don't get a scholarship."

Sage didn't think she imagined the way Len's body tightened, but Len kept her concentration entirely on her straw. Using her teeth, she pulled it free of the wrapper, then dropped it into her glass without ever using her hands. Kayla stared at her.

"Sage," Hannah said, reaching for a napkin, "I wanted to—" But her elbow clipped Len's water, knocking it clean off the table. "Oh, sorry!" The plastic cup clattered against the tiled floor, sending liquid flying. Hannah hopped up, grabbing napkins, and began cleaning the mess. Len, who'd looked paralyzed at first, reached for the napkin dispenser.

She took double what Hannah had grabbed, but instead of squatting down to help, she dropped the napkins to the ground and pushed them around with the toe of her boot.

Hannah stood and took her wet bundle to the trash, leaving Len standing above a mound of dirtied, sopping napkins. Len hesitated, seemed to decide something, then took her fork and tray—still filled with untouched food—down to the floor, using the utensil to push wet mass onto the tray.

"What are you doing?" Kayla asked. "Aren't you going to eat?"

Len continued pushing the napkins onto the tray, her head shaking the slightest bit. "I'm not hungry."

"Why don't you just pick them up?" Kayla asked.

Len stood, the napkins amassed on her tray. "I—" She frowned, forehead pinched, unable to make eye contact.

"Sorry about that," Hannah said again, rejoining the table. "I can be such a klutz sometimes."

"I've got to go," Len said, turning so quickly she almost tripped over Hannah's feet. Her eyes met Sage's for the briefest moment. "Sorry."

"Len—" Sage called. But Len practically threw her tray onto the kitchen conveyer belt before bolting from the cafeteria.

Hannah slid back onto the bench. "What just happened?"

Kayla drew a long sip of chocolate milk through her straw. "Yeah, Sage," she said, "she's not that weird at all."

Sage clanked her silverware on her tray. Her appetite had fled along with Len. "Why'd you do that?"

"Do what?" Kayla looked genuinely confused. "I just asked a question."

Sage stood, trying to temper the gross, guilty feeling flaming through her. She'd thought inviting Len to join them would be kind, but it had totally blown up—because of her best friend, no less. She gathered her things.

"Where're you going?" Kayla asked.

As she dumped her tray, Ian caught her eye from one of the football tables, and she was suddenly thankful their lunch periods had lined up this semester. His eyes narrowed into a *You okay?* look, and she nodded. She pushed through the cafeteria door, leaving Kayla's calls to her unanswered.

* * *

Sage found Len in the back of the art room at a table squeezed between shelves full of drying clay sculptures and totally creepy papier-mâché masks. "Len?"

Len didn't look up. Her fingers swiped her eyes.

"Hey." Sage took off her backpack. "Sorry about back there. About"—her throat tightened—"Kayla." Sage wanted to make an excuse for her friend. Instead she said, "She was a jerk."

Len gave a small shrug, her hands busying themselves with a group of papers on top of a purple folder.

"What's that?" Sage asked.

"Nothing."

Sage sat next to Len, relieved she'd spoken. "It can't be nothing," she prodded. "Come on."

Len straightened the small stack. "It's the criterion for this photography scholarship, the Melford. I probably don't have a chance—"

"I've seen your photos," said Sage. "You have more than a chance." She reached out her hand. "Can I see?"

Len let her take the papers.

"This is for a full ride!" said Sage. Her eyes found the bolded qualifications section. "Applicants must be North Carolina residents, in good standing. Essays and recommendations twenty percent; portfolio makes up eighty percent and must include, yada, yada, lots of art stuff I don't understand . . ." She flipped over the paper. "Maximum of three awards per year. Scholarship may be applied to any four-year degree program in North Carolina." She looked up. "This is a nice deal."

Len nodded. "No one from Southview has ever won."

Sage couldn't help smiling. It was the kind of challenge she loved. "Then it will be even more impressive when you get one."

Len snorted, and Sage couldn't tell if she'd made Len more relaxed or stressed. Maybe she was like Hannah, who didn't fare well with too much pressure. Just in case, Sage added, "I mean, even if you don't get one, you are bound to get into a great program."

Len's face clouded. "It's like your friend said. College is expensive. If I don't get the Melford..." She collected the papers back into the folder. "I don't think I'll be going anywhere."

Sage's mouth fell open. "You can't hang your whole future on one scholarship! There must be loads out there, right? And loans—"

"My family can't take on more debt," Len said. "We just—can't."

"But—"

The door clicked, and Ms. Saffron entered the room, startling at the sight of them. "Len?" Her eyes moved to Sage quickly. "Hello. I don't think we've met?"

Sage stood up. "I'm Sage Zendasky."

"Ah. The volleyball player?"

Sage nodded, ignoring the jab in her chest.

"I hear you've got quite the future ahead of you," Ms. Saffron said. "I played in my day. Setter. Glad the sport is finally gaining some popularity in the States." Her eyes narrowed. "I don't love students in my classroom when I'm away. What are you two doing exactly?"

"Nothing," Len said, sounding not at all suspicious. "I just needed ... I mean Sage, um—"

"Len was showing me the requirements of the Melford Scholarship," Sage said smoothly. "I'm helping her."

"Is that so?" Ms. Saffron crossed her arms, amused. "And are you a photographer, Sage? Or an artist of any kind?"

Sage smiled. She liked Ms. Saffron already. "No, but I'm super with deadlines." She nodded toward Len. "I'm helping keep her on track."

Ms. Saffron arched her eyebrows, and whether she smelled bullshit or not, she clearly liked Sage's answer.

"Wonderful," Ms. Saffron said. "I was just telling Len yesterday she needs to stay on top of this. The first round is due in just over two weeks."

Sage nodded, like she was fully aware of this. Ms. Saffron eyed Len.

"You left class today before I could ask how those prompts are coming."

Len looked at the table, her hands clenched in her gloves. Ms. Saffron walked over and knelt beside her. "Len, I want to help you win this scholarship. I really think you could. But you've got two weeks to design a themed series that we can use for the application's first round, and if you're not even doing the prompts—"

"She is!" Sage blurted. "And they're great. She's been taking pics everywhere. Even under the bleachers at the football game." Her eyes went wide and knowing. "And it's gross under there."

"For *vertical*," Len piped in. Sage had no idea what that meant, but she gave a satisfied nod, like it was very impressive.

Ms. Saffron *did* look impressed and more than a bit relieved. "What an interesting viewpoint. I want to see those, definitely." Her nails, turquoise and glittery, drummed the table. "How are you doing, Len?" Her voice reminded Sage of a warm blanket.

Len dug her hands into her sweatshirt's pockets. "Fine. I'm good."

"Remember," Ms. Saffron said, "you can always talk to me." Her eyes slid to Sage, who looked away, unsure what was happening. "I'm always here."

Len nodded, and Ms. Saffron stood up, her eyes finding the clock above the door. "Now, ladies, I need to get ready for my next class, so if you don't mind—" She held out her hand for them to exit.

"You're a good liar," Len said as soon as they were out of earshot. Sage wrinkled her nose. "That didn't come out right," Len said quickly. "I meant thanks for saying that back there."

Sage nodded. "No worries."

"You should know, though, my prompts are crap."

"So take more pictures." Sage stopped at the stairwell. "My next class is upstairs."

"I'm down," said Len.

"Okay. Well, see you around, then." Sage leaned on the door handle.

"Wait!"

Sage turned.

"Did you mean what you said back there, about keeping me on track?" Len asked. "Or were you just, you know, saying that?"

Sage tucked a thumb under the strap of her backpack. "I mean, I am good with deadlines." She shrugged. "You want me to text you reminders or something?"

"I don't have a cell phone."

Sage blinked back her astonishment. Was she serious?

"We had to make some budget cuts," Len said, looking down, "a few months ago. My Nonni, um, grandmother—" Her voice cracked.

"No problem," Sage said. "I totally get it. Maybe I could, um, ask you every couple days or something? Or is there something else that would help?"

"Actually." Len looked up. "Maybe—"

The bell rang above them, setting off a stampede of fast-approaching. footsteps. "I used to hike on the Parkway," Len said. "All the time, with my sister. A lot of my best photos come from there, but I haven't been in a while, and, well, I know you have practice after school, but maybe after that?" She shrugged. "It would be nice not to go alone."

A couple students nudged past them, pushing them into the stairwell. "Oh," said Sage, "I love hiking."

Len smiled.

"But . . . I can't."

The smile collapsed. "Yeah, no problem."

Sage could tell she expected a reason, but Len knew about her diagnosis. There was no way Sage could tell her about tonight's tryout with the Hendersonville team. "I'm sorry," Sage said and was surprised to find she truly meant it. "Another time maybe?"

Len nodded quickly, slinking back into the hall. "Sure," she said. "No big deal. Forget it." The hallway pulsed and writhed with bodies, and before Sage could say another word, Len stepped into the crowd and was gone.

CHAPTER TWENTY-THREE

SAGE

SAGE TOLD COACH SHE HAD TO MISS PRACTICE DUE TO A cardiology appointment, which he totally bought. She rechecked the YMCA address as soon as she got into the Subaru. So far, that was the only positive to having a defective heart. Mom felt so bad for her that, after getting Dr. Friedman to clear Sage for driving, she gave Sage full access to the extra car.

Derek, the boy who'd answered the number on the flyer, had told her to meet the team in the gym at four p.m., so she was a good twenty minutes early.

She heard it before she saw it—the uneven rhythm of balls smacking the court—and walked in to discover the place filled with players. Of course. This must be open practice for the competing teams. She felt silly for thinking it would only be the team offering the tryout. They couldn't reserve the whole court.

Her phone buzzed from her bag.

Kayla: Where r u? Coach said you had appt??

Sage frowned, still annoyed with Kayla for upsetting Len. She switched off the phone and tossed her duffle near a group of bags against the wall. As she leaned into a hamstring stretch, the sounds of the gym sank into her. The thuds of volleyballs on skin, the calls from setters, the squeaks of shoes—they settled into her blood, pulsing beside her heart, and she had the distinct feeling that she'd been asleep for days and had suddenly awoken.

"Are you Sage?"

She turned at the voice, the same one from the phone. "Yeah."

"Excellent." The boy clasped her hand. "I'm Derek." He nodded around the court. "We've worn our team shirts so you can identify us."

He pointed to the service line, where two women wearing shirts identical to his—teal with white lettering—stood warming up. "Those two are Lucy and Flick. Both played at UNC Asheville. Flick's our player-coach and wicked smart. You can thank her for the tryout protocol you're about to go through." As if she knew Derek was talking about her, Flick tossed the ball, jumped, and served with a sharp wrist that clearly earned her the nickname. It was the fastest jumper Sage had ever seen in person.

Derek pointed to another teal-shirted woman by the net. "Ketia's our setter. She turned down a volleyball scholarship at App State for a full academic ride to UNCA." He nodded at the giant man who had just stepped up for his turn to attack. "And that," he said, "is Mountain."

Mountain, Sage estimated, was at least six feet ten inches, and it didn't escape her notice that all the players opposite him cleared the floor as he tossed the ball to Ketia.

"Mountain's from San Diego," Derek said. "Probably coulda gone pro if he hadn't wanted to be an engineer."

Mountain proceeded to drill the ball inside the ten-foot line.

"Daaamn," Sage said. To play alongside that kind of skill—it would be incredible.

"Yeah," said Derek, misreading her excitement for nerves. "He gave the last guy that tried out a bloody nose; but that kid, well, he was subpar. I'm sure you'll do much better."

A smile played at her lips. Derek was trying to scare her, to gauge her grace under pressure. "What about you?" Sage asked, licking her palm and swiping it across the bottom of her Asics for traction. "What's your story?"

"Not as much of a pedigree, I'm afraid," he said. "I'm a senior at UNCA. Ketia got me playing when we met a few years ago, and I got, you might say, obsessed. You ready?"

Sage nodded.

Derek cupped his hands around his mouth. "TEALs, gather up!" His teammates looked over, their eyes moving past him to Sage. Most of them smiled, but they were the kind of smiles that said they weren't expecting much. Lucy gave Mountain a look, and Sage knew what it meant. What kind of high schooler would be available for a rec league in mid-season? But Sage didn't mind. With her name in the Asheville paper so often over the past couple years, she hadn't gotten underestimated by anyone in a while. A thrill itched through her, shutting out the whisper that had nagged her all day—*Was this safe? Could she actually die?*

Sage cracked her knuckles. The thing about Russian roulette, she reminded herself, was that most of the time, you won.

"Come on," Derek said. "Let's see what you've got."

* * *

They put her through the paces. And despite her multi-day break, Sage felt as if no time had passed at all. Her ankle had healed, she was back to full potential, and she was born to do this.

No one said anything, but she saw the tiny changes in their expressions with each drill. Derek's expression went from humoring to intent as he peppered with her to warm up. Flick raised her eyebrows when Sage nailed her jump serves. After an attack drill, Lucy looked at Mountain again, though this time her eyes were pleased.

When Sage had successfully dug Mountain's serve, Ketia laughed out loud. "That's enough for me," she said. "Flick?"

Flick motioned for her teammates to join her, and Sage had a moment to take stock as they huddled. Far from breathless, the drills had energized her. She felt buoyant, a volleyball Wonder

Woman who could play forever. Something that made her this happy, that felt this incredible, it couldn't be wrong, could it? The world couldn't be that cruel.

The team walked up to her, Flick leading the rest. "It's Sage, right?"

Sage nodded.

Flick crossed her arms. "You're not terrible."

Sage bit down a smile. Flick was a lot like her own coach, and though the words didn't sound like much, she knew they were a compliment. "Thanks."

Mountain stared down at her. "You really in high school?"

"I am."

"So why aren't you on a team again?"

Sage shrugged. "Grades."

Lucy folded her arms. "You're better than some of UNCA's girls," she said. "You probably coulda played there. Too bad about your grades."

"But good for us," said Mountain, clapping her on the shoulder. "Welcome to the team, Tiny."

Sage almost snorted, until she realized that for the first time in her life, she *was* the smallest player on her team. She'd thought Ketia was also five-eleven, but no. Standing right next to her, it was clear the setter was a good inch taller.

"Not yet," Flick said, holding up her hand and slicing through Sage's ease. "Mondays and Wednesdays are all-player open practices like this, three thirty to six thirty. Games are Friday evenings, starting at seven. You can be here? On time, every time?"

Sage nodded. "Yes."

"Occasionally I call team meetings, impromptu. Not required, but suggested."

"Strongly suggested," Mountain coughed.

"Are those in the evenings?" Sage asked.

Flick nodded. "Derek has your number?"

"I do," Derek said. "I'll add it to the group text."

Flick's dark eyes locked on Sage's. "This isn't just some silly rec league, understand? They're doing a state tournament this year, and the winners of all A leagues advance." She took a micro-step toward Sage. "I want that spot." She looked around. "*We* want that spot. And if we win the next two games, we get it."

Sage struggled to keep her face smooth. It was like the universe was giving her a sign, showing her she'd made the right choice. She could get her state title after all.

"I won't let you down," she promised.

Flick stared at her a moment longer. "We're counting on you now." She held out her hand. "Welcome to the team."

CHAPTER TWENTY-FOUR

LEN

LEN USED HER PHOTOGRAPHY PROMPT ASSIGNMENT FROM Ms. Saffron as the excuse to bolt right before Fauna's nightly phone call.

"Gravity, Reflection, Part of a Whole." She muttered the prompt words like a mantra as she crossed the rear school parking lot. She would have something to show Ms. Saffron tomorrow if it killed her.

Len had wanted to drive the Parkway, hoping the change of scenery would light her muse, but Dad said they didn't have gas to waste and Mom refused to let her bike on the blind curves. So she was stuck walking, like always, her camera looped around her neck should inspiration strike.

A large boulder marked the entrance to the back lot; it was spray-painted with Southview's blue and silver colors and an all-caps message about how this year's seniors were kick ass.

Original. When Len was a kid, she used to dream about the day she'd help paint the rock for her class—she was pretty sure she had a journal with doodling ideas somewhere—but now the whole ritual seemed pathetic. What a waste of time and paint to decorate something only so it could be vandalized the following year, as if your words and images had never existed, or, worse, didn't matter. She started toward the rock, but stopped at the grass's edge. It needed mowing. Who knew what she might step in?

A crow landed on the rock, tilting its head in sharp movements, and cawed at her.

"You're right," she said. "It might work for *Part of a Whole*." She snapped a picture, then turned quickly. The last thing she needed was someone from school overhearing her talking to a bird. Luckily, the only person around was a jogger wearing earbuds. Len looked back to the crow, to tell him they were safe, but it had already flown away, embarrassed to be seen with her.

Like Sage, Len thought, when she'd suggested they hike together. Sourness prickled through her, bitter as a vitamin on an empty stomach. She couldn't believe she'd thought Sage might actually want to hang out with her again. The coffee shop had been a fluke, a distraction because Sage had been upset and needed to get away. But Sage had come to check on her after lunch, had stuck up for her with Ms. Saffron, and Len couldn't stop the hope that bubbled up, that maybe Sage wasn't just being a good human. Maybe they could be friends.

She crossed the library lot that abutted the school's back parking area, crossed the road, and entered the picturesque neighborhood of Biltmore Woods. A lot of her classmates lived here, she knew, and she often wished she could ask what they used them for, all those rooms.

She pointed her camera—not at the houses, which, though magazine beautiful, were uninteresting for precisely the same reason. Instead, she zoomed in on smaller, often overlooked things: the street lamps; the tiny bark bits that littered the forest edges just beyond the neighborhood; the trees whose branches shaded the sidewalks.

Trees, she thought suddenly. They could be her theme. Trees and parts of trees. She could do some cool things with acorn patterns, with rings.

Talk about unoriginal, a voice in her head whispered, and it was immediately joined by the echo of Ms. Saffron's condemnation: *sterile*.

She pushed the memory away, snapping images at random. *Better done messy than not at all*, that's what Nonni used to say. Just get photos for the prompts. That was today's mission. That would be good enough.

As she walked home, dusk draped its sad fingers over every corner of the world. Len distracted herself from it by focusing on the ground in front of her, on not stepping on anything that might dirty her boots.

"Someone called for you," Dad said as she entered the house. Len stopped at the edge of the living room where her parents sat together on the sofa.

"You mean Fauna?"

"No," Mom said, her tone short. "I think she's given up on you."

The shame Len felt at disappointing her, at disappointing Fauna, was overshadowed by curiosity. "Who called then?" she asked Dad.

He finished a line in his sketchbook. "Sage someone. Strange last name." He held up a piece of paper. "She left her number. Asked you to call her back."

When Len tried to take the paper, Dad held on, catching her eyes. "Did you get some good photos?"

She nodded. Before he could say anything else, she tugged away the paper, grabbed the cordless from its base in the kitchen, and hurried to her room.

There was a moment when she didn't know if she could call. What if she was humiliated again? But then—what if Sage was having another panic attack? What if she needed her? Before she could talk herself out of it, Len dialed.

"Hey, Len!"

Sage's recognition caught her off guard. "Oh. Uh, hi."

"What's up?"

"Um, nothing." Len frowned, confused. "My dad said you called?"

"Yeah. He said you were out taking pictures. That's awesome!" Her voice was brighter than Len had ever heard it. Almost chipper. "Did you get some good stuff for your prompts?"

"Maybe." Len couldn't believe she'd remembered. "Were you . . . um . . . calling to check up on my progress?"

"Yes and no. I wanted to see if tomorrow would work for a hike? I checked and the weather's supposed to be nice. Sorry I couldn't go today."

Len's mouth opened and closed wordlessly.

"Hello?"

"I'm here," Len said, taking a deep breath. "Listen, it was really nice what you did today, but"—she shook her head, even though Sage couldn't see—"I don't need pity, okay, so if you just feel sorry for me—"

Silence.

Len waited for the click of a hang up, but it didn't come. Finally, Sage said, "I don't feel sorry for you." There was an edge to her words that wasn't there before. "I mean, I do, but not in the way you mean it. I feel sorry because I know you're sad, even though I don't know why. And honestly . . . Damn, you're right. I *do* say that word a lot."

Len smiled.

"Anyway, I feel like something is *wrong*, Len. Like maybe something happened to you, something bad. And it's fine if you don't want to tell me. But, I don't know . . ."

Len gripped the phone tighter, unable to answer.

"After what I told you the other day"—Sage's voice went higher than normal—"I get what you mean about not wanting pity." The phone crackled. "I'm talking to myself, aren't I? If you don't want to go—"

"Will it just be me and you?" Len asked.

"Who else?" Sage began. "Oh. You're worried about Kayla."

Len's mind couldn't stop replaying it, the way Kayla had looked at her as she pushed the paper towels onto her tray. The judgment in her voice when she'd asked Len what she was doing.

"It will just be you and me," Sage said.

Len nodded. "Okay."

CHAPTER TWENTY-FIVE

SAGE

AFTER LAST NIGHT'S SUCCESSFUL TRYOUT, SAGE FELT almost herself again. Enough, anyway, to concentrate on classes and fend off her friends' concern.

"How was your appointment?" Ella asked as she, Sage, and Kayla walked their usual route to practice after school.

Sage's jaw tightened. "Good," she said. "You know, as expected."

Kayla caught Sage's eye. She'd asked the same question that morning, but left it alone when Sage answered "fine" in a way that clearly meant she didn't want to talk about it.

"Did they say when you can play again?" Ella asked.

Sage called back the killer attacks she'd made last night, the respect she'd earned from talented college players. The triumph of it dulled the ache brought on by Ella's question. "Not yet, but they said I'll know soon." Her phone buzzed as she swung open the gym door.

Flick: Team meeting tonight. 7 pm. Patton Park.

"Ooo," said Ella. "Why the grin? Text crush?"

"What? No. It's nothing."

"Fine," said Ella teasingly. "Keep your little secret. We'll find out soon enough." As Ella headed for the locker room, Kayla grabbed Sage's arm, holding her back. "Are you bullshitting me?" she whispered. "Do you actually have more tests?"

Sage keep her face even, but her voice came out hollow and disjointed. "Why would I lie about that?"

Kayla released her arm. "I've been wondering that myself."

Sage matched her hard gaze, but she couldn't speak. Kayla stepped toward the locker room, then turned back suddenly, her eyes locking again on Sage's. "I don't know how to help you," she said. "Tell me what I can do."

Disappointment flooded Sage, like someone had shot it through her veins. "Tell you?"

"Yes. What do you need? Tell me how to help you."

You're my best friend! Sage shouted in her head. *You're just supposed to know.*

"Sage?"

It hurt to see Kayla desperate, imploring. But Sage couldn't answer her. It changed things, Kayla's not knowing. Somehow, in some ineffable but heartbreakingly real way, things between them had shifted.

"It's fine," Sage managed at last. "I'm okay. You're helping."
She swallowed the knot in her throat and went to help Hannah
tighten the net.

* * *

Sage's game face got her through practice. Coach let her help
lead warm-ups, as usual, though she wasn't allowed to do any
of them, which was humiliating. When Coach told her that he
couldn't even let her pepper with Kayla, Sage was sure something inside her withered up and died.

Still, her game face didn't waver. Her body control was so
great, in fact, that she numbed her whole self, doing whatever
she was asked—brainstorming plays with Coach, advising the
JVers on their attack approaches, and then sitting the bench
as her teammates ran through drills—all with the emotion of
a zombie.

I'm on the A team, she reminded herself, as she watched her
replacement shank a serve into the stands. *We're going to win
the championship. We're going to win a state title.*

She closed her eyes, reviewing the play names Flick had
given her after practice the day before. *I can still matter.*

At four thirty, when practice shifted to scrimmaging, it
dawned on Sage that there was no way she could hike with
Len *and* attend the meeting, not if she stayed until the end of
practice. Her lip curled unconsciously. And why should she do
that? She might be a captain, but she wasn't going to interfere

with Coach's instructions during the scrimmage. And Len had been so excited about hiking. If Sage called it off again, without explanation, she'd be hurt for sure.

Hand on her stomach, Sage asked Coach if she could go home, pleading a stomachache. And of course he let her. She was a liability now, and her dad was a lawyer. The realization sent a physical pang through her gut, and Sage pretended not to see Kayla's eyes follow her as she beelined out of the gym.

This time, Len answered the door on the first knock.

CHAPTER TWENTY-SIX

LEN

SAGE DIDN'T LOOK GREAT.

"Practice is over already?" Len asked.

Sage shrugged. "You ready?" There was an urgency in her face.

Len followed her to the Subaru that was parked in the drive, camera bag bouncing against her side. She couldn't make it add up, the way Sage had sounded last night on the phone—breathless and ecstatic—and the way she moved now, jerky and desperate. Something didn't jibe.

"Do you have a spot you like to go?" Sage's voice was sharp, all business, as Len slipped into the passenger side. "A favorite hike or something?" She started the car.

Len buckled her seatbelt, careful not to let the bag slip to the floor. "It doesn't really matter." Sage accidentally revved the car, cursed, then released the parking brake. The car kicked up stones as she backed out.

Len clutched her bag tighter. She knew better than to ask if everything was okay, even if she hadn't already known about Sage's heart. Still, she needed to say something. It was one of the loneliest pains, she knew, when people recognized hurt but pretended they didn't. When they ignored it simply because they didn't know what to say.

"So, uh . . ." She floundered a bit as Sage's face creased into a frown. "You had a good day yesterday?"

Sage flicked on the signal, turned onto the main road. "What do you mean?" Her voice betrayed a twinge of panic.

Len stared out the window so Sage's clipped expression couldn't intimidate her. "You sounded really happy on the phone, so I thought . . ." She chose her words slowly, carefully. "Maybe something good had happened? Some good news?" She turned back to Sage, who had hunched over the steering wheel, hands perfectly positioned at ten and two. It probably wasn't the smartest thing Len had ever done, driving with someone whose heart might give out at any moment. But then, probably better to die in a car crash, head-on with a tractor trailer, than suffer the crippling demise of childhood dementia.

"Yesterday was a good day," Sage mumbled. The traffic lights all glowed green, blessing their journey, and they flew down the four-lane in no time.

And then there was a semi, exactly like Len had envisioned, like she had somehow called it to them. Len shut her eyes, because how could she keep denying it? Manifestations were real. The truck was proof. *Just don't think*, she told herself. *Don't think anything bad. Nothing bad. Our lives depend on it.*

By the time she opened her eyes again, they were passing the arboretum, climbing up to the Parkway. It surprised her that Sage hadn't said anything, hadn't wondered why her eyes were clamped closed for what must have been several minutes. But Sage seemed lost inside herself.

At the stop sign, Sage finally glanced at her. "Actually," she said, "if you don't care, I have an idea." A motorcycle whizzed down from the mountain, followed by a train of cars. "There's this place," Sage said. "I go there when I'm feeling, um, not myself and, I don't know. It sounds kinda dumb, but I think it helps." She shrugged.

"Sounds like I should live there," Len said, and Sage laughed, her veil of irritation fluttering just a bit. The last car zoomed in front of them and Sage jetted onto the Parkway, the sudden acceleration pressing Len back into the leather seat. Sage punched a button, illuminating SIRIUS ALT NATION in boxy, calculator letters on the screen, and music flooded the car.

Sage's shoulders twitched, then bounced, her lips pursed. Len wondered if she was having some kind of fit.

"Are you okay?"

"Oh." Sage flushed. "Yeah." The twitching stopped, and her shoulders slumped forward. "I was singing." There was a shade of mortification in her tone. "In my head."

"You can sing," Len said. "I don't mind."

Sage shook her head. "I'm bad," she said. "I don't look bad in front of people." She clamped her mouth shut and cranked the volume louder.

Len turned back to her window, remembering, with a pang of embarrassment, the undeniable relief in Mom's face when Len had mentioned the hiking excursion.

"I'm so happy you're making friends," she'd said, practically radiant.

Friends. Len sneaked a glance at Sage, wondering if the word fit them, or if they were more like two lost people who, when with each other, weren't quite as lost anymore. Was that the definition of friendship? It seemed a bit bleak, even for Len.

The car climbed higher and higher, until finally Sage slowed, the *tick tick* of the car's blinker cutting in to Len's thoughts.

"There's a trail here?" Len asked.

"Uh huh." Sage parked on the tiny pull off, barely large enough for one vehicle.

"Does it connect to a lookout?"

"Not a lookout." Sage cut the engine. "Something much better."

They got out, Sage leaving her keys in the cup holder, the door unlocked. Len finally located the tiny indentation in the woods. The path looked overgrown and too small to be part of the official trails kept up by the park service.

"How did you even find this?"

Sage grabbed a long-sleeve T-shirt from the trunk. "Accident." She slipped the shirt—Southview Volleyball—over her head. "We took a wrong turn on another trail. I'm not sure where it ultimately ends up. I've never gone the whole way." She shut the trunk with a thud and headed toward the path, slightly muddled with wisps of fallen cloud. "Come on."

The mist often descended quickly in the mountains. Tourists hated the way it muted views for their Instagram posts, but Len had always felt at home in the mist. Especially this kind, thin enough to let you see twenty feet or so ahead before it shrouded the distance. "Hang on a sec," she told Sage as she tugged out and assembled her camera. She snapped a few test shots, then a few more, to calibrate the light settings. "Okay," she said. "Ready."

After several silent minutes, Sage stepped off the path.

"What are you doing?"

"It's this way," Sage said. "The spot I was telling you about."

"You mean, off the trail?"

Sage turned around. "Is that a problem?"

Len surveyed the long, tangled weeds and briar thickets on either side of Sage.

"You just have to mash them down," Sage said, as if reading her thoughts. "Most of them are broken already from when we were here last time."

Len didn't ask who "we" was, but she had a pretty good idea.

"Are you coming?"

Len took a deep breath and nodded. She couldn't go back now. And it was okay. Sage was in there in only shorts, the edges of vines clipping her skin, and she was fine. She wasn't even worried. Len used to explore places like this all the time. She could do it again. She *would* do it.

She placed one foot off the path. Then another. *Don't think,* she commanded her brain. That proved impossible, though, so she concentrated on imaging a bright, protective light surrounding her body, keeping her safe.

"See that oak?" Sage pointed. "Just there? That's where we're going."

Len nodded, ignoring the sweat skidding down her neck and back. She snapped a few photos, then ducked low to avoid a grapevine, which Sage had lifted without a thought. Finally, Sage stopped, holding out her arm so Len wouldn't walk past her.

Several feet beyond Sage, Len saw that the ground fell away completely. The chasm ran left and right as far as she could make out, but it wasn't particularly wide, at least not here. A huge, fallen tree, its thick, vein-like roots exposed and dangling, crossed the divide right in front of them. A knot of entwined roots formed steps, as if they had been created specifically for that purpose.

"This is it," Sage said, her hand sweeping toward the fallen tree. "This is the bridge."

Sage pulled herself onto the roots steps, using a higher root for balance. "Careful," she told Len. She tested a spot with her foot before stepping on it with her full weight. "There're a few rotten parts."

Len inched over to the drop off, but all she saw was an ocean of fog. "How far down does that go?"

Sage shrugged. "Far enough to matter."

You shouldn't do this, Len thought, at the same time she knew that she would. That she wanted to. She secured her camera around her neck and pulled herself up.

"There're seats over here," Sage said. "Or sort-of seats. Come on."

Len found her way to where Sage had draped herself in a crook of overlapping branches, and squeezed herself into a similar nook. The branch she leaned against swayed slightly.

Sage tipped her head back, eyes closed. Len stuck her camera through the tree's crevices, snapping images from all angles—close-ups of the bark; of tiny beetles, which she fended off with a stick when they got too near; of the leaf patterns above them and the mossed-over rocks that peeked through the mist below. As she adjusted her lens, her boot nicked a piece of bark. It dropped silently into the abyss. Len peered over a little farther. It would be so easy, she thought, to move just a few inches forward. To let herself tip over and fall.

Her body shuddered, scared by her brain, and she jerked backward.

Sage opened her eyes. "Everything okay?"

Heat rushed Len's whole body. *Don't tell. Don't let her know you're crazy.* But Len couldn't help it. It was so tiring, keeping this to herself. She was so tired of feeling tired.

"I was thinking," Len began, "and this, uh, it might sound crazy, because I *do not* want to jump off a cliff or anything, really. But sometimes . . ." Her eyes strayed over the tree bridge. "Sometimes I wonder what it would feel like. And how easily I could do it. Jump. You know?"

Sage frowned.

"It's stupid," Len said. "Forget it."

"No," Sage said. "I've felt that way, too."

"You have?"

"Yeah." Sage pulled her knees to her chest. "Just like you said, I don't *want* to jump, but I feel like, if I'm there too long, near the edge, maybe I will."

"Yes!" Len said. "Exactly."

"It makes me feel a bit better, actually," Sage said, "knowing I'm not the only one." She cocked her head. "Don't you think it's strange that we've both felt that way? Like, is it a thing? Some kind of universal feeling?"

Len's relief at Sage's admission was too large to give much thought to the question. Maybe she wasn't so alone after all. Whatever was happening to her—whatever was overtaking her brain—maybe she could fight it. Like the man Dad told her about. The brain was powerful—humans only understood ten percent of it, after all. She just needed to try harder, to will it into submission. She wanted her *self* back. Her real self.

"I mean, where would it come from?" Sage continued. "If we don't *want* to jump, why would our brains give us that feeling?" She rested her head on her pulled-up knees. "I would love to know."

Len didn't really want to talk about brains. Instead, she asked a question she hadn't even realized had been in her mind until it slipped out: "Do you believe in an energy force? Something that, uh, kind of unites the universe?"

Sage turned her head, still resting on her knees, to look at her. "What do you mean? Like, God?"

Len shifted. "Not exactly, although I guess maybe it's what some people mean by God." Len's family had never been religious in the typical sense. "My parents call it the Life Force. I think in Chinese philosophy there's something called *qi* that's similar—that's what my dad said." She shrugged. "Sometimes I think I feel it connecting things. Connecting people."

Sage stayed quiet, and for a moment Len worried she'd offended her. What if she was uber religious and thought Len was some kind of heathen? What had she been thinking, asking a question like that? She was so stupid sometimes. But then Sage smiled. "Life Force sounds a little woo-woo for me. But do you mean like The Force in *Star Wars*? Because I'm totally into that."

Len smiled. "Yeah, I guess so. Something like that."

A breeze rippled the leaves like wind chimes, then whirled stronger, sending a low, eerie whistle through the crevice below them. It was just the way sound worked, how wind created ghostly calls when channeled through tight spaces, but Sage and Len still looked at each other, wide-eyed.

"Whoa," Sage whispered. "That was weird."

"A sign?" Len whispered back.

"I don't know if I'd go that far," Sage said, "but it was cool anyway." Another gust whipped up, and this time Sage played along, rising to her knees, arms spreading. "Take it in, Len!" She giggled, clearly self-conscious, but then, slowly, her face changed. Relaxed.

It was happening, Len realized, right in front of her. The energy force Dad was always going on about—it was flowing right there and Sage was tapping into it, soaking it in.

Len turned her face up, the wind catching her hair, tugging strands of it free. But it wasn't enough, the light touch on her face. She needed more. Her whole body craved it.

In a fierce impulse, Len peeled off her gloves. The wind kissed the chapped skin of her hands. It was delicious. Mirroring Sage, she lifted onto her knees, eyes closed.

How had she survived without this for so long—the taste of the world on her bare skin, its wildness rippling through her. Part of her shouted, *Danger!* But no. She could do this. She could beat down those thoughts. She could win.

"Oh!" Sage said. "Your gloves!"

Len opened her eyes, smiling, pleased that Sage had realized what a big deal removing them was for her. But Sage wasn't looking at her hands.

"There!" Sage pointed, and Len turned just in time to see the wind whisk one of her gloves along the trunk.

"No!" Len dived after it, but too late. The glove skipped farther, then turned, airborne, and dropped into the chasm. Len's hands dug at the bark to maintain her balance. Something wet and mushy soaked under her nails. A beetle grazed her fingertip.

A guttural cry scraped out of her, and she yanked her hand skyward, her fingers covered with dark pieces of who-knew-what. She shrieked, a shrill, almost unnatural wail.

"What?" Sage asked. "What is it?"

Len pushed herself up and staggered forward, practically diving back to the ground. She dragged her hand through the grass. Some of the dark pieces fell off, but her hand was still filthy and now she'd touched the germ-ridden ground.

Don't do this, she willed herself. *You were so close.* But then she was screaming, a feral, horrible sound. She heard her name, and there was Sage beside her, her face creased and terrified.

"It's okay—" Sage started.

"Does this look okay to you?" Len screamed, and Sage stepped back. Len shook her head, shook it so wildly her hair tumbled loose, the whole unbrushed mess of it, covering her neck and shoulders. She bent over, stomach threatening to empty, and gagged, all while managing to keep her unclean hand away from the rest of her body.

"It's only a panic attack," Sage said, like she was some expert now. Len's body convulsed and she stumbled, her knees buckling. She screamed again as her hands and knees hit the ground. *I'm going to disintegrate*, she thought wildly, lungs burning. *Whatever's happening, I can't take it. I'm going to splinter and fall apart.*

Twigs cracked, then footsteps, and Len couldn't believe Sage was still here, that she hadn't abandoned her like the freak show she was. She wouldn't have blamed her. She should have known not to get close to anyone after Nadia. But that was

Len's problem. She wasn't careful enough. She was *never* careful enough. If she had been, this wouldn't be happening. If she was careful, she wouldn't have ruined her family's lives.

"Len?" Sage's voice was unsettled, but firm. It was not—Len registered—disgusted.

Len hiccupped, sniffling. She couldn't touch anything. She would be down here forever, trapped in a warped version of child's pose. Maybe this was where she would die.

"Can you hear me?" Sage bent down, and Len met her eyes. Everything was still, the forest silent except for her labored breathing. Even the wind had fled her.

"Please," Len whimpered. "Get it off."

CHAPTER TWENTY-SEVEN

SAGE

LEN HAD LOST HER SHIT.

No, Sage reminded herself. It was a panic attack, like the one Sage had had after the game. Now Len needed strength, and strength was Sage's specialty.

Sage inched closer. Len, still on her hands and knees, held her left arm out at an odd angle, like it was an unwanted growth. She spoke, garbled and unintelligible.

"Here," Sage said. "Let me help you."

Len jerked back. "Don't touch my hands."

"What?"

"Can you—" Len was visibly shaking. Sage grabbed her elbow without any protest from Len and helped her stand. Len held her hands out, zombie-like.

"I'm here," Sage said. "What do you need?"

Len's face twisted. "I'm sorry." She was battling with something Sage couldn't see. That was clear.

"It's okay," Sage said. Her heart twinged with pity, but also with more fascination than she cared to admit.

"My bag." Len's voice broke, but at least it was louder. "There're wipes." She stretched her hand out farther. "Help me clean my hand."

Sage swallowed. "Your bag is on your back," she said slowly. "Right there."

Len wouldn't meet her eyes. "Please," she said. "My hands . . . I can't . . . I can't touch my bag." A tear rolled down her cheek. "*Please.*"

This was more than a panic attack, Sage realized. This was something else. Sage's body tightened, but her game face stayed even, her take-charge instincts kicking in. She stepped behind Len and unzipped her camera bag, careful not to let anything spill. She found a travel dispenser of antibacterial wipes.

"Here," she said, holding them out.

Len stared at the ground. "Can you please wipe my hands off?" The words came out in a rush. She shut her eyes tight, her whole face scrunched, then opened them again. "I know it's weird, but please?"

Sage suppressed the urge to let her mouth fall open. *This is more than weird,* she thought. *Way, way more.* Something was seriously wrong. Something about Len was broken.

"Please," Len echoed.

Sage took a deep, steadying breath. She didn't particularly want to clean someone else's hands with wipes. Kayla's voice nudged into her. *Clean your own damn hands. I'm out.*

Len's eyes remained fixed on the ground. Sage pulled out a fistful of wipes.

"Is this why you freaked out?" she asked quietly, because it was too uncomfortable to do this in silence, to pull dirt and tree debris from the finger pads of another person. "I thought it was because you lost a glove, but was it because you touched something?"

Len's eyes focused on Sage's movements. "I don't like dirt."

That might be an understatement, Sage thought. She'd gotten most of the dirt off, but took another wipe from the package and ran it over each of Len's fingers again, the way the manicurists massaged each finger bone when she and Mom went to the salon.

"I'm sorry," Len muttered again.

"It's okay."

"No," Len said. "It's not okay. I ruined it."

Sage looked up. "Ruined what?"

"Everything."

Sage waited for her to elaborate, but instead Len pulled her hands away. "Okay," she said, studying her palms. "That's good." She stuffed her hands into the front pocket of her sweatshirt, relief visibly transforming her. "Thank you."

Sage nodded. "Okay, I guess . . . um . . ."

"Definitely," Len said. "Let's go home."

* * *

Len didn't speak as they wound back down the Parkway. But Sage couldn't stop herself. "In the picture," she said, "the one in your room, you aren't wearing gloves."

Len hugged her bag to her chest. Sage noticed she was careful not to let any part of it touch the grass stains on her knees.

"And that picture," Sage continued, "you said it was from last year. That's not that long ago."

Silence.

"Look," Sage said, "we can pretend nothing happened if you want, but we both know what happened back there wasn't normal. That wasn't just a panic attack."

Len made a show of turning to the passenger window.

Sage tried again. "When did you first start—?"

"I don't know," Len snapped, which made Sage think that, in fact, she did.

Sage gripped the steering wheel tighter. "Why'd you want to go hiking if you don't like getting dirty?"

Len put a hand to her temple. "I love hiking." Her voice was thin. "Or loved. I wanted to still be able to do it. But I think it's getting worse."

Dread crawled into Sage's chest, dry and scratchy. "*What* is getting worse?"

Len still wouldn't look at her. "You don't want to know."

When they pulled into Len's driveway, Len muttered a quick "thanks" and jumped out before Sage could say anything else.

"Hey!" Sage cut the engine and jumped out to follow her. Len turned, surprised.

"I, um, need to go the bathroom," Sage said.

Len frowned. "Okay." She jiggled the lock and the door open. "Back there, you remember?" She pointed through the kitchen. "First door on the right."

"Thanks." Sage found herself in the small, green-tiled bathroom that probably hadn't been renovated since the seventies. She hadn't noticed before, but the shower curtain was whale themed. Several bottles of essential oils lined the mirror, as well as four different types of gemstones. Sage's eyebrows rose. She couldn't really get a read on the Madders. She waited several moments, stalling, then washed her hands.

As soon as she returned, Len moved past her with a quick "you can let yourself out, yeah?" and it hit Sage that that must be the only bathroom in the house. The bathroom door shut, and Sage found herself alone in the tiny kitchen. A quick look around told her there was no one else home. Somewhere, wind chimes clinked, but the sound was soon drowned out by running water. Shower water. The hand wipes apparently hadn't been good enough.

Sage sat down at the table. There was no way she could leave Len alone, not after the major freak-out she'd just had. She pulled out her phone. The first phrase she Googled—*freaks out if gets dirty*—yielded a bunch of hits about the wrong kind of dirty.

"Ugh," Sage muttered, deleting the results.

Wears gloves all the time didn't fare much better. She scrolled through each hit, but none of them offered any kind of explanation. Sage slumped back in the chair. There had to be an answer somewhere, but she couldn't figure out how to ask the question. She didn't have the right words.

She sat up, because that was it. It was just like her Lit teacher had said last year every time someone suggested a research essay topic: *It's not specific enough. How will you research that?*

Sage reopened the Google app, replaying Len's despair over and over. *Be specific.* She bit her cheek and typed: *severe panic attack from dirt.*

These hits were much more on target, offering the difference between panic attacks, panic disorders, and anxiety attacks. Sage's eyes widened. Who knew they were different? She almost clicked on the first hit, but no, it wasn't really what she needed. She thumbed down further, skimming the summaries of each one.

"Come on," she breathed. "I don't know how else to explain it." She scrolled again. There had to be something else. Something she was missing.

Suddenly, as she was about to clear the search and start again, a phrase caught her eye: *contamination fear.*

"You're still here."

Sage's head shot up. Len stood in the kitchen doorway, fingering the neck of a new sweatshirt with her gloved hands. *How many gloves did the girl own?* The pink towel wrapping her wet hair slipped slightly. She couldn't quite meet Sage's eyes. "Why?"

Sage made a face. "Um, I don't know, to make sure you're okay?"

Len's mouth pinched, like she couldn't understand the answer.

"What happened, Len?" Sage stood and took a small step forward, the linoleum creaking beneath her. "What happened to you?"

Len's hand shot up, freezing her. "Don't," she said. "Please, don't."

Sage wasn't sure she was doing the right thing, but not getting Len to talk felt worse. She took a breath. "I never had a panic attack before," she said. "Not once in my whole life. Until I found out . . . until my life changed. Forever."

Len's lip trembled with the effort of holding herself together. Sage recognized that look.

"Something happened to me," Sage said. "Something must have happened to you."

"If they knew," Len started, and it was like she was talking to someone else, someone far away. Then she blinked and her focus returned to Sage. "You wouldn't understand."

"I had to wipe dirt off your fingers, Len. Try me."

The words cracked something in Len, the tremble in her lips overtaking her body. She stepped forward, stumbling to reach one of the chairs. The towel holding her hair unraveled and dropped to the floor. "I didn't mean to." Sage took her elbow, cold seeping into her as drops from Len's wet hair fell on her arm. "But it was me," Len said. "It was my fault."

Sage guided her to the seat, then crouched beside her.

"What?" Sage asked. "I won't tell, I swear," she added when Len whimpered like a wounded dog. "It's okay."

That made Len look at her, and Sage saw the instant her resolve gave way. Whatever she'd been fighting, it had won. Resignation cracked her face.

"My sister, Fauna," Len said. "Her baby. I think I killed her."

CHAPTER TWENTY-EIGHT

LEN

SAGE'S HAND DROPPED OFF THE CHAIR. "WHAT DO YOU mean, you *think* you killed her?"

Len couldn't answer. She scanned Sage's face for a hint of disgust or fear, but even now, after hearing the horrible truth, it was extraordinary how Sage kept her cool. What Len wouldn't give for an ounce of that superpower.

"It doesn't seem like something you could be unsure about," Sage added.

"It was me," Len said. "It had to be."

Sage dropped into the chair opposite Len. "Okay," she said. "Tell me what happened. From the beginning."

Len held on to the edge of the small table, trying to find the right words in her head. "My sister, Fauna, she and Diane, her wife, they live in Atlanta. And they tried to have a baby for a long time. Years." She took a tight breath. "Fauna wanted to carry—she's always dreamed about it, ever since she was little.

But the regular fertility stuff, it wasn't working, and the other treatment—some kind of shots and the way they have to remove your eggs—" She made a face. "It was expensive. Really expensive. They pooled all their savings, and it still wasn't enough, so Mom and Dad helped, and my Nonni, she used a bunch of her savings, too, though we didn't realize that's where it was coming from or I don't think Fauna would have taken it."

Len stopped, unsure how or if she could continue. Sage stayed still, only nodding to show she was listening. For some reason, that nod helped her keep going.

"Anyway, they were going through all this stuff, and nothing was working, and Fauna had two miscarriages, which are apparently awful, and she was kind of a mess and they almost gave up, but then . . ." Her hand lifted. "It happened. One of the last zygotes took and Fauna had Nadia." She wiped her nose. "Right before Christmas, last year. It was the best Christmas, Sage. Everyone was so happy. I can't remember ever being happier in my life." She covered her face. Sage's hand landed softly on her arm, squeezing gently.

"And they didn't have any money for babysitters, and you know, having a newborn is exhausting. So for Fauna's birthday my mom told her to come to Asheville so she and Diane could go out and have a nice evening. We'd watch the baby." Len kept her gaze fixed on the table.

"And they were so happy, and so grateful," she went on. "We put the Pack 'n Play in my room because it's farthest from the living room, the house noises, and Dad's paint smells."

She couldn't speak for a long while, just shook her head slowly in her hands.

"What happened then?" Sage asked.

Len lifted her face, finally. "My mom fed Nadia and put her down and we had a monitor, and she woke up right around nine. And I rubbed her back just like Fauna showed me, and I—" Her voice cracked. "I told her I loved her." Tears dropped onto the table. "She was breathing."

Sage's hand had gone still. Len closed her eyes, but she was shocked to find she *wanted* to keep talking. She looked at Sage. "Fauna texted me and I said everything was great and that Nadia was fine, so they decided to catch a late movie. Dad was painting, and Mom was here, too, and I checked on the baby a couple times, and she was breathing. Every time. I *swear*. We were watching TV, an old *Simpsons* episode. Dad called it distasteful, but we kept watching." She sniffed. "Then I went to my room and . . . and . . ."

She could have stopped. Sage didn't prompt her again. But Len needed to finish. She needed to confess. "Something didn't feel right that time, as soon as I walked in. There was a feeling in the air or something. So I turned on the light and . . . her face . . ." She swallowed. "I must have screamed. I don't know. She was all blue. So blue."

Sage made a small choking sound, and her hand flew to her mouth.

For the first time, the whole sentence bloomed in Len's head. For the first time, she might be able to say it out loud. It seemed important, somehow, to speak it. "She was dead."

Her mind wound back, and she was there again, living it, the sirens and crying and blueness. And screaming. So much screaming.

There was a hand on her back, a voice.

Len's eyes refocused. Sage was bent in front of her, talking. "You didn't do anything wrong."

Len blinked at her. Was she stupid? Hadn't she been listening? "My niece was dying in my bedroom while I was watching cartoons. If I'd just gone back there sooner . . ." Her voice disintegrated, because it was too painful. Imagining what might have been.

"You did everything you were supposed to do." Sage said. "Sometimes stuff—terrible stuff—like that . . . it just happens."

Len took the paper towel Sage offered. "They called it sudden infant death syndrome."

Sage nodded. "I've heard of it," she said. "SIDS."

"They say that when they don't know the cause," Len said. "Healthy babies don't just die for no reason."

"It still wasn't your fault."

"You don't get it," Len snapped. "I *made* it happen. I manifested it."

"Manifested?" Sage frowned. "What are you talking about?"

Len struggled for the right words, because she knew how it would sound. But she also knew it was true. "Manifest, you know? Make things happen with energy? There's no way it was a coincidence."

"Slow down," Sage said. "I need more information."

Len pinched the bridge of her nose. "Fauna and Diane," she said, "they looked so terrible that day, like they hadn't slept since Nadia was born. And they were kind of fighting, and I don't know, I had this thought—this really powerful thought— about how maybe the baby wasn't a good thing. Maybe it would mess up their lives, their relationship." She covered her mouth. "Two hours later, Nadia was dead."

Sage went very still. When she finally spoke, her words were slow and even. "So you think that because you had a thought, you somehow killed Nadia?" She shook her head. "That's impossible."

Tears leaked down Len's face. She didn't even try to stop them. "How can you say that? You're an *athlete*. You know how important thoughts are!"

"What?"

227

"Don't you visualize making plays?" Len said. "Don't you imagine your success in your mind so you can will it into being? There's *science* that shows how doing those things helps performance. And I've seen you play. You always spin the ball and let it bounce one time before you serve. Because you believe that matters, don't you? You believe you'll only serve well if you do that."

Sage didn't answer, and Len could tell she was getting through to her, at least a little.

"And what about people whose positive thinking helps them get better?" Len persisted. "My dad just told me about someone with cancer—*terminal* cancer!—who only had a couple weeks to live and then started this whole meditation thing and is healed. Positive thinking can heal people! Why wouldn't the reverse be true?"

"But that's . . ." Sage was clearly struggling for a response. "That's not the same thing. Come on, Len. You really think you have the power to kill people with your *mind*?"

"I wasn't careful enough," Len said. "Nadia was so young. So tiny and fragile. I must have messed up the Life Force, the *qi* or plain old Force or whatever you want to call it. I put negative energy into the air. I created an imbalance. It's the only explanation!"

Sage stood and walked to the counter. She ripped off more paper towels. "You didn't do anything wrong, okay?" she said, bringing them to Len. "What you're talking about, it doesn't work like that."

Len took a towel, crumpled it. Had she really expected Sage to believe her? *Yes*, she thought bitterly.

"I'm gonna lie down," Len said.

Sage followed her to the sofa. "Are your parents coming home soon?" she asked. "Do you know?"

Len curled into a tight ball. "Mom's visiting Nonni, and Dad must be painting. They'll be home by seven, though." She buried her face in her hands. "Fauna calls at seven."

Sage glanced at her phone. That was still forty minutes away. "Okay," she said. "I saw some tea on the counter." She bit her lip. "Should I make some?"

"Whatever," Len mumbled. Why didn't her brain come with an off button? She imagined pushing it, jabbing it, until her thoughts evaporated and gave her peace.

Soft sounds came from the kitchen—cabinets opening. Mugs set on the counter. Why was Sage still here? She rolled over, facing the back of the sofa, and imagined pressing the button, over and over, until finally, mercifully, it worked.

CHAPTER TWENTY-NINE

SAGE

SAGE HELD A CRACKED MUG OF TEA AS SHE STOOD OVER Len, wondering what to do. Sage had been in the kitchen less than three minutes, but Len was definitely asleep. She'd never have her mouth open like that if she was faking.

Sage placed the mug on the end table, moving a small notepad to one side. It was like Len had literally shut down—like her system had short-circuited.

She sat on the cushion beside Len's feet, trying to process everything she'd heard. No wonder Len was a mess. Having a baby die in her bedroom and thinking it was her fault.

She glanced sideways at the small ball that was Len. She couldn't really believe she'd killed her niece just by her thoughts, could she? And none of what she'd said, awful as it was, explained why she hated dirt to the point of a mental breakdown, or why she covered herself head to foot so as not to let her bare skin touch anything dirty.

A tiny clock on the wall tick-ticked into Sage's thoughts. She had to leave soon to make the team meeting, and she couldn't miss the very first thing Flick asked of her. Not after what Flick had said yesterday. But she needed to talk to Len's parents. Len had said she was getting worse, and maybe, if Len had been hiding it from them, they didn't realize how badly she needed help.

Len shivered. Sage found a throw blanket tucked into a basket beside a plaid arm chair and draped it over the sleeping girl. She waited seven more minutes, hoping one of Len's parents would come home. When they didn't, she grabbed the notepad next to Len's tea and scribbled a message with a pen she found in the kitchen. She debated detailing Len's breakdown at the tree bridge, but she wasn't sure how to describe it.

She decided to keep it simple.

Dear Len's mom and dad—
I'm worried about Len. She told me about her niece. (I'm so sorry.)
I think Len is still having a really hard time.
—Sage (Len's friend)

It was bare-bones, but if Sage's mom got a note like that, it would be enough to make her check in with Sage—to help her.

She wedged the note between the kitchen landline's base and the wall so that Len's parents wouldn't miss it when Fauna called, if they didn't notice it before. There was a chance Len would wake and find it first, but Sage doubted it. She seemed completely wiped.

Sage checked on Len one more time, texted Mom that she was working at the library for a while, and then slipped out the door.

* * *

"Team meeting" actually meant team run. Sage pulled into the Patton Park parking lot just as the others were about to take off.

"You made it," Flick said as she joined the group.

"I told you," Sage said. "I won't let you down."

Flick nodded, and Sage recognized that look—it was one she'd received so many times from Coach. Approval. Acceptance. Trust.

Dr. Friedman's warnings crept over her, but she pushed them down. She was in excellent shape. If her heart rate got too fast, she would stop. She knew her boundaries.

"We'll be back in a few," Flick said to a green Ford Focus, and only then did Sage notice there was a man behind the open window in the driver's seat. "That's Jon," Flick said to Sage, sensing her confusion. "The teammate you replaced." Jon gave her a small wave and went back to reading his phone. "The usual," Flick said to the rest of them, starting the jog.

"It's only about a mile," Ketia told Sage as they fell into step. "Just to keep us in shape."

Sage looked over her shoulder, back to the Focus. "Jon still comes to the team meetings?" she asked. "That's dedication."

She almost added "for a rec league," but then remembered what Flick had told her that first day. *This isn't just some silly rec league.*

"Yeah," said Ketia. She grinned. "He also happens to be Flick's husband, so there's that."

It only took a couple hundred yards for Flick, Lucy, and Derek to pull ahead. Sage resisted her urge to keep pace with them; she was used to being in the lead. Instead, she took slow, steady breaths and checked the heart rate function on her Fitbit.

"Not gonna lie," Mountain said, his large sneakers slapping the cement with a gate that betrayed he was not a runner. "You surprised us, Tiny."

"Yeah?" Sage said. "Why's that?"

"We had three people try out over the weekend," Ketia said. "All of them were personally invited by one of us." She pursed her lips. "None of them was good enough for Flick."

Pride surged inside Sage, which she hid by glancing at the Fitbit again. They'd already gone a quarter of a mile. This was fine. Mountain was so slow they were barely running.

"You okay?" Ketia asked.

"Yeah." Sage forced herself to stop checking her heart rate. "I was just checking my markers for the week."

"Oh," Mountain said. "Anybody talk to you about a uniform yet?"

Sage shook her head.

"Lucy has the extras," Ketia said. "They might be a little big, though. You could tie it."

"I don't mind," Sage said. "The teal color's nice. Usually rec team shirts are hideous."

"You need some lucky socks, too," Mountain said. "We got any extra, Ketia? We've never lost since we got those rainbow socks."

Ketia nodded. "Lucy and I both have extra. I'll bring mine tomorrow."

She was starting to sweat, but Sage got a sudden chill. "You really think that matters?" she asked. "Everyone wearing the same socks?"

Mountain shrugged. "Can't hurt, can it?"

Sage couldn't help remembering Len's comment about her serve. How she linked the ritual to mind control, to having the ability to *kill a baby*. Nausea roiled her stomach. "I don't know."

They rounded a curve, and the parking lot came back into view.

"What do you mean?" Ketia asked.

Sage hesitated. She'd only just met these people, but she felt a strong need to tell someone what Len had said, to see if anyone else could make sense of it.

"My friend," Sage began, "she said something today about this stuff, and I don't know."

"What did she say?" asked Mountain.

"I didn't really understand it all. But basically she's worried she can hurt people by, um, having bad thoughts."

Ketia went bug-eyed. Mountain frowned.

"And not just that," said Sage. "There's other things. She wears gloves every day and she freaks out about dirt."

"I'm no doctor," Mountain said, his breath coming heavier. "But it sounds like this thing my cousin has—OCD."

"Obsessive compulsive disorder?" said Ketia.

"Yeah, that's it. My cousin's had it since he was a teenager, but I never knew till last year. He hid it pretty good."

"OCD," Sage said. "That's, like, when you're a super neat freak and stuff?"

Mountain shook his head. "I don't know much about it, to be honest. But the way my cousin explained it, it can be really different person to person." He took a couple ragged breaths.

"He never cared too much about dirt, but he had this weird thing with numbers." His face scrunched, thinking. "It had a name, something about magic."

"Magic?" Ketia said, her voice pitching higher. "Are you for real right now?"

"Yeah, for real." Mountain snapped his fingers. "Magical thinking! That's what it's called. But my cousin also said it was OCD, so I don't know."

"What's magical thinking?" said Sage.

"Look, you're asking the wrong person," Mountain said. "I just try to be there for him. We were tight growing up." He frowned. "He always had a few weird habits, but I just thought that was him. I feel bad not knowing how much he was struggling."

Sage ran over the odd things she'd seen Len doing and made a mental note to Google *magical thinking*. Her heart twinged, and she stopped instinctively. Ketia and Mountain both paused, jogging in place.

"You okay?" Ketia asked.

"Cramp," Sage improvised, flexing her leg. "I'm fine."

"Damn heat," said Mountain. "Think you're dehydrated?"

"Is there a problem?"

All three of them turned at Flick's voice. She and the others waited in the parking lot, where Lucy and Derek stood stretching. Jon was out of the car now, leaning against it, and Sage noticed a brace around his knee. Ketia took off at a sprint, but Mountain bellowed, "Running sucks!" and thankfully resumed the same pace. Sage fast-walked the rest of the way.

Flick met them with small sheets of paper, which she passed out to the three of them while Lucy rummaged through the back of her car. When she returned, holding a teal shirt, Flick said, "I made some more game notes last night, and Jon had an idea for tweaking the Cardinal play."

"We were just talking about shirts," Ketia said as Lucy tossed Sage the jersey. "I'll bring you the socks tomorrow."

"No one's going to know Sage," Flick continued, "which is a huge advantage for us, provided she pulls her weight." Her gaze lingered on Sage. "Our game plan is going to be basically the same—"

Sage put two fingers to her throat, gauging her pulse. *You're fine, you're fine,* she told herself. Any minute now it'd return to normal.

Ketia nudged her arm, and Sage realized everyone was looking at her.

"Sorry," she said. "What was that?"

Flick's eyes narrowed. "Do you have any *questions*?"

"Oh. No." She stared at the paper, which outlined a few different plays, but nothing tricky. "No questions."

Flick nodded. "Right. Get a good night's rest everyone. See you tomorrow, no later than six fifteen."

Mountain saluted her. Sage hesitated, then trailed him across the lot. When they were out of earshot of the others, she called to him. "Hey, Mountain?"

He turned.

"I was just wondering . . . if my friend does have something like that magical thinking or whatever, what helped your cousin? I mean, is he okay?" As soon as she asked it, she realized how personal the question was. "Sorry, it's none of my business. But . . . I'm worried. What should I do?"

A sadness crossed Mountain's face. "Things like that," he said, "they're tough, you know? I don't know all the details, but my aunt—I know it was rough for her, seeing her son go through that." He gave a small shrug. "Sometimes the toughest part is getting the person to admit there's a problem."

"I think my friend knows," said Sage.

"Good." He nodded. "That's good. But knowing's one thing. Admitting—that's something else."

"I don't understand."

"I mean, you can't do it for them." Mountain opened the driver's door of his Jeep. "They have to *let* you help them. They have to want it, you know?"

Sage wasn't sure she did, but she nodded anyway.

"Wish I could be more help."

"No," Sage said. "That was definitely helpful. Really."

Mountain nodded. "Till tomorrow, Tiny."

CHAPTER THIRTY

LEN

LEN WOKE TO A SOUND. IT STOPPED BEFORE SHE COULD place it, but the damage was done—the haven of sleep was breached, and her consciousness streamed in. She strained her ears, her brain slowly registering other noises: steady drips from the kitchen tap, her parents' whispers, the calming whir of the fan near the front door.

It took her a disoriented second to place herself on the sofa. Under a blanket. To reconstruct how she'd gotten there.

Sage.

Len opened her eyes, but closed them quickly as she remembered. Everything. She'd told Sage everything.

Footsteps thudded close by and she sensed movement on the other side of her eyelids. A hand touched her arm.

"Lennie?"

No. She wanted to sleep. Everything was fine in sleep. Sleep was safe.

"Len?" her mom said again, gently shaking her. "Wake up, sweetie. Diane wants to talk to you."

Len's eyes leapt open. "Diane?" She sat up, pulling her damp hair away from where it had matted against her neck. "Why?"

"Why don't you find out?" Dad suggested. He stood in the kitchen, holding the receiver. The final wisps of slumber lifted from Len's brain.

She stood and shuffled slowly to the kitchen, one arm tingly from the way she'd slept. She had so many excuses ready for why she couldn't talk to Fauna. But Diane? She couldn't think of a single one.

She took the receiver. "Hello?"

"Len! Hey, thanks for talking to me."

She hadn't heard Diane's voice in months, but she knew immediately the tone was off.

"What's going on?" Len asked.

"I'll get right to it." The phone crackled as Diane took a breath. "Why won't you talk to Fauna anymore?"

The question punched Len's breath away. *Because I killed her baby. Your baby.* Len steadied herself against the doorframe. "I . . . I talk to her." Her voice pitched unnaturally high.

"You haven't talked to her in, like, six weeks."

"I've been—"

"Yeah, you're always out when she calls. Convenient."
Diane's voice cracked, and the annoyance in it made Len feel
like garbage. "She needs you, Lennie. She needs her sister."

Tell them.

Len closed her eyes.

Tell them!

"They'll hate me," Len whispered, before realizing she was
speaking aloud.

"What?"

Len's head went fuzzy. She needed to sit down. Instead, she
made a deal with the universe. *If Fauna is there, I'll tell her.* The
receiver cut into her ear. "Is, uh, Fauna around?"

"No," Diane said. "That's why I'm calling now. She told me
not to. Said everyone grieves in their own way."

Len didn't know what to feel. Her body stayed numb. "How
is she?"

"A mess," Diane said. "We're both—" her voice choked off
and Len was pretty sure she put down the phone. "I should go,"
Diane said finally. "Maybe answer next time she calls, yeah?
And actually talk to her?"

Before Len could respond, the line went dead. She held
on to the receiver until the phone dial sounded so angry she
couldn't stand it anymore.

"Lennie?"

Dad stood at the door to the meditation room, motioning Len toward him. "We need to talk," he said, not upset, but determined.

There was nothing Len wanted less at the moment than a talk with Dad. She had done far too much talking already—it had probably cost her her only friend—but she followed him into the meditation room anyway. Mom was gone. She must have slipped past Len while she was on the phone.

Dad scratched the back of his head. "Have a seat, sweetie."

"I don't want to talk about the phone call, Dad. Diane and I—"

"I don't want to talk about that, either," Dad said. "I want to talk about this." He held up a scrap of paper. Len stepped closer. It was a note. From Sage.

"Your friend seems pretty worried about you."

Len's numbness bled out, leaving her cold. "I told her today. About Nadia."

Dad reached for Len's shoulder, but she moved away, hugging herself instead.

"Look," he said, "I know this has been hard on you. It's been hard on us all. We all loved that little girl." A deep line creased the center of his forehead. "But Mom and I, we're worried." His voice fell. "You've got to get a grip, Len. You're not the one who lost a baby."

Len took a step back, like he'd slapped her.

"Fauna and Diane need us right now. We've got to be there for them."

If he said anything else, Len didn't hear it. The room started to spin and she couldn't catch her breath. She stumbled and Dad's arm was there.

Len tried to speak, but it came out all muddled and she was pretty sure she was crying. *Just ride the wave,* she told herself. *Let the panic wear itself out.*

"I think . . ." She swallowed a sob, but it leaked out anyway, ugly bursts of tears and sound. She wiped her face on her sleeve. "I think there's something wrong with me."

Dad pulled her close and this time she let him. "No, sweetie, no," he said. "There's nothing wrong with you. This is an awful time, but you're strong." His chin rested on her head. "Mom and I know how strong you are, how strong you've always been, and we're so proud of you for that."

Len nodded into his shirt. She hadn't realized how much she needed to hear those words.

"You're strong enough to get through this," Dad went on. "*And* to help your sister. You know that, right?"

She nodded more, crying until the panic drained away. The hug felt good. She wished she had more hugs, but that would mean more touching and everything was so dirty. People were so dirty. Had Dad even showered today?

She released him, even though she didn't want to. Why couldn't she stop thinking—*stop worrying*—for just one second? It was exhausting.

"Do you really believe that thoughts have power?" she asked, wiping wet streaks from her face. "Like, real power?"

He squinted at her, and she didn't think she imagined the disappointment. "Look, Len," he said. "There're all kinds of things in this world we can't control. Too many. Our thoughts are one of the few things we can. And every day, science reveals more and more about the power of positivity and our mind's ability to impact our bodies and our experiences." His eyes went wide with fascination. "I think that all speaks for itself, don't you?"

Len stared at the rug beneath her. There was a stain just to the left of her right foot. She hadn't stepped on it, had she? Maybe she should Lysol her boots again.

"Len," Dad said quietly, "have you been meditating at all?"

She shook her head.

"You know it will help, don't you? You've felt it work before?"

"Yeah," she said. "I know. You're right."

Dad checked to make sure Mom wasn't in the adjoining family room before turning back to Len. "There's something else," he said, his voice much lower now. "Mom doesn't like to talk about it. She doesn't want to upset you more, but Nonni . . ." He rubbed his face. "She's not doing well. And between that and Fauna, plus all the usual crap she deals with at work, your mom—" He glanced out of the room again, and for the first time in Len's recent memory, he looked scared.

Len looked toward the back of the house, the cold spreading out to her hands and feet. "Is Mom okay?"

Dad nodded a tad too forcefully. "She's okay. Just a little distracted, you know? Talking to Fauna each night, absorbing all that pain." He took a deep breath. "Mom is an empath, and, well, it's just a lot. I need your help, Lennie," he said. "We've got to be the strong ones."

Len nodded.

"Thatta girl." He gave her a quick smile. "I knew you wouldn't let me down."

CHAPTER THIRTY-ONE

SAGE

LEN DIDN'T SHOW UP IN THE CAFETERIA ON FRIDAY, AND Sage discovered her leaving the art room just as the lunch period ended. Ms. Saffron, Len explained, had agreed to let her eat there while she worked on the Melford Scholarship.

"That's great," Sage said, but Len wouldn't quite meet her eyes. Sage lowered her voice. "Look, about yesterday," she said, "you don't need to feel—"

"I'm feeling much better," Len cut in, and the plea in her tone was so strong Sage understood not to mention it again. Secretly, she wondered if speaking her fears had helped Len see how irrational they were, because something about Len had changed overnight. She was embarrassed, Sage could tell, but Len also seemed more determined somehow, like something inside her had been set ablaze. Sage wanted so badly to ask about it.

Instead she said, "Okay, well, I'm glad." Then the bell rang, and Len was gone.

Sage might have dwelled more on the conversation had her first Hendersonville match not been mere hours away, but her attention and body were both hyped up for the game. She even sat through practice with less numbness than usual. Everyone—her parents included—was going to the away football game, so she didn't have a single worry about being found out.

After the second opinion results and her freak-out at the last game, her parents hadn't blinked an eye when she told them she wasn't going to any football games for a while. Mom had offered to stay with her, but Sage had convinced her she needed some time to herself.

"You sure you don't want to come?" Kayla asked after Coach dismissed them. "We don't have to sit with the others, if you don't want."

"You go ahead," Sage said.

Kayla frowned. "I'm not sure it's good for you to be by yourself."

"I'll be fine," said Sage. "Really. Text me about anything good, okay?"

There was something about the way Kayla nodded, the way her mouth never fully settled into one expression, that made Sage uneasy. "What?"

Kayla broke eye contact. "Nothing. If you're sure you want to be alone."

Sage nodded, barely able to contain her excitement. She held up the side of her fist, but Kayla had already started walking away.

* * *

The nerves took Sage by surprise. It was only a rec league tournament, she told herself, because she couldn't think too deeply on what it really was—her last chance to win a state title and the dream she'd harbored since she was a child. Her heart might have ruined every other dream, but she refused to let it have this one.

It took exactly three plays for everyone in the gym to recognize the caliber of Sage Zendasky. Set up for a cross court attack, Sage rotated her body mid-jump, deceiving the defense, and smashed the ball down the sideline. Lucy and Mountain let out simultaneous bellows of glee. Jon whooped from the bench. Even Flick flashed her a smile.

Sage went temporarily light-headed with the ecstasy of belonging—of doing what she was built to do.

"Pulling your weight," Flick said as she passed Sage on the way to serve. "Keep it up."

Sage nodded before sinking into her stance. God, she had missed this. The pull of her muscles as she waited on the balls of her feet, the rush from unloading her full force into the ball. Her body pulsed so fast with endorphins she could taste them.

For the briefest moment she wondered if it was a mistake. If she really was playing Russian roulette with her life.

She sunk lower, quads almost perpendicular to the floor. This was no mistake. Not when it was the only thing that made her feel like herself.

Flick served an ace and that was pretty much it. The opposing purple-shirted team was decent, but not entirely cohesive as a group—and the three-game match lasted barely an hour.

"Good work tonight, people," Flick told everyone as they debriefed after the game. "But we can't lose focus. Next week won't be anything like this."

Lucy ground a fist into her palm. "Next week is personal."

Sage wanted to ask what she meant, but the line of Flick's mouth told her now wasn't the right time. Flick handed out more papers. Plays with new names.

"Memorize for Monday," Flick said. "See you then."

* * *

It was a relief coming home to an empty house. Ian's game wouldn't end for at least forty minutes, and since it was all the way across town, Sage had a good hour and a half left to herself. She tossed her keys onto the island, hesitating at the small mason jar of sunflowers that had appeared since she'd left that morning. A note leaned against them. It read simply "I love you, Mom."

Sage's jaw muscles twitched. It was such a *sweet* gesture, and she knew Mom meant only to help, to bring a small piece of light to Sage's darkness. How was Mom supposed to know that the flowers, simply by reminding Sage of why she was given them, made Sage feel worse?

Her phone buzzed. As if Mom had sensed Sage's thoughts, she'd sent a text:

You OK?

Sage moved the flowers to the sunroom, where she didn't have to look at them, and dropped the note into the recycling bin. Her phone buzzed again with the same text. *Fine* she sent back, then tossed her phone onto the counter and raided the fridge, settling on a bag of baby carrots and a hummus pack. Another buzz. Mom again. Sage took the phone to the couch.

You want me to come home?

Nah. I'm good.

Already the adrenaline was leaving her, her good mood slipping away. But she couldn't help herself. She typed:

How's Ian doing?

After a moment, Mom sent back two high-five emojis. Sage stared at them, trying to cipher out an underlying message. Two weeks ago, Mom would have sent a paragraph response to that question, detailing every kick and why Ian was or was not doing well.

Not anymore. Sage's whole body went hot. No one would ever treat her the same again.

Not true, she realized. Len wasn't weird around her. Well, not weirder than she was anyway, and shit, she'd forgotten to Google that term Tiny had mentioned.

She opened her phone's browser and thumb typed into the search bar:

magical thinking OCD

"Holy—" Sage breathed, because the results seemed endless. How had she never heard about it before? She crunched a carrot and settled back into the cushions, clicking article after article. It seemed that almost everyone engaged in some kind of magical thinking. Len had been right—magical thinking *was* prevalent in sports, but most people accepted limitations. Most people, for instance, would still wear "lucky socks" again even if their team lost while they had them on, because they could separate the magical element from reality. Sometimes, though, magical thinking spun out of control. That's when it could grow into a form of OCD.

Sage clicked onto a site that detailed the brain and its wiring, how thought patterns were established chemically, and how the brain could literally rewire itself. The stuff that OCD sufferers believed—that loved ones would die if they didn't do everything a certain number of times; that the mere thought of a disease could make them sick with it; that wearing the same clothes they had on for a funeral could cause another death—it seemed so outlandish to Sage, so irrational, that it was nearly impossible for her to fathom. Were these sites even real?

She double-checked the sources. Some of them were random people's blog posts, but others were definitely legit: the National Institute of Health, *Psychology Today* magazine, the International OCD Foundation.

It was absolutely *real*, as was explained by one particularly helpful article written for family members of OCD suffers. Even if Len's supposed ability to kill someone with negative thoughts was only imagined, her *belief* in that ability and the fear that came with it was so real that it changed both her body chemistry and the neurological pathways in her brain.

Sage checked herself, realizing she was devouring the articles with a kind of hungry fascination. She should feel *sorry* for Len, not intrigued as if she were some kind of science experiment. And Sage did feel sorry. She felt awful. This disease sounded miserable—the way it could warp and control your mind. But—she couldn't help it—it was also downright enthralling.

Why hadn't they learned about this kind of stuff in Psych class last year? There'd been big units on moral development, body language, and theories of intelligence—those kind of things. She vaguely remembered a brief discussion about mental health that focused on eating disorders, and they'd been given a phone number for a suicide hotline. But there was nothing about this.

Sage crunched one of the carrots in two. She'd often heard Dr. Surrage complain to her parents about the people who came into her office with self-diagnoses from the internet.

Still, the symptoms aligned so perfectly with what she'd witnessed in Len, and with what Len had told her. She didn't want to scare her, but what if she was right and Len's brain was sick? Her heart pounded with something awfully close to excitement, because this could solve everything for Len. A couple articles had mentioned something called cognitive behavioral therapy and a bunch of medicines that doctors could prescribe to help manage OCD. Len probably didn't know about these options, though.

She punched Len's house number into her phone.

A busy signal met her ears. "Are you kidding me?" Sage said aloud. She didn't even know it was possible not to have call waiting. She was about to dial again when she heard the click and whir of the garage door.

Sage tore off the sofa, spilling carrots everywhere, and raced up the stairs.

"Sage!" Mom called from downstairs. "Honey?"

Sage sent her mom a text.

Sage: In bed. Headache.

She barely had time to jump under her sheets, still in her game clothes, before Mom stuck her head around her door frame.

"Hey, baby."

Sage smiled weakly, her fingers clamped on to the sheet right below her chin. There was no reason Mom would pull back the sheet, but if she saw the uniform, Sage's volleyball dream would be over.

Mom sat beside her, her weight pulling one side of the sheet down slightly, and put a hand on Sage's head. "You feel clammy." Fear crossed her face. "Have you been sweating?"

"I'm fine," Sage said, willing her to leave so she could change clothes. She rolled over. "I'm tired, Mom, okay? I just want to sleep."

Mom sat quietly for what seemed like forever. "You know you can talk to me, right, Sage?" Her hand rubbed Sage's shoulder. "About anything."

"Um, yeah, Mom. Thanks."

"Or maybe you'd like to talk to someone else?" Mom said quieter. "Dr. Surrage gave me some names."

She could not be serious. As if talking to anyone could help her heart become normal. "I'm good, Mom," Sage said.

"It's just—"

"Mom! I'm fine." Then, in a flash of genius, she looked up and added, "Thanks for the flowers."

"Oh," Mom said, her relief bursting out in a smile. "You're welcome."

It gutted Sage, Mom's desperation to help an un-helpable situation. Sage turned away again, wanting only to be alone. "Is there any way," she asked quietly, "you could make me some chicken soup?"

"Of course, baby." Her tone was grateful at the chance to help. Sage closed her eyes, and the bed lightened as Mom stood up. "Coming right up."

CHAPTER THIRTY-TWO

SAGE

THE NEXT MORNING, SAGE WOKE TO KNOCKING. SHE stretched, squinting against the sunlight striping her face, and peered at the alarm on her nightstand. Just after nine a.m. It was still strange not getting up for her regular Saturday morning run, but at least she'd had last night's game. Otherwise, the inactivity would be almost unbearable.

Another knock. Sage pulled the comforter over her face just as Mom poked her head around the door.

"You awake?" Mom asked. "Some of your teammates are downstairs."

"What?" Sage threw back the blankets and sat up. "Who? Why?"

"Kayla, Ella, the whole crew." Mom shrugged. "They said they were here to see you." Her hand lingered on the door. "Should I send them up?"

"No." Sage fell back against her pillows, trying to imagine what could have possibly drawn her friends here so early. Especially Kayla, notorious for her hatred of weekend mornings. She kicked her sheets out of the way. "Tell them I'll be right down."

* * *

"Hi!" Ella said brightly as Sage appeared at the bottom of the stairs. The others added hellos from behind her.

"What's going on?" Sage asked slowly.

"We just wanted to hang out," said Hannah, way more bubbly than usual. "You know, see how you're doing."

Lyz and Nina nodded, their smiles a touch too bright.

Sage darted a look at Kayla, but her best friend stared hard at the floor. Sage's neck prickled, the same way it did when she knew Ian was about to scare her from behind a corner.

"Why don't you ladies take the sunroom?" Mom suggested, corralling them into the expansive addition Sage's parents had added last summer. "And you're welcome to stay for bagels. I'm just running out to get some." She shut the glass door behind her.

Kayla stood beside one of the floor-to-ceiling windows, staring intently at the forest that was Sage's backyard. The rest of the team crammed onto the long cream-colored sofa against the wall. Sage grimaced at the jar of sunflowers centered on the side table next to it. When she didn't sit, Ella got up and led her to the delicate floral loveseat, the one no one ever actually used, and sat beside her.

"What's going on?" Sage asked again. She spoke to Kayla's back, but it was Ella who answered. Her plastered smile faded.

"We wanted to let you know," she said, and looked toward the others, who nodded encouragingly from the sofa, "that we're here for you." She glanced at Kayla, who had finally turned to face the group. "Whatever happens with those extra tests. Even"—she scooted closer to Sage—"if it's the worst."

Sage fought back a sense of dizziness. Kayla wouldn't have said anything, not when Sage had specifically asked her not to. The girls on the sofa suddenly looked uncomfortable.

"Kayla?" Her voice was more a scrape than a sound. "What did you tell them?"

Kayla's chin lifted. "I told them you had more tests," she said. *"That's what you told me."* They locked eyes for a moment, and Sage saw it as clear as bold type across her face: Kayla knew there were no more tests. Why had she ever tried to fool someone who knew her so well?

Kayla's stubbornness gave a bit. "People need to know," she said softly.

"Stop." Sage stood up. "Stop talking."

"There are rumors, Sage, everywhere," said Kayla. "You must be deaf not to hear them."

Why did she sound so sad? Sage couldn't stand it. Kayla took a small step forward, and it was there, in every move of her friend's body. Her whole presence reeked of it—*pity*.

Sage's stomach spasmed, like she might hurl. She'd told Kayla not to pity her. She'd *told her*.

Kayla took another step. "They deserve to know what's going on," she said, glancing at the rest of the team. "We all do."

Kayla was close enough to punch. Sage envisioned it, her fist connecting with jawbone. Every muscle in Sage's body strained against the movement, her hands clenched by her side. She *would* regain control of herself. Of the situation. Her mind fought wildly for a response.

"Sage," Nina said. "Do you have a heart condition?"

Every eye in the room flew to Nina, then back to Sage. Ella covered her face with her hands.

Sage dragged her eyes to Kayla. "I trusted you."

"She didn't tell us," Nina said, and Sage forced her gaze away from Kayla's crumpled face. "This guy I know," Nina continued, "from my old school. He can't play sports anymore. Like, at all. He passed out during football practice." She didn't add "like you," but it was there, in all of her teammates' faces.

As Sage tried to think what to say, a stray leaf, still vibrant green, floated down outside the window. It wasn't fair, Sage thought. Why had that particular leaf dropped so early, its life cut so much shorter than the others? What had it done to deserve that?

"Sage?" Ella stood up beside her. "Look, you take as much time as you need. We'll go, okay?" The others began to stand, too. "We didn't mean to make you feel worse, really—"

"I can't play," Sage said. "You're right." Everyone in the room froze. "I can't ever play again."

Sage understood their shock. No matter how strongly you suspected something, it couldn't completely seem real until you knew it for sure. But she would be strong for them, like always. "My heart is too thick, apparently. Bad genes." She dug her nails into her closed palm, pretending she was discussing someone else as she looked right at Kayla. "If my heart rate gets too high, there's a chance . . ."

"You could die," Nina said, and Hannah gasped. "Same thing with my friend."

Sage felt her nerve unraveling. "I don't want to talk about it."

There was a flurry of sound as her teammates said things they probably thought were helpful:

Let us know what we can do.

I'm so sorry.

Is there anything you need?

You'll always be part of our team.

You can still coach, right?

Sage focused on the trees outside, thick with leaves still in their proper places.

"You'll call us, right, if you need anything?" Hannah asked. "If there's something we can do?"

Sage blinked, coming back to what was happening around her. Her friends were leaving. Of course they were. It wasn't like her body language was asking them to stay. Still, she couldn't help remembering Len's response to the same news. How she hadn't flitted around nervously, like Sage's devastation might be catching. How she'd stayed. "Sure," Sage whispered.

Ella gave her a hug. "It sucks," she said into Sage's ear. "How life isn't fair." Sage's throat threatened to close; she swallowed to make sure she still could.

"And you're being absolutely heroic about it,"—Ella's voice lowered so it was barely audible—"especially with Kayla's offer and all."

Sage jerked back, and Ella's face went panicky. "She did tell you, right? She told us all last night, so I assumed—"

"Of course she told me," Sage lied.

Ella relaxed. "I mean, I'm sure you're happy for her, but I know UNC was one of your top choices."

Sage's eyes zeroed in on a dark knot in the hardwood floor, her head giving the barest nod. She didn't even try to speak.

"You're the strongest person I know, Sage," said Ella. "If anyone can get through this, it's you."

Sage listened to Ella's footsteps, to the front door opening and closing. Someone tapped her arm. Kayla stood in front of her. "I'm sorry," Kayla said. "I told them to give you space, but—"

"You got the offer," Sage cut in.

"Oh." Kayla stuck her hands deep in the pocket of her hoodie. "That."

"*That*," Sage repeated, letting her anger flare. Because if she was angry, then she wouldn't cry. And she *would not* cry.

"You told everyone but me?" Sage accused.

"I thought . . . look, I didn't want to hurt you."

Sage couldn't keep the disgust from her voice. "Did you think I wouldn't find out?" she spat. "How long were you gonna keep it a secret?"

Kayla's face hardened. "You're one to talk about keeping secrets. Why did you tell me you had more tests?"

Sage didn't have a good answer, which pissed her off even more. "You have no idea—"

"You're right!" Kayla said. "You barely talk to me anymore, and I know you're going through a lot and you're messed up about it, but I'm trying to help you!"

Sage's jaw dropped. "I'm messed up?" How could Kayla, her *supposed* best friend, say that when Sage had done nothing but hold herself together since learning about her heart?

"That's not what I meant," Kayla said, tears dampening her lashes. Kayla, who never cried, whose heart worked perfectly, and who had just earned a full volleyball scholarship to a Division 1 program. Whose life was going to be everything she ever imagined it would be.

Sage's anger surged higher. Poor Kayla, who couldn't understand why maybe Sage didn't feel like confiding every tiny thing to her at the moment. Poor Kayla, whose biggest dreams were gonna come true.

Kayla wiped her eyes. "All I've ever been trying to do is help you."

"Well, you're doing a shit-tacular job of it!" Sage had to get out of here. Away from Kayla, away from everyone. "Ian!" She tore up the steps. "Ian!"

Her brother stuck his head outside his door. "You okay?"

"Kayla needs a ride home. Tell Mom and Dad I went to the outlets for some shoes or something. Say, I don't know, one of my favorite sandals broke."

His forehead crinkled. "Why can't you—"

"Look, just do this for me, okay? Please."

Before her diagnosis, Ian would have put up a major argument. He would have told her about the countless better things he had to do than drive her friend home. Instead, he studied her for a moment and frowned, but nodded.

"Ian'll take you home," Sage told Kayla, bounding down the steps past her.

"Where are you going?" Kayla called after her, but Sage had already slammed the door.

CHAPTER THIRTY-THREE

LEN

LEN KNEW IMMEDIATELY THAT SOMETHING WAS WRONG.

"You wanna come in?" she asked Sage, who had shown up at her doorstep. Len was still in her pajamas.

"I need to go on a drive," Sage said. "Anywhere." She shifted her weight, her hands fidgeting a hair tie around her wrist. "Can you come?"

"Um, maybe. Let me check." She couldn't believe Sage still wanted to hang out with her after yesterday, but she didn't question it.

Ten minutes later, Len was dressed in her usual outfit and Sage's car was speeding along the highway. Len checked the battery life on her camera for the fifth time.

Sage took a hard turn and something tumbled along the back floor, catching Len's eye. A vibrant orange shoe lay on the floor. One of Sage's volleyball shoes. It must have rolled out from under the seat.

Len turned down the radio, which Sage had blaring with an all-women punk band that was a little hard for Len's tastes. "Where should we go?"

"Doesn't matter," Sage said, passing a silver minivan with an *I used to be cool* bumper sticker on the back window. "I just want to drive."

Len watched the speedometer tick up. They were going fifteen miles over the speed limit. Eighteen. Twenty. Len laid the camera on her lap. "You gonna tell me what happened?"

"Huh?"

"You're upset. You gonna tell me why?"

The car slowed suddenly, as if Sage had only just realized she'd been speeding. "My team came to my house today." She tightened her grip on the steering wheel. "They know about my heart condition. That it's permanent."

Len pulled at the tip of her gloved pinky. "You hadn't told them yet?"

Sage shot a look at her, before refocusing on the road.

"All I mean is, they had to find out sometime, right?"

"It wasn't how I wanted to tell them," Sage said. "And Kayla—" Her eyes went dark, and Len recognized her expression, the look of shutting out memories. "It doesn't matter," Sage said.

Len pushed her luck. "Sounds like it matters."

Sage cursed. Then again. She nodded at the blue sign listing food options at the next exit and put on her turn signal. "I'm gonna grab some coffee. You want anything?"

"No thanks." Len watched Sage from the corner of her eye. For the first time, she didn't see Sage as a tragic superstar. Yeah, she was spectacular at volleyball, but she was also a regular person, anxious about something that had happened with her friends.

Len switched her camera on, then off again. She'd grown accustomed to doubting herself, mistrusting almost every single thought. But she couldn't squash the certainty rooting in her bones: Sage Zendasky, epitome of strength and success, might actually not be okay. She might even need some kind of professional help.

As Sage pulled into the McDonald's drive-through line, Len realized she'd never heard Sage talk about anything other than volleyball. That didn't seem completely healthy.

"So," Len said, "what's your senior project about?"

Sage's mouth became a hard line. "Talk about a random question."

Len shrugged.

Sage rolled down her window. "Yeah, I'll take a small coffee. Just cream, thanks. Nope, that's it." She inched the car forward. Len waited. Finally, Sage said, "I'm doing it on physical therapy and sports medicine. I have a mentorship set up with Coach for the spring." She shrugged. "It's an easy way to fulfill that requirement."

The way she said it made Len ask, "But is it want you want to do?"

Sage let out a short, barking laugh. "I *want* to be a pro volleyball player. But that's not happening, is it?" The woman at the window traded a coffee cup for Sage's change.

"Don't look at me like that," Sage said, as she pulled back onto the road. "I don't need pity."

"I'm not pitying you," Len said, though she totally was. She faced the windshield, worrying the strap of her camera. "You think maybe you will go into physical therapy now?"

Sage took a deep swig of coffee and wiped her mouth with the back of her hand. "My whole life," she said, "I've always known I was going to do something I *loved*. Something that made me excited to get up every single day." Coffee sloshed over the cup's edge and she cursed, sucking brown liquid from her hand. "I don't exactly see physical therapy giving me that." Her voice tightened.

"Maybe the mentorship will help," Len offered. "It might be better than you think."

"Maybe." Sage pulled up to a red light, and her whole manner changed. "I tried to call you last night, but I couldn't get through."

"Oh." Len's breath caught. "My sister calls a lot."

Sage drummed the steering wheel. "Do you know anything about OCD?" she blurted. The light turned green. "Obsessive compulsive disorder?"

"Um, a little, I guess. It makes people do things over and over, right? Like they have to do things a certain number of times?"

"It's more than that. It covers a lot of stuff, actually." Sage's eyes slid to Len. "I think you might have it."

Len's chest convulsed like something had slammed into her. "That's not what I have."

"Hear me out."

"No!" Len shouted. "I know what's wrong with me." She turned to the window, crumpling.

"You do?"

"I want to go home."

"Len—"

"Take me home, Sage."

"No."

Len whipped back to her. "What do you mean, *no*?"

"You said you know what's wrong. Tell me."

Len shook her head. She'd been so stupid. Why had she gotten in the car? Sage hadn't wanted her company at all. Len was just a problem to her, a mind puzzle to distract from her own misery. Len covered her face, desperate to hide her mortification. "Why won't you just take me home?"

"Because." Sage made a sudden sharp turn, forcing Len to grab the handle above the door. "If you go home, you'll be miserable and beat yourself up over something that's not your fault at all." The car bounced as it hit the edge of the curb before finally coming to rest in a Walgreens parking lot.

Len closed her eyes. She was so, so tired of fighting what was happening to her. Of keeping it a secret. "I have childhood dementia." She glanced at Sage, who wasn't even trying to hide her horror.

The roar of traffic filled the car. "What is that?" asked Sage.

"Just what it sounds like. It's rare, but that's life, right?" Len took a deep breath, then told Sage everything. About Nonni and how her mind had slowly come unraveled. How the same thing was happening to Len, she was sure of it, and how Jamie had treated a patient who was just ten years old. How Nonni didn't recognize them and Mom cried at night when she thought Len was asleep. How Len couldn't bear to tell her parents, because Mom cried enough, and they wouldn't be able to afford treatment anyway, and she'd found a letter saying they'd missed last month's rent.

"Shit," Sage said, finally. "I'm sorry. About all of that." Her head tipped back against the seat. "It just . . . shit."

It was such a ridiculous understatement that Len laughed—a small sound at first, but it rippled into a half-crying belly laugh. Sage looked at her like she was slightly insane, which she supposed she was, because nothing was funny. But she'd gotten a taste of it, the laughter, and it was delicious, like spring water after an all-day mountain hike. It fed something in her she hadn't realized was hungry. She wished she could laugh forever.

"See," Len said, because Sage was still looking at her like she was nuts. "I'm losing my mind."

She thought that might make Sage laugh, too, but Sage just sat back, drumming the steering wheel again. She reminded Len of a falcon, like the one she'd seen with Nonni several years ago on a hike at Chimney Rock. Peregrine, that was it. Nonni had almost fainted at their luck.

Nonni had shown her a close-up photo later, and Len had been struck by the bird's fierce countenance and its intense, piercing concentration. Sage's face held the same, calculating look.

Sage turned to her. "So, you haven't been diagnosed with this childhood dementia thing, right? You just think you have it?"

Len bristled. "Dementia is genetic. I have all the symptoms. And there's no cure." Her voice caught, but she was out of tears. "We don't have health insurance. All a diagnosis would do is mess up my family worse." She looked out the passenger window. "I've caused too much pain already."

"Here's the thing," Sage said, and Len turned back to her. She ran a hand over her dark messy hair. "You said this type of dementia is super rare, right?"

"Fifty thousand people have it." The stat had been bouncing around Len's head ever since she'd first looked up the disease.

"Fifty thousand people *in the world*? Out of, like, eight billion?"

Len stiffened. "You don't believe me."

"It's not that. Listen. You said your symptoms match up with dementia. But I really feel like they match up with OCD, which is way more common."

"I don't have OCD!"

"Len." Sage's voice was soft. "You had me wipe mud off your hands. Because you couldn't do it yourself."

Shame gushed through Len. It closed off her throat, leaked out her pores.

"There's this thing I read about," Sage went on. "Contamination fear—"

Len must have looked bad, really bad, because Sage stopped talking midsentence.

"This is why you picked me up?" Len asked. "To make me feel like this? As bad as you?"

Sage recoiled. "Of course not—"

Len's mouth felt caked with mud, her lips dry and crumbly. "Something is happening to me. And yeah, I don't like to get dirty, but it's more than that." She touched her head. "It's hard to process things sometimes. A lot. And I forget things. I get confused. And . . . scared." She hugged herself. It was awful saying this out loud, admitting it. "It's hard to explain, but I'm the one that lives in my own head, okay?"

Sage looked over the steering wheel at the traffic that whipped by on the road in front of them. "Yeah," she whispered. "Okay."

A horrible thought attacked Len. "You won't tell anyone this, right? I told you this in confidence. And anyway, I'm doing better now. I think, um, I just needed to get it out, you know?"

Sage frowned, and panic seized Len. If Sage told anyone, her parents would find out about Nadia, and so would Fauna. She couldn't hurt them again. And what if she was force-fed drugs for the rest of her life or placed in some kind of institution?

"I'll show you," Len said. "I'll prove I can control it." She swallowed. "Let's go hiking again."

Sage raised an eyebrow, and Len could tell she was remembering what happened last time. "I'm not sure—"

"I can do it," Len said. "Anywhere. You choose." Her heart pounded in her ears.

"Okay," Sage said, in a voice that was overly nonchalant. "How about Graveyard Fields?"

The name flooded Len with memories, dozens and dozens, all of them with Fauna. Len kept herself very still. Sage knew this. She'd seen the photo of Len and Fauna on her wall. This was some kind of test, and Len *would* pass it, because Dad was right: she *was* a strong woman, and she would will herself to do whatever she needed to convince Sage. To keep her from telling.

She counted a slow breath in, a slow breath out.

"Great." Len pretended to adjust something on her camera. "Let's go."

* * *

The parking lot at the Fields was full, of course, being Saturday. Sage circled the lot twice, then managed to wedge the car between a Ford Focus and a group of motorcycles. The calm that overtook Len surprised her. She hadn't been here since Fauna had revealed her pregnancy, and after Nadia died, she had no intention of ever coming back.

"Ready?" Sage asked, climbing out.

Len swung open the car door. She could do this. She *was* strong. "Yes." She looped her camera around her neck and followed Sage to the stone steps that led down to the paved trailhead.

As usual, the air was almost ten degrees cooler up here. Sage had slipped on a thin wind jacket she'd grabbed from the back, which, from the style, Len guessed belonged to Sage's mom. But Len found the sixty-five-degree air perfect. She followed Sage halfway down the steep steps, then paused, inhaling a huge gulp of pine- and rhododendron-scented air. The last bit of tightness in her chest loosened.

A twentysomething couple approached, returning to the parking lot. Sage passed them and kept going, entering a sea of rhododendron, but Len gave wide berth to the German Shepherd by their side. Then she surveyed the landscape through her lens. Some of the trees were already turning up here, their edges fringed with specks of sunset gold. The whole hilly expanse shimmered.

Len didn't think so much about angles or the themed series that she had less and less time to create. She just shot. She'd needed space and Sage had given it to her without being asked. She descended the remaining stairs and snapped a quick photo of Sage engulfed in a mountainous twist of rhododendron. If someone had asked her yesterday what a friend was, she might have given any number of answers. A person who likes you despite your weirdness—perhaps because of it. A person who sticks up for you, who doesn't go to parties that they were invited to but you were snubbed from. Who helps if you ask, no matter what. She adjusted the f-stop and sneaked another picture of Sage.

But there was another facet of friendship, Len realized. Something she hadn't really considered before, but that suddenly struck her as essential. Regular friends should do all those things, sure, but there was also maybe a different kind of friendship, a deeper kind. A kind Len felt certain she'd never had with anyone besides Fauna and had believed didn't exist outside of sisterhood.

She angled her head back and snapped a picture of branches and sky, catching just enough of the sun's edge to make the foliage glow.

This deeper kind of friend knew what you needed sometimes before you did. And they gave it to you without needing to be asked.

She swiveled her lens back to Sage. Were they real friends now, maybe even that deeper kind?

Sage looked up. "Get anything good?" she called.

Len walked over to her and turned the camera around so Sage could see. As she flipped through the images, a seed of excitement planted in her belly. Some of them weren't too bad.

"Wait." Sage stuck her hand out. "Is that me?"

Len nodded. "It was a cool visual, like the rhododendron was devouring you." She looked up. "Is that okay?"

Sage squinted. "Not devouring me." She pointed at the image. "See how my hand's there. It's like I'm making it grow." She wiggled her eyebrows, and Len laughed.

"You have a good laugh," Sage said. "It's crackly. Like fire."

It was an odd compliment, but Len liked it. Sometimes Sage seemed as offbeat as she was.

"I think I needed to come here," Len said suddenly.

Sage pulled the sleeves of the wind jacket over her hands and rubbed them together.

"I didn't want to come back," Len said. "I haven't, since—"

Sage nodded.

"But it's okay," Len said. "I didn't think it would be."

Sage rocked back on her heels. "So do you want to go on to the Fields, then? It's my favorite part."

Len looked down the path, remembering the last time she'd walked it, full to bursting with joy. "That's where my sister told me," she said quietly. "About Nadia. That she was gonna have a baby girl."

As if on cue, child laughs came from the parking area. Len's nose began to sting.

"We don't have to go," Sage said. "We can hike somewhere else."

"No," Len said. "I can do it." She repositioned her camera and slipped her hands into her pockets. She'd made a promise to Dad and she intended to keep it. "I want to."

They passed through the rest of the rhododendron thicket in silence, pausing on the bridge overlooking a small creek so Len could snap some photos. The wind was stronger on the bridge. It whipped Len's hair loose and burrowed into the gap at the neck of her sweatshirt. A few yards ahead of her, Sage shivered, but Len wasn't cold at all. For once, she felt okay. Good, even.

She let her camera rest on its strap and closed her eyes. The soft water gurgles, the heady scent of leaves and bark, the gentle touch of sun, even the cool wind on her lips—all of it alone was ordinary, and yet somehow the combination felt magical. *An ordinary magic*, she thought. *Maybe this was the Life Force.*

Len wasn't entirely sure she understood the concept in the same way as her parents. Really, she wasn't sure what she understood or believed, and it was almost too much to think about at times. But she couldn't deny that there was *something* about places like this, so remote and wild that not even cell signals could penetrate them. She took another breath, this time visualizing a soft white light coming from the trees and rhododendron. It spread out, enveloping her before melting into her skin, soft and buttery, like Mom's favorite homemade lotion.

"Len?" Sage said. "You okay?"

"Yeah." Len blinked, soaking in the feeling of steadiness. Pride burst through her, and she made a mental note to tell Dad about the successful visualization.

They went left at the fork, away from the crowded Lower Falls, and climbed a set of wooden steps. When the trail became grass and earth, Len didn't let herself stop. She imagined the white light again, a protective bubble, and plowed onto the dirt trail, astonished at her own fearlessness. She was doing this. She *could* control her fear.

"It's so beautiful," Sage breathed.

They were walking straight toward it, the place immortalized in Len's photograph. The place she first learned Nadia's name. Len's breathing shortened, and she looked down. Huge mistake. The dirt trail was littered with bits of debris and dark matter. What *was* it?

"Did you read *Wuthering Heights*?" Sage asked. "I always imagined the setting someplace like here. Well, maybe a little darker. More gloom, you know?"

Len grunted acknowledgment. Those were just normal dirt things, she told herself. Normal outside things. Normal people don't even notice them.

Somehow, Sage was still talking, "But if you ask me, Heathcliff is a total possessive, abusive psycho. How can anyone find that romantic?" Len's attention faded out. Animals died out here. She could have stepped on a piece of dead animal. What if it had rabies? How long did rabies last? Could she get rabies if she touched her boot? Could she bring it back to her house?

Len stopped, her heart pounding so heavily it hurt. She tried to call back the white light. She was safe. She wasn't touching anything. Her *boots* were touching things. She could clean her boots. She could Lysol the shit out of them.

Sage turned around. "What do you think? Are you—?"

Len watched Sage take her in. Watched understanding click in her face. This is what Dad meant. *Get a grip, Len!* But as much as she wanted to, Len couldn't force herself to move.

Sage smiled. It was a new smile, though, one Len hadn't seen before. Gentler. Like she was looking at a fawn and wanted it to know she wouldn't hurt it. "Sorry," she said. "I talk a lot." As if that were the reason Len was frozen. "You just have to tell me to shut up. I won't mind. Ian does it all the time."

Len's mouth twitched in an attempted grin.

Sage walked back and stood shoulder to shoulder with Len, her attention focused on the landscape. "This is a nice spot," she said. "Do you want to take some pictures?"

Len blinked. Yes. She did want to take pictures. Slowly, the comforting pressure of the camera on her chest came back to her. She lifted the lens and starting shooting. Randomly. Nonsense photos. She would delete them all.

"I don't mind your talking," Len said quietly, the camera still covering her face.

They stood there for minutes, Len shooting the same image over and over while Sage pointed out interesting tree shapes in the distance and musing about different books she'd read.

Then, right after explaining why *Pride and Prejudice* was so much better than *Emma*, Sage said, "Kayla got a full scholarship offer yesterday. From one of my favorite programs."

Len lowered her camera. Sage kept her eyes on the horizon, like she was still talking about the landscape.

"She told the rest of the team," Sage continued. "I only found out when one of them mentioned it because she assumed I already knew."

"Maybe . . ." Len loathed defending Kayla, but she wanted to help Sage. "She probably didn't want to hurt you."

Sage looked at her. "By telling *everyone else*? Did she think she could keep it a secret?"

Len frowned. "You should have gotten that offer."

"Yes." Her eyes concentrated on the trees like they were the only thing that mattered.

"What if," Len said slowly, "she just didn't know how to tell you?"

Sage wiped her sleeve across her face. "Look!" she said. "Is that a groundhog? God, they're ugly."

Len snorted and lifted her camera again, snapping a few shots where Sage pointed. Her thoughts weren't spiraling anymore, she realized, and her breathing had returned to normal. She let the camera fall back around her neck. Maybe it wasn't the place that had calmed her. Or maybe the place wasn't the only reason. Maybe it was *Sage*.

Len adjusted the f-stop again. There was something about Sage, about the energy she exuded, that made Len feel stronger.

Maybe *that* was friendship. She nodded across the field. "Right over there," Len said. "That's where Fauna told me."

Sage looked at her. Len could tell that, if she were someone else, Sage would have hugged her. She was definitely a hugger. But Len didn't want her to—Sage touched way too many things for Len's comfort—and Sage must have intuited that. Still, she stood as close to Len as she could get without touching her, and somehow, in an ineffable but important way, that mattered.

* * *

After Sage dropped her off at home, Len felt better than she had in ages. She'd gotten some great photos. She possibly had a real friend. And, most important, she'd beaten her brain.

She rewarded herself with an extra-long shower and a mug of spicy ginger tea. After saying goodnight to her parents (Dad was thrilled to hear about the visualization), she decided to inspect her boots and see how much Lysol was required.

They were lying on the small rug near the front door with the other shoes. There was more mud on the soles than she'd imagined, and there was a faint odor to them as well. Her pulse surged. She must have stepped in something foul. She'd have to scrub them as well as Lysol. But what if she couldn't get rid of it all? What if the grossness touched her while she was cleaning? What if it fell off places she didn't see? She bit her lip. She loved those boots. Fauna had helped her pick them out.

"Lennie?" Dad called. "Everything okay?"

"I'm just checking something." Len grabbed her boots by the tops and took them into the kitchen, stuffing them into a plastic Walmart bag. She opened the cabinet, pausing. She only had one other good pair of shoes, and the boots had cost almost fifty dollars. She'd saved up for months.

She couldn't just stand here. Her parents would ask what she was doing. She didn't like how close the dirt was anyway, even though it was in a bag. Before she could overthink it, she took a deep breath, tied a knot in the bag's top, and stuffed the whole thing deep inside the trash.

CHAPTER THIRTY-FOUR

SAGE

LEN DID *NOT* HAVE CHILDHOOD DEMENTIA.

Any Google search that lasted longer than five minutes revealed as much, though Sage could see how Len might have convinced herself otherwise, if she'd only spent a few minutes confirming what she suspected.

Sage hitched up her backpack as she walked through Southview's nearly empty liberal arts hallway, telling herself she was doing the right thing. Google had explained that sufferers of severe OCD could hold on to and obsess about ideas, especially fatalistic ones, no matter how irrational they appeared to others and, this was the kicker, *despite being presented with logical evidence to the contrary.*

A shiver tingled Sage's spine, as it did every time she thought about the inner workings of the human brain. She'd only meant to spend an hour or so researching Len's supposed condition, but even after she'd ruled out childhood dementia for sure—Len would have shown signs since infancy and suffered from major neurological issues, like seizures—Sage had ended up spending most of Sunday reading articles about the brain.

She had also surreptitiously called Dr. Surrage, but that proved less helpful than expected. Dr. Surrage was a general practitioner so knew very little about the specifics of how severe OCD could manifest, but the main takeaway had been clear: as long as Len wasn't in danger, Sage couldn't do anything to help Len without Len getting on board herself.

The hallway forked, and Sage turned down the left corridor, hugging the folder containing the articles she'd printed. Her jaw ached, and she realized she was grinding her teeth. Was Len going to hate her for this?

It *was* a little curious that Len had rallied on the hike and then seemed okay—that she'd pressed on, braving the entire loop. Sage had to admit, she was impressed. If Len did have severe OCD, then that had been an incredible feat of strength. It suggested that Len was a true fighter and she was doing everything she could to combat the disease terrorizing her brain.

Everything, that is, except admitting she needed help. Mountain's words about the difference between knowing something was wrong and admitting it were proving all too true.

But there was no way Sage could sit by doing nothing while Len's brain slowly choked off her rationality.

Sage stopped in front of Ms. Lewis's psychology and sociology classroom, which she hadn't stepped into since last semester. Clearing her throat, she knocked and pushed open the door. Ms. Lewis sat at a table, waiting for her. "Good morning, Sage."

"Thank you so much for e-mailing me back," Sage said. "And coming in early to talk."

"Oh, I'm here much earlier than this every day." Ms. Lewis motioned for her to sit. "You said you wanted to talk about obsessive compulsive disorder? May I inquire why?"

Sage kept her face even. She understood it was a teacher's duty to refer students to the school counselor, but even if Len hadn't asked her to keep her secret, she would never be responsible for Len having to see that man. Everyone knew he was counting the days to retirement, and this was way out of his league anyway. He probably thought it was still okay to call people like Len "crazy."

"It's my friend," Sage said smoothly. "She lives in Madison County, but we talk all the time, and lately, I've just been, um, noticing some things." She explained Len's strange habits and the way she avoided dirt. "And apparently," Sage continued, "she had to have her friend wipe off her dirt-covered hands because she couldn't touch her backpack to get the wipes out."

Ms. Lewis's forehead folded into a deep crease.

"Also," said Sage, "her niece died from SIDS, and she thinks it's her fault, even though no one else does. I read that trauma can cause OCD, too." She leaned back in her chair, feeling winded. "So does that sound like OCD to you?"

Ms. Lewis shifted, clearly uncomfortable. "I'm not a certified psychologist. I can't make a diagnosis, unfortunately. The best thing you can do is encourage your friend to talk to a doctor."

Sage fought the urge to make her frustration visible. "My friend doesn't think she has OCD, which I read is a pretty common reaction among sufferers. How do I convince her that she needs to go see someone?"

Ms. Lewis let out a low whistle. "How to convince a person with mental health struggles to get treatment? You ask easy questions, don't you?"

"I tried to look it up, but I couldn't find a good answer."

Ms. Lewis crossed her legs. "That's because there isn't one, or at least one that works universally. Not that I know of." Her mouth turned down sadly. "You need trust, of course, but even with loved ones, it can be a long, arduous process. In some ways, these types of conditions are like an addiction—the brain is working on a similar kind of loop. Unfortunately, it can almost be like reasoning with an addict at times."

Sage slumped back against the hard plastic chair.

"I know that's not the answer you are looking for. If the situation gets too dire, her parents might have to intervene."

Sage didn't understand how Len's parents could fail to see there was something wrong, but apparently Len hid it well. "And if her parents don't?" she asked.

Ms. Lewis looked pained. "There's only so much you can do, Sage."

"That's not good enough." Sage opened the folder, like she might magically find an answer in the articles she'd already read.

"What are those?" Ms. Lewis asked.

"Articles. I thought if maybe I presented her with evidence . . ." Sage shrugged.

"May I see?"

Sage passed over the folder, watching as Ms. Lewis thumbed through the stapled papers. "There's a lot of good research here." Ms. Lewis held up an article. "Did you go on the library database to get this? JSTOR?"

Sage nodded.

"You must really care about your friend."

"I can't just do nothing! Besides, it's kind of fascinating, the way the brain can trick itself." Sage looked to the floor, embarrassed.

Ms. Lewis closed the folder and passed it back. "Last semester, in Intro to Psych, you never seemed that interested."

Sage stuffed the folder into her bag and stood, shrugging. "We didn't get into this kind of stuff."

"No," Ms. Lewis said. "I guess not." She ran a finger along the crack in the table. "Perhaps I should add OCD to the curriculum."

Sage nodded, barely able to conceal her disappointment. She really thought her teacher might be more help.

"In fact . . ." Ms. Lewis pursed her lips. "Do you have your senior seminar now?"

"Next semester," said Sage, confused by the sudden change of topic.

"I'm surprised, honestly, by the amount of new data you found. So many people have outdated ideas about it." She tilted her head. "An explanation with current therapies would make a marvelous senior project."

Sage shrank back. "I can't use my friend's pain as a project idea."

"Of course not. You wouldn't have to study OCD. There is an unlimited supply of neurological fascinations."

Sage hesitated. She wondered why she hadn't considered it before. "They told us last year we couldn't change our topics. And Coach is my mentor, anyway. He's already done the paperwork."

"Oh," said Ms. Lewis. "You want to be a physical therapist?"

Outside, heels clip-clopped down the hallway. Voices rose and fell. The clock above the door clicked off the seconds, steady as a beating heart.

"I think I'm all set with Coach," Sage said finally.

Ms. Lewis nodded, but didn't seem convinced. "Think on it," she said.

Sage's heart pounded so fiercely she didn't register the morning bell at first. She put a hand to her chest, thinking how tragically ironic it would be if she dropped dead right here. If her pulse was going to surge like this anyway, she might as well be playing volleyball.

Then students tumbled in, Ms. Lewis turned to greet them, and Sage slipped away.

* * *

Sage didn't even make it to her locker before her teammates swarmed her in the hall.

"How are you?"

"Did you get my texts?"

"How can we help?"

Panic swelled inside Sage, but before it could crest, Kayla pushed herself into the throng. "Give her some room," she said.

Sage shot her a grateful look, which Kayla's eyebrows acknowledged. For a moment it was like nothing had changed.

"Can we carry your stuff?" Hannah offered. "Are you allowed to lift things?"

Kayla put a hand to her forehead. Sage took a deep breath and told herself they meant well. "I can carry my stuff," she said. "But thanks."

Ella pulled her in close. "My mom says she has a great therapist if you need one."

"I'm good." Sage forced a tight smile. "But thank you. I'm okay, really."

Ella hugged her. "See you at lunch?"

"Um, yeah. Sure."

The team dispersed, giving Sage access to her locker. Kayla, however, stayed put, waiting for her like usual. Sage dug out a notebook and zipped it inside her bag.

"So," Kayla said, "about Saturday. Are we good?"

Sage closed her locker, twirling the lock away from the last digit of her combination. Her throat went thick and lumpy, but she swallowed the things she couldn't say and met Kayla's eyes. "Yeah. We're good."

Muscle memory made her hand twitch. This is where they'd fist bump. Sage hooked her hands under the straps of her backpack.

"Okay," Kayla said. "Cool."

They stepped into the stream of students.

"You wanna come over after practice?" Kayla asked.

A mix of guilt and relief jolted through Sage. "I can't," she said. "Not today."

Kayla nodded.

A few feet ahead of her, Sage caught sight of a familiar sweatshirt. "Len!"

The sweatshirt stopped. Turned. Len's eyes slid from Sage to Kayla.

"Did you go through the pictures?" Sage asked. "You should see them, Kayla, the new ones she took. They're really good."

Kayla gave a half smile, then looked away. Sage pushed down her disappointment and turned back to Len. "Do you have a series idea?"

"Maybe," said Len.

"We're gonna be late," Kayla said.

"See you," Len mumbled.

But Sage didn't wave bye as Len turned down the liberal arts corridor, too jarred by what she'd just noticed. For the first time since Sage had known her, Len wasn't wearing her boots.

CHAPTER THIRTY-FIVE

LEN

LEN HAD RECOGNIZED THE LOOK ON KAYLA'S FACE. MOST people would have read it as uncaring disinterest, but Len had used it too many times not to know it for what it was: the face of someone left out.

Len had vowed never to make anyone feel that way, although she couldn't deny it gave her delicious satisfaction, seeing someone who made her feel like an outsider every day forced to know what it felt like.

The thought gave her heartburn. Maybe she was no better than people like Kayla, people who kept up their status and sense of worth by stepping on those around them. Maybe she would do it, too, if the positons were reversed. And what if she had, at some point in the past, without even realizing?

It was an uncomfortable thought spiral, and she hurried into Photography to break out of it. The bell rang just as she reached Ms. Saffron's desk.

"I got them," Len said. "The prompt images. And a series idea, too."

Ms. Saffron beamed. "Wonderful. Can you come in at lunch to review?"

Len nodded, her body alive with an excitement she hadn't felt in so long that she almost didn't know it for what it was. But then, with a surge of energy, she recognized it: *possibility*.

* * *

"These are excellent!" Ms. Saffron said at lunch, flipping through the ten images Len had printed from the photo lab computer.

The praise made Len feel expanded, like her whole body was smiling.

"Hit me with your theme ideas."

Len flattened out the crinkled piece of paper she'd been carrying in her pocket, and which she'd continually added to all morning. "Well, at first I was thinking something abstract, something that's really hard to define with words."

"Such as?"

Len read the first idea from the paper. "Breath."

Ms. Saffron looked up, her head swaying slightly like she was bouncing the idea around her mind. "Interesting. Let's keep that as an option."

"I also like the idea of darkness, so I thought, what about a collection titled *Fragments of Dark*? I could get really metaphorical."

Ms. Saffron's nose wrinkled. "Too metaphorical maybe. You don't want to sound like you're trying too hard." She flipped to a new photograph. "Oh!" She tilted the picture, the one with Sage in the rhododendron, so Len could see. "I like this a lot."

"That's one of my favorites," said Len. Inspired by Sage's comment, she'd played with effects until it looked like light radiated from Sage's palm, pushing open digitally enhanced blooms.

"You haven't done many images with people, have you?"

Len shook her head as Ms. Saffron rifled through the rest of the pictures. Len had included another unenhanced photo of Sage in the hedge, and Ms. Saffron laid it alongside the first.

"There's a story in these two," she said, "more so than the others. In this one"—she pointed to the unenhanced image—"I love that the person isn't the focus. That she's almost a part of the landscape. Or maybe it's the fact that she *isn't* quite part of everything. She's trying but she doesn't quite fit in."

"Or maybe she's just about to fit in," Len said. "Or about to claim her power, like in this one." She pointed to the other picture. "She's on the edge. It could go either way, couldn't it?"

Ms. Saffron looked at her. "Yes. I suppose that's right." She turned back to the photo. "There's something about the not knowing that invites the viewer into the image. Is this subject on the edge of something good or something terrible?"

"Both, maybe," said Len. "It could be anything."

Ms. Saffron smiled. "I'm impressed, Len. Truly. These are stunning."

Len felt warm color rise to her cheeks. She slid her sweatshirt's cuffs over her gloved hands.

"I think you could create something really amazing if you played with this style," Ms. Saffron continued. "This way you've upended the usual presentation of a person—you just need a theme to tie it together." She looked back at the other pictures. "Did you say you had other theme ideas?"

Len did have a few, but she didn't like them anymore. Her brain spun with Ms. Saffron's praise and the serendipitous way the photos of Sage had come to be. "None I like that much," she admitted.

"There're four photos I think are perfect for submission," Ms. Saffron said, laying two others beside the rhododendron pictures. "I also pulled three from last semester's file that could work, if you need them." She handed the file to Len. "You'll either need the right theme to tie them together, or produce additional publishable-quality photos by next week. Do you think you can do that?"

Len nodded as the excitement, the *possibility*, flared hot and bright again.

"E-mail me as soon as you have a theme idea," Ms. Saffron said. "And with any more photos you think will work."

She clapped her hands. "I know you can do this, Len. This first round is to weed out the people who aren't really serious, and I know you can get through. You just have to buckle down, okay?"

Len slipped the photos into the folder Ms. Saffron gave her and placed it in her bag. "Thanks."

"Len," Ms. Saffron said as Len was about to leave, "you look more inspired lately." Len could tell what she really meant was *better.*

"Your friend," Ms. Saffron continued, "the volleyball player. Is she helping you?"

Len fingered the loose strap that dangled from her backpack. "Yeah," she said. "I think she is."

* * *

Len couldn't wait to tell Sage about the success of her photos. When school ended, she waited outside the gym, planning to catch Sage on her way to practice. She tucked herself into an out-of-the-way corner that gave her a perfect sightline to the entrance while avoiding getting trampled by end-of-day madness. Added bonus: since nobody walked in the corners, the tiles were remarkably clean.

It was still strange, the connection she felt to Sage, when they hadn't known each other that long. But Sage had seen the rawest, ugliest part of her and hadn't run screaming. Len hugged the folder with her photos tight against her chest.

"She's not here," a voice said, startling Len so much she almost dropped the folder. She turned to see Kayla, a duffle bag slung across her shoulder. "You're waiting for Sage, right?" Kayla folded her arms. She was even taller than Sage, and more solid, her shoulders definitively squarer. Len's first impulse was to escape, to get as far from Kayla as possible, but whatever had reawakened within her in the art room stirred again and quelled her initial burst of fear. She lifted her chin.

"Yes," Len said. "I need to show her something."

"She told us she had another checkup with her cardiologist." Kayla narrowed her eyes. "But I think that's bullshit."

Kayla's bluntness made Len hesitate. "Where else would she be?"

"Dunno." Kayla's muscled shoulders lifted. "But you guys are so chummy now. Why don't you tell me?"

Len's head tilted. Was Kayla—powerful, fear-inducing Kayla—jealous? Of *her*?

"I have no idea." When Kayla's stare didn't waver, she added, "I wouldn't be waiting for her if I knew she wasn't here, would I?"

Kayla frowned, but her posture relaxed, her gaze moving to the gym door. She looked pissed, but beneath that, Len recognized something else: worry.

Len risked a step forward. "You really think she's not at an appointment?"

Kayla looked surprised, like she'd already forgotten Len was there. "Forget it," Kayla muttered, and stalked into the gym.

Len stared after her. Shoe squeaks and the pounding of volleyballs swelled then quieted as the gym door opened and closed. Why would Sage have lied about an appointment? Was she in some kind of trouble?

She placed the photo folder into her bag and booked it out of the school.

CHAPTER THIRTY-SIX

SAGE

KAYLA WAS SUSPICIOUS.

The doubt in her eyes when Sage told her she was missing practice for yet another checkup had been unmistakable.

Sage stuffed the duffle filled with her school clothes into the same locker she'd used for last Friday's game and headed toward the Y's gym. The championship game was this Friday. She only had to hold Kayla off for four more days.

Her shoelace came undone, and she bent to fix it. Unless they won, of course. Which they would. They had to.

"Hey, Tiny."

Ketia stood in front of her. Sage made a face at the nickname.

Ketia grinned. "So it's not the best or most original name." She clapped Sage's shoulder. "But you should be flattered. Trust me."

Sage didn't need to ask what she meant. Nicknames; inside jokes; small, good-natured pokes at one another. It was all part of team culture. It meant she was one of them.

She followed Ketia to the gym, where the rest of her team was already going through drills. Sage smiled. *Her* team. She supposed Tiny wasn't such a bad name after all.

"You two!" Flick called to them. "Get over here, you're late!"

"Are we late?" Sage asked under her breath.

"We're not early," said Ketia, "and that's late in Flick-world."

"Don't leave the service line until you've landed all six spots," Flick told Sage. "Ketia, I want you practicing tips, especially between P2 and P3, the Pumpkins' weak spot." Before she could say anything else, a ball zoomed between them, inches from Flick's face. She whirled around. "Derek, what did I tell you about your form?"

"The Pumpkins?" Sage asked as Flick darted off to chastise Derek. She grabbed a stray ball from the ground.

"The team we're playing for the championship," said Ketia. "They have orange shirts." Her smile was quickly replaced by seriousness. "There's history there."

Sage remembered what Flick had said after the last game. "What kind of history?" She followed Ketia to the line for spiking drills.

"You know Flick and Lucy played college ball?"

Sage nodded.

"Well, one of the Pumpkins played at the same time, was a captain just like Flick. Her team kept Flick's team from the Division title three years in a row."

"Damn."

"Mm hmm," said Ketia. "There is bad blood, ya know what I mean? And add the state qualifier on top of that?" She whistled. "It's gonna be tense, Tiny. You better be ready."

* * *

Sage knew something was wrong as soon as she entered the house. Dad was waiting for her at the kitchen island. She'd changed back into her school clothes at the Y and left her duffle in the trunk, but he stared at her like he'd caught her red-handed.

"So," he said, "how was the appointment?"

Sage's mouth fell open. "Dad—"

"Do *not* lie to me," he said. "Your friend called a little while ago, someone named Len? She wanted to see how your appointment went." Sage clamped her mouth shut, her brain scrambling for excuses.

"You can imagine my surprise," he said, "to learn you had a cardiology appointment I didn't know about." Dad stood up. "Where were you, Sage?"

She swallowed, her body still buzzing with adrenaline.

"Sage!"

"I went on a walk."

Dad snorted. "A walk?"

"Yes. I walked around the school and then went to the library, just to get away. I had to." She met his eyes. "Do you have any idea what it's like, sitting there, watching my friends do the thing I love more than anything and not being able to play?"

"You are still the captain of that team, Sage. They need you there. For encouragement. For support."

Sage gaped at him. Did Dad not want to understand her? Or was he simply not able to? How had Len put it in the coffee shop that day, when Sage explained why she didn't want to tell anyone about her heart? *You're afraid they can't handle it. And then you'll have to hold their disappointment, too.*

Dad looked away from her gaze, like he'd sensed her thoughts. The air between them practically shivered with his unease. With his disappointment. It didn't matter that he was disappointed *for* her. She had enough disappointment for a lifetime.

She thought again of Len in the coffee shop, absorbing the horribleness of Sage's situation without blinking. Led hadn't looked away in discomfort or offered advice. Or even tried to change the subject. She'd made space for Sage's discomfort, not the other way around.

Sage's nose crinkled. It was a different kind of strength, she realized—the ability to face a bleakness you couldn't fix. She was certain not many people possessed it.

"I have homework," she said.

Dad rubbed his chin. "I know this isn't what you wanted," he said quietly. "And I wish . . ." His voice hitched and he met her eyes again. "But this is life, and we have to deal with it. We have to move on."

Move on.

They were such simple words, and so small. Sage held the words in her mind, let them echo through her. She could almost taste them.

Bile rose in her throat.

"Homework," she repeated, starting past him. This time he let her through.

CHAPTER THIRTY-SEVEN

LEN

LEN'S HEART SURGED AS SHE TOOK THE PHONE'S RECEIVER
from Dad. If Sage was calling, that meant she was okay.
"Sage? Hi!"

"You called my parents?"

"Oh." Len turned away from her dad, her voice low. Sage was
clearly pissed. "I was worried. Kayla said—"

"So you're listening to Kayla now?"

"What? No . . ." Len's words stumbled around her tongue,
until she remembered Sage's note. "And how can you be upset
anyway? *You* left a note for *my* parents."

The phone remained silent for a long moment. Finally, Sage
huffed into it. "Next time, just call my cell, okay? My parents"—
she let out another deep exhale—"they complicate things."

Len knew what that was like. "I don't have your cell."

"I called you—"

"Landline, remember? No caller ID."

"Right." Sage gave her the number.

"Thanks," said Len, then paused. She'd been so excited to tell Sage about Ms. Saffron's reaction to the photos, but now things felt off. But it had been such a good day. She couldn't let it end like this, all awkward and uncomfortable. "Ms. Saffron loved the photos," she said in a rush, then poured out everything the teacher had told her. "If I can figure out the theme and create a few more photos, I might actually get through the first round."

"That's great," Sage said, although it sounded like she wasn't really listening. The spark that had flared during Len's talk with Ms. Saffron sputtered.

"There's something I wanted to talk to you about," Sage said. "I found out some interesting stuff about OCD."

Anger curled Len's toes. "I went to the Fields with you!" she said. "I proved I was okay. You said you'd drop it."

"I know, but—"

"We made a deal."

"Your boots, Len! Where are your boots? Have you worn them at all since the hike?"

Len paused a breath too long. "Of course."

"When?"

Len's fingertips burned from squeezing the phone, and why was she crying? Maybe, Len thought, she actually hated Sage.

"I gotta go."

"Len—"

"I think Fauna's trying to call." She hung up the phone with a clunk, then lifted it back off the receiver for a few minutes, just in case Sage tried to call back. Her head hurt. Her *brain* hurt. Her thoughts went all tangled and blurred.

She took off her gloves, washed her hands, washed them again, and climbed into the safety of bed.

CHAPTER THIRTY-EIGHT

SAGE

SAGE HAD PUSHED TOO HARD WITH LEN. IT HAD BEEN clear on the phone, but also in the way that Len avoided Sage over the next few days. Sage hated that she'd messed up, but she had more immediate concerns. It was Kayla's stupid suspicion that led to Len's calling in the first place, so Sage needed to deal with that pronto.

Immediately after calling Len on Monday night, Sage had called Kayla and admitted that, although she had weekly cardiology checkups on Wednesdays for two months (lie), on Monday she just hadn't felt up to watching practice, not when she couldn't participate (sort of true), so she'd skipped (completely true).

Kayla had bought it completely, and even had given Sage a hug the next day at school. "I knew it was something like that," she'd said. "No shame in needing some space." And while the lie didn't feel awesome, it made everyone happy. Kayla didn't need to worry about Sage, and Sage knew Kayla would cover for her after that.

More concerning was that Mom had actually scheduled a real follow-up appointment with Dr. Friedman for after school on Wednesday, and had already taken off work to attend, which meant there was no way Sage could sneak off to Hendersonville for practice afterward. Although she begged Mom to reschedule, she failed to give a convincing enough answer as to why. "That's the only time they have that fits when I can take off," Mom said. "And I have questions for him." So that was that.

Sage finally brought herself to send her rec team a group text Wednesday at lunch.

> I'm so sorry, but I can't make tonight. Will be there Friday for sure.

Less than five minutes later, her cell phone rang. It was Flick. Sage stepped out of the cafeteria and answered. "Hello?"

"You made a commitment!" Flick said.

"I know." Sage had the lie ready and forced herself to spit it out. "There's a funeral. I'm sorry." Sage hated using that excuse, but it was the only thing she could think of that Flick couldn't question. And technically, she didn't say she was *going*.

Flick swore. "I'm sorry. I hope your family's okay."

"Yeah," Sage said, feeling like the biggest jerk in the universe. "They're okay."

"Friday determines who goes to the state championship," Flick said. "You understand that, right?"

"Yes," Sage said.

"And it's an earlier start time, remember. Four p.m."

"I'll be there."

"We have to win," Flick said. "You need to bring your A-plus game. Your A-plus-plus game!"

"I know," Sage said. "I will." She heard the resignation in Flick's sigh.

"All right. See you Friday."

As she pulled the phone from her ear, Sage caught sight of Len walking to Ms. Saffron's classroom and called out to her.

Len stopped. Turned. Waited.

Sage wanted to tell her about the Hendersonville games, about how her parents were being so dumb about her appointments. Even the smallest truth—that she missed her. Instead, she said, "How's it going?"

Len's face stayed even. "Fine."

"You have a theme yet?"

"Not yet." Len looked at the floor, at the toes of her off-brand sneakers.

"I'm sure you'll figure it out," Sage said. "Do you wanna come eat? I'm just heading back in."

Len didn't even look up. "No," she said. "Thanks."

Sage stayed in the hallway until Len was out of sight. She wanted to scream. She wanted to throw something. She wanted to hit a volleyball.

Friday could not come soon enough.

When the championship game day finally arrived, Sage almost couldn't stand how long everything took—the drawn-out minutes of classes, the never-ending lunch chatter about weekend plans, even walking with Kayla and Ella to the gym after school. All of it seemed to happen in slow motion. She couldn't believe she'd had to miss Wednesday's practice for what turned out to be more of the same. Mom had asked question after question, but Dr. Friedman always came back to the same points: Sage was doing as well as anyone with hypertrophic cardiomyopathy could do. As long as she listened to her body and didn't push it too hard, she'd be okay.

Ella opened the gym door. Sage told herself she'd count to two hundred before making an excuse to leave. As soon as they stepped onto the gym floor, though, Kayla grabbed Sage's arm. "Hold on," she whispered. "I need to tell you something." Ella continued to the locker room.

Perfect, thought Sage. No need to wait to two hundred. They were alone, and she could tell Kayla she wasn't feeling well and slip out to Hendersonville before anyone else asked questions.

"I think I'm getting an offer from Penn," Kayla blurted.

Sage froze. Everything—her legs, her brain, her mouth—went completely inert.

"They called yesterday," Kayla added quickly. "Last night. I didn't know how to tell you. I know it's your dream school, or it was, but . . ." Her face flushed with guilt, or maybe excitement.

"They're sending a scout to practice today." Kayla's fist tightened around the strap of her duffle. "After Saturday, and what you said, well, I knew you'd want to know. I wanted to tell you." She looked almost petrified, like Sage might slug her. Sage might have, too, if she'd had any feeling in her arms.

"Coach sent them my tapes, too," Kayla added when Sage didn't speak. "Last summer. Same time as yours." Her eyes dragged to the floor, but she snapped them back up again. "I didn't realize until last week, after Thursday's game. Coach told me they'd shown interest. I guess someone was at the game Tuesday, too."

Sage's mind flashed back. Kayla *had* been a beast on Tuesday, the obvious MVP in their four-game takedown of Erwin. Of course, Kayla's spike opportunities had increased exponentially with Sage's absence.

Kayla took in a quick gulp of air, as if she'd been holding her breath. "They like me for outside hitter." She said it quietly, a confession, and it took every ounce of Sage's strength to knit her face into a placid expression, to keep standing. If anyone on their team deserved a Penn scholarship, it was Sage. And she would have earned it, too. Outside hitter was *her* position. It should have been *her* scholarship. Kayla knew it as well as she did—it was all over her traitorous, guilt-ridden face.

Sage envisioned herself made of steel, an immovable, impenetrable building. She could not topple. She could not fall on the ground in complete despair. It was against the laws of physics.

"Sage?" Kayla prompted. "Say something. Please."

A volleyball hit Sage in the leg. It seemed absurd that her teammates were warming up only a few yards away, joking and goofing off, while her best friend was stabbing her through her treacherous, defective heart. It was bad enough to have your life's dream categorically stripped from you. To have it handed to your best friend *because of that* . . .

"Sage?" Kayla repeated.

"I have to go," Sage said.

"What? Wait!"

"Tell Coach I'm sick, okay? You can do that at least, right?" She pushed through the gym door. The sunlight flooding the hallway was blinding.

"Sage!"

Sage put her hands on her head. She could handle this. She *could*. She just needed to process.

Kayla was at her heels.

"Don't," Sage said, her voice tight with the effort of speaking. "Don't follow me."

But Kayla's footsteps didn't slow. They followed Sage onto the pavement. To the parking lot. Through the grass.

"Please," Sage said, more a whimper than a word. Kayla didn't hear, but Sage couldn't force another sound out, her effort consumed by her desire not to do anything she'd regret.

Kayla's footsteps stayed close, mashing the gravel that led to the track around the football field. "We have to talk," Kayla said.

Sage clamped her hands over her ears.

"This isn't healthy!" Kayla shouted. "We need to deal with this."

We! As if Kayla ever dealt with anything. Sage dealt with things, and she let Kayla in on the benefits. Sage was the one who found those isometrics that added three inches to Kayla's jump. Sage was the one who insisted they work out in the summers to strengthen their upper bodies. Sage was the one who had researched twenty-eight Division 1 teams over the past two years.

"I know it sucks," Kayla began.

Sage stopped. She turned, her duffle thudding to the ground.

"It *sucks*?" she repeated. "Is that how you'd describe it? Me losing everything I worked for my entire life? That it *sucks*?"

Life was an unfair piece of shit, but Sage could at least set the record straight.

"I gave everything to this sport," Sage said. "I *love* it. And you—" She lifted her hands.

Kayla stiffened. "And me, what?"

"You eat Reese's Pieces for lunch!"

Kayla's nostrils flared. "What does that have to do with anything?"

"It means you don't care!" Sage shouted. "Not like I do." Her fury whirled inside her, drumming against her ears. "That was *my* scholarship. You know it was. *I* deserved it."

It felt good to say the words, but she regretted them instantly.

Kayla was shaking. "You think I haven't worked my ass off, too?" she accused. "I've always been second to you, Sage, and that was fine. But that doesn't mean I'm not damn good, too."

Sage hadn't thought it was possible to feel any worse, but somehow she managed it. "Kayla—"

"No." Kayla held up her hand. "I'm sorry your heart is screwed up. It's total shit that this happened to you, that you can't play." Her eyes went glossy. "But that doesn't mean you get to treat people like garbage."

Sage opened her mouth, but Kayla was already walking away.

"I told you not to follow me!" Sage screamed after her. She sank into a squat, hands clutching her head.

Pull it together, Sage.

She didn't have time for this. She needed to get to her car. People were counting on her. But she couldn't show up like this, either. She had to bring her best.

Her legs twitched with pent-up energy, and she stood, checking her phone. She had plenty of time. She surveyed the grassy field used for extra parking. A quick dash to the end of it would clear her head.

Or kill you.

Sage's heart beat faster. No, Dr. Friedman had just said at the checkup that moderate exercise was okay, as long as she listened to her body. As long as she didn't ignore any signs. She took a step, then halted. Theoretically, sprinting could kill her. But so could riding in a car. She turned to pick up her bag, then changed her mind again and swiveled back, her hand tracking the pulse in her chest. If she didn't release some energy, she'd probably have a heart attack anyway.

She took off.

"Sage?" someone called.

Sage's too-thick heart sank. The voice was Len's.

"Oh, my God," Len cried. "Sage, stop!"

Sage sprinted faster, faster than she'd run in weeks. Faster than she'd maybe ever run again. It wasn't fair. None of this was fair. Why'd Len have to live so close to school? Why'd she have to see her? The universe really did hate her.

"Sage!" Len's voice filled her head, which went light, just for a second.

Sage stopped and screamed. Len ran up to her, camera tight in her gloved fingers. Panic lined every inch of her, though for once she didn't seem to be constantly watching where she stepped.

"What are you doing?" Sage yelled when Len caught up to her. Her head was clearer. The sprint had worked.

"Me?" Len's eyes bulged, cartoon style. "You're doing the one thing that could *kill* you! What were you thinking?"

Sage squared her body with Len's, staring down at her. "Actually, there are quite a few things that could kill me. A car crash, for instance. Falling off a bridge. Overdosing on sleeping pills."

Len blinked, open mouthed. "Are you taking sleeping pills?"

"What? No." Sage rubbed her head. "I was making a point."

Len's stare was unnerving. "Why were you running?"

"Because I was pissed!" Sage said. "Forget it. It was one run. Not even. One forty-yard dash." She turned and headed back to her bag.

Behind her, Len inhaled sharply. "Oh!" she said. "The shoes."

"What?" Sage glanced down at her blue Asics, her practice pair, then back to Len, who looked like she was working something out in her mind.

"You're playing volleyball."

The phone slipped from Sage's fingers, and she stopped, fumbling to catch it. "What are you talking about? Practice is right now. I'm clearly not there."

"That's not what I mean."

Sage had never seen Len so focused. She *knew*. Sage could see it in her eyes, in the confident stance of her body. Sage did the only thing she could think of. She went on the offensive. "What, are you stalking me now?"

Len took a step back, her face suddenly unsure. "Stalking? What?"

"That's it, isn't it?" accused Sage. "You followed me to Hendersonville and you don't think that's stalking? That's the definition of stalking!"

"What are you even talking about?"

Sage's mouth made a thin line. "Nothing. Forget it. I'm going home." She grabbed her duffle.

"Sage." Len's voice stabbed into her. "I think you need help."

She whirled back to Len. "Me?" she seethed. "All your weird shit and you have the nerve to say *I'm* the one who needs help?" She stepped close to Len, pulling herself up and glaring down at her. "You can't control things with your mind, Len! *You can't kill babies with thoughts.* And if you really believe that, then you're as crazy as everybody says."

Something in Len's face cracked. Sage's bravado rushed out with her breath. "I didn't mean—"

"Forget it," Len said, already speed walking away.

"Len! Come on, I'm sorry!" Sage started to go after her, but she couldn't be late for the game. She cursed and wrapped her arms around herself. It was okay. She'd fix it, right after her team won the game. A couple of hours wouldn't kill anyone. She dug out her keys and hightailed it to her car.

CHAPTER THIRTY-NINE

LEN

LEN BARELY REMEMBERED THE DRIVE TO THE TREE BRIDGE.
She wasn't even sure why she'd come, but she'd needed to get away, far away, and it was as good a place as any.

She slammed the door of Nonni's truck—its metal thud a rip in the tree fabric surrounding her—and found the path, crashing down it before she could change her mind.

Of course she knew why she'd come. Why even bother to pretend? She stuffed her shaking, gloved hands deep into her sweatshirt's front pocket. Last time, this place had beaten her. Last time, she'd completely freaked out and she was sick of it, sick to death of not having control of her own brain, of her own thoughts. She remembered how she'd asked, no *begged*, Sage to wipe off her hands because she'd lost all shame and she was a total loser and none of this was fair and she was just. so. angry.

The tree bridge appeared ahead of her, a taunt. She passed the spot where she'd cowered, frozen, while Sage had wiped down her hands, the sick slime of mortification ooz-ing back over her. "Enough," she spat to the ground. It felt good, powerful even. Like one of Dad's mantras. *Manifest your truth.*

She stepped onto the bridge, teetering slightly to get her balance, and moved to the middle. *"Enough!"* The scream sent two birds scattering from the branches above her. She screamed again. And again. Over and over, until her throat ached.

Sage's words snaked through her: *OCD. I think you might have it. You're as crazy as everyone says.*

She'd show Sage. She'd show everyone.

Slowly, one finger at a time, she pulled off her gloves.

Len exhaled, long and slow, forcing down the slimy shame that threatened to overpower her. Her dad was right. She *was* strong. She could do this. And something internal told her that if she touched the bark, if she proved she could do it, even if she didn't want to, then things would be better. She'd have regained control. She'd have beaten her own mind.

Carefully, she crouched low, her left hand hovering inches away from the fallen trunk. There were tiny pieces of things covering it.

No, not just things. Grime and disease. Shoes had stepped on this tree, carrying God knows what, and—

"Shut *up!*" she yelled, and slammed her hand hard against the crinkled wood.

For the first second, a rapturous joy came over her. She'd done it! She was okay. She still had control.

Then she started shaking.

"No," she whispered, but there was no one to hear, no one to help. Len stood, her hand outstretched. This had been such a mistake—she was always making such huge mistakes.

Her pulse banged in her ears, and it was *so loud.* She took a breath. She could drive one handed. She could make it home without her hand touching anything. It was fine. Everything was fine. She imagined dousing her palm with soap—scrubbing and running it under the hot tap water. Her body ached for the relief.

She was almost to the end of the bridge when she started crying. This place had beaten her again. Furious, she slammed her foot hard onto the trunk. Too late, she remembered the rot.

Her foot broke through.

If she hadn't needed to keep her right hand clean, it would have been fine. She'd have braced herself with both palms, regained her footing, and gone on climbing down. Instead, she curled her right hand away, desperate not to touch the bark, and that threw her off balance. She screamed as she tilted over the bridge, her shoes trying to find purchase. At the last second, she whipped her right arm out, grabbing on to a branch and keeping herself from toppling into the rock-lined chasm below.

Righting herself, she scrambled back to the grass, tears streaking her cheeks and catching in the corners of her mouth. She stared down at her hands, her jeans, and the side of her shirt, all covered in dirt and wood rot, and cried harder. Her brain, her stupid messed-up brain, had almost killed her.

Somewhere—so far she couldn't even place the direction— came the piercing, familiar cry of a blue jay. The harsh call was one of the things Nonni loved about the bird. *It says its mind,* she'd told Len. *Don't matter how loud you are. A blue jay'll make sure you hear.*

Len wiped her cheek against her shoulder. "I hear you, Nonni," she whispered. She couldn't do this anymore, not alone. Sage was right; dementia or OCD, whatever was going on with her, it was too big to keep to herself. Len hiccupped, a ridiculous sound considering she'd almost just died, alone, in the middle of the woods.

At some point (she didn't actually remember starting to walk), Len began the hike back to the car. There was nothing she could do about it—she'd have to get the car dirty. She'd get some Lysol wipes and clean the whole thing down once she got home. And then her brain rerouted, rewound to her confrontation with Sage, because she had been on to something, hadn't she, before their fight?

Why had Sage mentioned Hendersonville? Len was the one that went there, not Sage.

Slowly, an idea unfurled in her mind. It was wispy, first, like morning fog. But the more steps she took, the more solid the idea became.

The day Kayla cornered Len by the gym, Kayla had thought Sage was lying about why she'd missed practice. And the orange Asics—Sage's game shoes—that Len had seen in Sage's car. Len hadn't thought anything about it at the time, but then she'd noticed that Sage had different practice shoes. She dipped under a low branch. It might not mean anything. But what if the orange Asics were in the car because Sage had been using them? Len started to run, unable to shake the dread building along with her fuzzy, half-formulated suspicion. She didn't know exactly what Sage was up to, but she had a horrible feeling she hadn't gone home.

When she reached the pickup, Len hesitated for only a moment, then shoved her grime-covered hand at the door handle and yanked it open. Some part of her noticed that whatever the malfunction in her brain was, her panic for Sage had overridden it, at least temporarily.

She threw the truck into drive and U-turned back onto the Parkway. She wished Sage could see her, covered in muck, both hands firmly on the wheel. Len wanted to claw the dirt off her body. She dreamed again of soap, of scrubbing her hands, her whole self, of taking a shower forever.

Her hands tightened around the steering wheel, warming with sweat. She was a hot mess, literally, but somehow, she was doing it. She was doing it for Sage.

A biker appeared on the road, and she slowed, tailing him until she had enough of an opening to pass. The speedometer ticked its way back up. Her mom always told her that it was the other drivers she was concerned about, but today, Len was that "other driver." Distracted, half-crying, she put all the focus she could muster on getting safely back to her driveway.

The truck had barely parked before Len leapt out. The shower beckoned her, but she tore herself away from the idea, allowing only a couple minutes of hand washing before pulling on new gloves and grabbing the phone from the kitchen.

Sage's cell went straight to voicemail, and no one picked up at her house. Len cursed and booted up her laptop. She opened Google, punching in *volleyball Hendersonville*. A huge list of school schedules came up, so she added *recreational*, but that turned up a ton of hits, too. She scanned several sites before thinking to add in the date. A new heading popped up: *Hendersonville YMCA, A-league championships. Today.*

"No," Len whispered. "No, no, no." Sage knew the risks. She wouldn't—

Of course she would. Hadn't Len just caught her sprinting?

The urge to bathe was so great that Len groaned as she forced herself in the opposite direction, to the front door, to Nonni's truck.

She paused. She couldn't drive, not like this, not with her mind short-circuiting because she couldn't drench herself in soap. It had been risky to drive on the Parkway, but she'd had no other choice. But now—

Something pulled her attention behind her and she turned. The school.

"Stupid Force," she said and starting running.

* * *

Kayla stood at the net, facing away from the gym door. Even from the back she oozed intimidation, but Len didn't have time for skittishness. She forced her voice to boom: *"Kayla!"*

The gym went quiet as every eye focused on her. Even the coach stopped talking. "It's an emergency," she called, and to her astonishment, Kayla trotted over.

"What's wrong?" she asked. Then, her eyes taking in Len's dirtied clothes, she added, "What happened to you?"

"It's Sage," Len said. "I think she's in trouble."

Kayla's natural confidence fell away, her face paling. "What kind of trouble?"

"I think she's playing volleyball. Like, seriously playing. Right now."

"What?"

"I'll explain on the way," Len said. "Come on."

"The way where?" Kayla asked. "Slow down."

"Hendersonville. At least, I think."

"You think or you know?"

"I think I know. Come *on*, I need you to drive. And help me talk to her."

Kayla held up her hands. "I don't even have a car!"

"I do," Len said. "*Please*. We're wasting time."

"Kayla?" Coach was beside them now. "You need to get back out there." His eyes were wide and incredulous. "Your scout came a long way."

"You know what could happen, right?" Len said, snapping Kayla's attention back to her. "If she plays full out?"

Kayla turned to her coach. "Tell the scout I'm sorry," she said. "I have to go."

Kayla pulled Len out the door, letting it close on Coach's protests. "Okay, Madder. Lead the way."

CHAPTER FORTY

SAGE

"THAT'S THE ONE," KETIA TOLD SAGE AS THE CAPTAINS shook hands before the game. "The setter. She kept Flick and Lucy's college team from the title game." Ketia shot Sage a look. "I don't wanna stick around if we lose this match."

"We can't think about *not losing*," Sage said, repeating one of Coach's truisms. "We think about winning."

Mountain clapped her shoulder. "And that's what we're gonna do. For Flick. For Lucy. For all of us."

Flick joined them at the service line, calling a quick huddle. "This is it," she whispered. "We win this, we advance." She glanced at the orange-shirted team on the opposite side of the net. "They're good. They're experienced, and they want it," she said. "We have to want it more."

As they piled their hands on top of each other, Sage was sure her teammates must feel the want burning out of her. Her whole body ached with it.

"Do we want this?" Flick challenged.

The team nodded. Murmured. The referee blew her whistle.

"I said, *do we want this?*"

This time the team answered with one voice. The power of it sent a thrill up Sage's spine.

Flick's grin was fierce. "Then let's take it."

Ketia caught Sage's arm as they moved to position. "I miss Jon," she admitted. "But I'm glad we found you. You were born for this."

Sage smiled and sank into her defensive stance, offering a silent *thank you* to the universe. She couldn't have asked for a clearer sign that she was meant to play, that she was right to take this risk.

The match was intense from the first play, and much too close for comfort. The Pumpkins, while not quite as sharp offensively, were exceptional at defense, and Sage couldn't push another of Coach's mantras out of her head—*defense wins games.*

The teams split the first two games. The third went five extra points, but Sage's team eventually took it and rode that momentum to a steady lead in the fourth. But a long hit by Derek set off a string of errors, letting the Pumpkins eke out a 22–20 victory to force a fifth, and final, game.

As Flick gave a quick pep talk about reclaiming momentum, Sage downed the last remaining drops in her water bottle. Her head felt light, maybe even a little dizzy. She sat on one of the metal chairs that served as a bench.

Ketia toed her shoe. "You okay?"

Sage nodded, wondering what she looked like that made Ketia ask. She *was* fine, just a little hot. The pace had been non-stop. She took her pulse. A little quick, but not crazy. She could do this. She wished she had more water, though.

"Tiny, you ready?" Flick called.

Sage looked up to see the rest of the team, hands on top of one another, waiting for her. She stood, adding her hand to the pile.

"Bring everything," Flick commanded. "It's all or nothing now."

The game started promisingly enough, with Sage's team taking a quick 4–2 lead, but a series of long volleys kept things close at 9–6.

When Ketia served an ace to give them a four-point advantage, Sage started to feel like she might vomit. She told herself it made sense. She'd missed Wednesday's practice and hadn't played a game this intense in two weeks; she was no longer conditioned for it.

Only five more points. Five more points and she'd be on a championship team, headed to states. Sage wasn't sure if her head suddenly felt stuffy or if it was the high of the realization—a long-held dream finally coming to fruition. She sucked in a breath. Maybe she did feel a little wobbly. And what if the sick feeling was caused by her heart condition? She could pull back, just a little.

That's when things began to crumble.

Mountain lost an easy point when he touched the net, and then Ketia was called for back-to-back questionable lifts. Flick almost lost her mind over the calls and was lucky to get off with a warning, but the energy had shifted. The Pumpkins were back in it, 9–10.

Flick clapped her hands, like she could wake her team up with sound. "Let's *go*," she ordered. "Let's do this." She pointed at Sage, who realized Flick had seen something that let her know Sage was the server's target. Sage sank low, ready. The ball went up and over right toward Sage, then suddenly veered to the left.

It was one of the craziest floaters Sage had ever seen, and she realized three things in the same nanosecond:

She could maybe reach the ball if she sprawled.

She still might not reach it.

She really, truly didn't feel well.

"Short!" Flick screamed, and for the first time since junior high, Sage was caught motionless, her instincts dulled by indecision.

The ball hit the floor in front of her.

The Pumpkin bench whooped as the scoreboard ticked 10–10. "Time out!" Flick thundered. She whirled on Sage before they'd even made it off the court. "What was that?"

Sage blinked. "I'm sorry."

"Her floaters always go left! I just told you that in the huddle!"

Sage stared at her. Had she really said that? Why couldn't Sage remember?

Ketia put a calming hand on Flick's shoulder. "This isn't helping," she said. "What's our play?"

Flick drew a few scribbles on her whiteboard. "I want a short set just left of middle, here. If that's not available, run Cardinal, got it? When we get the ball back, thirty-two can't handle a jump serve—" She met Sage's eyes. "You're up next. Your jump serves can put this thing away, understand?"

Sage nodded, her arms already aching for the ball and the chance to redeem herself. The whistle sounded the end of the time out.

"Let's finish this," Flick said, "on our terms."

"You got this, Tiny," Mountain told Sage. "Don't take Flick personally."

"It's fine," she said. "My coach is the same way."

Mountain frowned. "What coach?"

But then the ball was served, and there was no time to argue. The Pumpkins eked out another point before Mountain's spike almost took the face off the guy in the back row, giving the serve to Sage.

Flick handed her the ball. "Show 'em what you're made of, Tiny. And bring us home." She held out her fist to Sage, who bumped it. "Remember," Flick whispered. "Jumper to thirty-two. Position five."

Sage never looked at position five—she'd practiced this serve so many times she didn't need to. When the ref signaled, she let her body take over, sending the ball directly to thirty-two, who shanked it into the wall.

Sage's teammates whooped.

This time Sage stared down her target before the serve, just for fun. Again, he shanked. The scoreboard flipped to 13–12.

Ketia ran back to high-five her. "That's the way, Tiny," she said. "One at a time."

Sage's heartbeat crawled to her temples.

The ball rolled past her, and Sage bought a few seconds as she slowly walked to retrieve it. When had it gotten so hot in here? Had the heat kicked on? She wondered if maybe she should do a regular overhand serve to save some energy, but when she stepped close to the serving line, Flick shook her head. She signaled another jump serve.

For the first time, Sage thought maybe she should tell her team about her heart. Maybe she was tempting fate too strongly. Sweat dripped down her hairline, pooling at the dip in her throat. She was so close, though. Two points to advance to states. Two points to prove beyond all doubt that she didn't just belong on this team; it *needed* her.

The whistle sounded before Sage was ready, so her toss went high. She compensated, straining to make solid contact, but at least she got the ball over. The Pumpkins set up an attack, but Mountain and Derek's block was so perfect that even Flick roared in triumph as the ball dropped back on the Pumpkins' side. Her teammates' cheers made Sage's thoughts flicker, thin and flimsy.

"One more," Flick told her, walking the ball to her. "And we're going to states."

Sage pinched the bridge of her nose. "Why aren't they calling time out?"

"They don't have any left. And we've only got one." Flick's eyes narrowed. "Are you okay? Sage?"

"I'm fine."

Again, a small voice inside said maybe it was time to stop, but she closed her mind to it. She hadn't worked her whole life to be robbed of her only dream and two different championships to boot.

She swallowed the saliva gathering in her mouth, pretending it was water. The whistle sounded, and she tossed the ball into the air.

"Nooo!"

For a nanosecond Sage thought her mind had revolted, her fear somehow voicing itself aloud. It confused her just enough that she hesitated and gave in to her impulse not to jump. The ball dropped to the floor.

It's fine, she told herself. She still had her one re-serve. But as she stepped forward to retrieve the ball, someone cried, *"Stop!"* at the same time another voice said her name. Sage faltered, because it wasn't possible. Len and Kayla ran toward the court, waving frantically.

"Step back." The referee waved them off.

"Do you know them?" Flick asked, incredulous. Sage glared at her so-called friends, trying to steal this last triumph from her. How were they even here, *together*?

"One more point," she told them, frantic.

"Don't do this," Len said from the sidelines.

"Please!" added Kayla. "It's not worth it!"

"What are they talking about?" Ketia asked.

"Sage?" Flick stood next to the referee. "Do we need a timeout?"

"No!" If she stopped now, it was over.

"I'll tell them!" said Kayla.

In a breath Sage was at the sidelines, her face inches from Kayla's and Len's. "This is *my* choice," she said. Then, because she couldn't let them ruin her final chance, she changed tactics. "*Please*, don't take this away from me."

The referee's whistle sounded. "Delay warning," she called. "Continue play or service and point is forfeited."

"Sage!" Flick was near hysterics.

"But your life—" Len started.

"This *is* my life," Sage said. The ref whistled again, beginning the eight-second countdown she had to serve.

"Tiny!" Mountain roared, and Sage scrambled into position, visualizing her jump, the ball soaring over the net. The small voice crept in again: *Stop.*

Her hands slapped the ball. Only one more jump.

That's the other thing about Russian roulette, the voice said. *All it ever takes is one.*

"Five seconds," Flick croaked. Sage lifted the ball.

"I'll get help!" Len cried. "If you stop, right now, I'll get help."

Sage wanted to scream. Len *needed* help. But it wasn't fair to ask her like this, to make it conditional. And now she'd waited too long to jump serve.

"Serve the ball!" Ketia commanded.

She could still serve overhand. It only took a second.

She needs help. Len needs serious help.

Her vision went blurry. Her heartbeat raged against every vein in her body.

I need help, too.

Sage lowered the ball. "Time-out," she told Flick, who immediately signaled the referee. Sage sagged to the ground, relief bursting through her vision in tiny dark spots. Footsteps padded around her. Then she was standing, supported by Mountain and Ketia, who were saying things she couldn't understand.

She found her balance, walked herself off the court, and vomited.

"Oh, my God!" Ketia said. Someone called for a janitor.

"What is happening?" Flick demanded. Sage collapsed onto one of the metal folding chairs. Jon passed her his water bottle, but it was several moments before she could collect herself enough to speak. She thought Len and Kayla would be there, explaining everything, but she didn't see them anywhere.

That was odd, but for the better. She needed to do this alone.

"I have a heart condition," Sage said. "That's what's keeping me from my school team, not grades."

Several teammates—maybe all of them—swore.

"You don't mean . . ." Ketia's voice trailed off.

"Yeah," Sage said. "My heart could stop at any second."

"Jesus Christ," said Mountain. He looked toward the ref. "Call an ambulance!"

"No!" said Sage.

"Keep drinking," Jon told her.

Sage's eyes went wide. "Are you still on the roster?" she asked Jon. She turned to Flick. "Can you sub him in?"

Ketia threw up her hands. "She's still worried about the game!"

"Just one serve," Sage told Jon. "You can do that, right?"

Jon looked at Flick, who for once didn't seem to know what to say.

"You have to win," Sage told her.

"I'll be useless in the backcourt," said Jon. "But I can get the ball over."

Flick, rubbing her head, walked over to the ref's platform.

"What can we do?" Ketia asked Sage.

"Nothing." She took another drink and elevated her feet onto the chair beside her.

"Okay," Flick said, returning. "An ambulance is on its way."

"*What?*" cried Sage.

Flick glared at her. "You almost killed yourself, and you think we wouldn't call a medic?" She was clearly pissed. "I didn't need to anyway. Your friends already had. At least they have some sense." She jutted her chin at Jon. "Substitution is made." She stomped back to the court, where the ref was talking to the Pumpkins' captain.

Sage couldn't blame Flick for being angry. For the first time she imagined how Flick—or any of them—would feel if something had happened to her. She took another long pull from the water bottle.

"You better not die on us," Mountain told Sage as the ref signaled both teams back to the floor. "'Cause when I get back here, I'm gonna kill you."

Sage gave him a weak smile.

It was over quickly, and after everything, decidedly anticlimactic. Jon served underhanded, the Pumpkins returned, but Mountain made a successful block, ending the match.

Ketia and Mountain high-fived, but Flick didn't even clap. Guilt knotted inside Sage. Flick had wanted this win so badly, and now she couldn't even celebrate it.

After the teams shook hands, Flick marched up to Sage. "You know you're not playing states, right?"

Sage blanched. "Um, yeah."

The doors burst open, and two paramedics rushed inside, pulling a stretcher. Len and Kayla joined them. Sage covered her face.

"Hey." Flick knelt beside her. "We wouldn't be going if you hadn't helped. Understand?"

Sage nodded.

"*If* your parents contact me with permission, you can join us. As inactive, of course." She gave Sage a quick, tight hug.

"Here she is," Kayla said frantically, leading the medics to where Sage sat.

The EMT approached Sage. "Miss, just relax. How are you feeling?"

Sage frowned. "I've been better."

"Scale of one to ten?"

"I don't know," Sage said. "I'm feeling a little better now. Five?"

The other medic, a woman with tight dark curls, took Sage's pulse and blood pressure. "She's stable," she told her partner. To Sage she said, "We're going to lift you now."

"You mean—?" Sage gaped at the stretcher.

"We're coming with you." Kayla grabbed her hand. "They told us we could."

The woman said, "I'm going to lift under your knees, okay? He'll lift under your arms."

Soon Sage was on the stretcher with Len and Kayla hurrying alongside her, her teammates' voices trailing behind them. Only Ketia's came through clear: "We love you, Tiny! I'll call!"

Outside, the medics opened the door of the ambulance. "You ladies can sit on that bench there," said the man. "I need the one on the left." Sage heard thuds and clunks as her friends scrambled inside. Then she was airborne, sliding into the van. The woman climbed into the driver's seat.

"This is mortifying," Sage said as the man hooked her up to a heart monitor.

"Sage!" Kayla said. "You almost died. *Again!* Please, get over yourself."

Sage might have been irritated, but Kayla's comment had made Len smile. For the first time, Sage got a good look at her, at her clothes and face covered with grime. "Len!" She couldn't believe what she was seeing. "You're *filthy*."

"Yeah." Silent tears mixed with the grime, and Sage wondered how she could stand it, being that dirty. She must be in torture. *For you, idiot*, Sage realized. *She's doing it for you.*

Sage felt her own tears welling up, and this time she didn't stop them. "You're really brave," she told Len. "Hella brave. I'm gonna help you, okay?"

"What's she talking about?" Kayla turned to Len. "Why do *you* need help?"

Sage started to answer for her, but, shockingly, Len beat her to it. "Something's wrong with my brain," Len said, and the words weren't even a whisper. "It makes me . . . not myself."

Kayla glanced at Sage, who nodded. She turned back to Len. "You mean, like, what? You're sick or something?"

Len nodded. "Something like that."

Kayla kept silent, no doubt realizing what that meant; she'd been mocking a sick person. Her mouth twisted guiltily. She could be an asshole, like anyone could, but she wasn't a bad human. Not at her core.

"I'm sorry," Kayla told Len. "I just—I'm sorry."

Len nodded, the barest trace of a smile in her eyes.

"Wait," Sage said, so suddenly her heart rate ticked up on the monitor. "Wasn't the Penn scout coming today?"

"Kayla left," Len said. "As soon as I told her you needed help."

"It doesn't matter," Kayla said. "Scouts can come back. But you . . ." Her voice hitched. "You're more important anyway."

The medic interrupted them to reposition a wire, which was good because Sage couldn't speak. When he sat back, Sage held out her hand. Kayla took it.

"Thank you," Sage whispered, "both of you. I'm sorry. I said terrible things to you—"

"It's okay," Len said.

Kayla nodded. "We all messed up." She pulled her hand away and held it up, making a fist. Sage smiled and bumped it, pinky side. She extended her fist to Len.

"Um," Len said.

"Come on," Sage said. "You have your gloves on." Len looked a little pained, but she bumped back. She even held her first out to Kayla, who barely hesitated before returning the gesture. Sage beamed at both of them.

"We're almost there," said the medic. "Your parents will be able to see you once you're admitted."

Sage's heart rate increased again. "My parents? Do you have to—?"

"We already called them," Len said as the medic nodded.

Sage's eyes widened in horror. "They're gonna put me in therapy for sure."

"You *need* therapy," said Len.

Sage closed her eyes.

"You said you'd help me," Len went on. "And I need it. But so do you."

Sage looked up at her, because she was right. Each of them knew it.

"We'll get help," Len said. "Both of us."

Sage swallowed. "Both of us," she echoed. "Together."

CHAPTER FORTY-ONE

LEN

LEN STARED UP AT THE MODEST TOWNHOUSE TUCKED slightly back from the narrow Atlanta side street. It was tall— three stories—but thin, like it was continuously holding its breath.

Sage cut the engine, and Len pulled on her gloves. As payment for Sage driving her, she'd agreed not to wear the gloves in the car. If Sage got her way, Len would be starting something called cognitive behavioral therapy in the next couple weeks, and Sage thought it would help if Len started prepping. There were still some hoops to get through, but when Sage learned Len had almost died at the tree bridge, she'd been in full fixer mode for the past forty-eight hours.

Sage had called Dr. Surrage at home yesterday, and over speakerphone she and Len told her about Len's symptoms, how they were getting increasingly severe, but that Len had no way to pay for therapy. Dr. Surrage said there were some options available through a local children's nonprofit to get Len evaluated and into some sort of pay-as-you're-able therapy. There were only a few spots, but with Dr. Surrage as a reference, they were hopeful Len could get in.

"Len?" Sage prompted, bringing her mind back to the townhouse in front of her. "You ready?"

Len unbuckled her seatbelt. "I don't think I'll ever be ready," she said. "But I'm going in."

Sage nodded. "You know that's the definition of courage, right?"

Len fought not to roll her eyes and climbed out, grabbing her camera bag. She took the five steps to the front stoop quickly, Sage at her heels, and—forcing herself not to run away like she wanted to—pushed the doorbell instead.

A dog barked, and footsteps padded inside the house. Then the door opened and Fauna was there, smiling and near tears at the same time. "You're here!" she said. "You actually made it." She went to hug Len, then stopped as Len pulled back. "Right. No hugging. You told me yesterday. Sorry. Come in, come in!" She held out a hand to Sage. "I'm Fauna."

Len slipped past her sister as Sage introduced herself, making up for Len's social ineptitude. Diane stood a few feet away at the edge of the sofa, cradling their terrier mutt. She gave Len a small wave. "Thank you for coming," she mouthed to Len.

"This is my wife, Diane," Fauna told Sage, leading her into the living room. "And our dog, Fezzywig."

"We call him Fezzy," said Diane.

Sage ruffled Fezzy's ears. "He's the cutest."

"Want something to drink?" asked Fauna. "We have tea or soda. And coffee. Water, too, of course."

"I'm good, thanks," said Sage.

"You sure?" Diane pushed back the black twists of hair that draped across her eyes. "Fauna got me an espresso maker for my birthday, and I make a mean cinnamon latte. Or, if you're adventurous, I can whip up my special ginger-and-secret-spice cortado."

Sage peered into the kitchen, a warm space full of green plants and sunflower yellow walls. "I don't know what that is, but I'm always adventurous." Diane laughed and led her away, chatting like they were already friends. It amazed Len how easily social banter came for Sage, even with people she'd just met. She longed for it, the carelessness of not constantly examining her surroundings and not flinching when someone took her arm. Len took a slow breath. Maybe someday it would be easy for her, too.

"So," Fauna said, her voice high and nervous, "you wanted to talk. I'm so glad." Her eyes welled, but she blinked hard, clearing them. "You wanna sit down?"

Len looked to the steps. "Would it be okay if we went upstairs? It's just . . . I want to make sure we're alone."

"Oh." Fauna clasped her necklace, Nadia's birthstone. "Okay. Our bedroom is kind of a mess, but we can go to the rec room, if that's okay?"

Len followed her upstairs, past the closed door of the guest room—what used to be the nursery—and into the small bonus space that housed a spare sofa, desk, and elliptical. She perched on the edge of the sofa, and Fauna took the cushion beside her, a tight, unsure smile on her face.

It was strange and a little sad, her sister clearly not knowing how to act around her anymore. But Len had brought it upon herself.

"What is it?" Fauna asked, because she'd never been able to sit long in silence. She was like Sage that way, Len realized.

Len's throat went dry as dirt. She couldn't do this. She couldn't. Then Sage's laugh floated up through the floorboards, a reminder of the promise they'd made each other. Sage was here, wasn't she? She had her back.

"I . . ." The word croaked out of her. Fauna rubbed her necklace.

Len gathered the strength inside her. It was time. "The night Nadia died," she said, "right before it happened—"

Tears burst over Fauna's cheeks, like Len knew they would. She felt her own prick behind her eyes, but forced herself to keep going.

"I had this thought," Len said, "this really powerful thought. I didn't mean to, but you and Diane were so stressed and tired, and everything seemed like it was going wrong, and I—" Her voice cracked. "I thought maybe Nadia shouldn't have been born, that maybe things would have been better—" Tears caught in the corners of her mouth. "I didn't *mean* to, because what kind of person thinks that?" She pushed her fingers into her temples. "But I *did*. And Nadia was in *my* room, and it must have been all the negative energy in there—" Her voice went unnaturally high. "I think Nadia died because of me." She was sobbing now, ugly sobbing, and she slowed because she had to remain intelligible. "I'm sorry, Fauna. I'm so, so sorry."

Fauna had slumped inward, her arms wrapped tightly around herself, and she rocked gently, eyes closed.

It was happening—the thing Len had tried desperately to avoid, the reason she had slowly stopped taking Fauna's calls. Fauna was reliving that night—all the agony of it. Because of Len.

Her sister whimpered, and no one could ever hate Len more than she despised herself at that moment. Then Fauna opened her eyes—red and hard and fierce—and grabbed Len's shoulders. "You listen to me," she said. "You had nothing to do with Nadia's death. Understand?"

Len couldn't have heard right. "But—"

"*Listen!*" Fauna commanded, and she actually shook Len, her hands gripping so tightly they hurt. Then Fauna pulled Len against her, rocking Len as she'd rocked herself, her tears dampening Len's hair and face.

"I'm sorry," Len said, over and over, as Fauna hugged her and Len hugged her back, and for some reason it was okay, the hugging, like Fauna was an extension of herself. But Fauna wasn't understanding. She needed to understand.

"Dad told me about this guy," she said into Fauna's shoulder, and repeated the story. "Why wouldn't negative thoughts have as much power?"

Fauna leaned back, her face swollen and sad. "Some of our parents' ideas," she said, "especially Dad's"—her face scrunched—"well, I think there's real value in some of them—meditation and visualizations. Positivity mantras. Those things can be important to people, and helpful, to a point." She took Len's gloved hands in hers. "But they're like anything else, you know? Too much reliance on them . . . it throws you out of balance."

"It was my fault, though," Len said. "I can *feel* it." She pressed a hand into her chest. "In my soul."

Fauna's eyes glossed again. "Do you think I didn't think the same thing, Lennie? That I still don't? That if Diane and I hadn't gone out that night, if one little thing had changed and kept us from leaving, then our baby would still be alive?"

Len's mouth opened, then closed, shame sucking the air from her lungs. She *hadn't* thought about that, not at all. She shook her head violently. "It wasn't your fault."

Fauna's eyes shifted beyond Len, and Len turned to see where they landed: a photo she hadn't noticed on the desk—a close-up of Nadia sporting a white onesie that read *One month*. It would have been taken just a couple weeks before she died. The thought of her, of what could have been, made Len's lungs feel close to collapsing.

"Terrible things happen sometimes," Fauna whispered. "Terrible, terrible things." Len took her sister's hand, which had gone slack and lifeless. The pressure seemed to revive her. "I'm learning," Fauna said, "that you have to face them, though. You have to go through all the darkness." Her eyes stayed glued to Nadia's picture. "If you don't, it will devour you."

They stared at the photo, together, for a long time. Then Len said, like a secret, "Sage thinks I have this disorder. OCD."

Fauna's eyes slid back to her, their unasked question toppling the wall Len had worked so hard to build around her secrets, and everything spilled out. How Len thought she had childhood dementia. How she didn't want to worry Mom, who was breaking apart. How the blue jay had come and led her to Nonni, to the idea of dementia in the first place. How she'd met Sage, whose dreams had been stolen, and they'd somehow become friends. How Len agreed to get help if Sage did, and how their pledge had been what finally got Len here.

"There's this doctor," Len said, her eyes drifting back to Nadia. "Sage knows her, and I guess she knows people in the hospital. They can get me a low-cost evaluation. I didn't even know that was possible."

Fauna squeezed her hand, nodding. "I've started grief therapy," she said. "It's . . . hard. Maybe the hardest thing I've ever done, besides losing Nadia." She stood up and walked to the desk. "Every day my arms feel empty. I don't think that will ever go away." Her fingers grazed the lines of Nadia's face. "But the therapy helps. And meeting other moms who've . . ." Her words choked off. "Anyway, somehow, talking helps."

Len pushed herself up. "I've been a terrible sister," she said. "I'm sorry."

Fauna tucked her lips together, but they twisted anyway, and she slumped to the floor, the photo clutched against her heart. Len knelt beside her, holding her as tightly as she sometimes had to hold herself.

"Don't stop talking to me again, okay?" said Fauna. "Please. And don't stop talking about her." She squeezed the picture frame. "Everyone tries to distract me. Mom wants to talk about anything else, but I *need* to talk about her. I need people to remember. The therapy has helped me see: that's the only thing that helps."

Len hugged her tighter. It seemed counterintuitive because she'd always heard you weren't supposed to dwell on sadness. But Fauna's words resonated, too. She *had* felt better when she'd talked to Sage. Like, by saying the words out loud, she'd let something go. Not the sadness, of course. That would be there forever. But maybe, just maybe, she'd released a tiny bit of its power over her.

"I'm sorry I'm not there," Fauna said, "to help with Nonni." She wiped her face. "I don't think Mom or Dad, or any of us, really, were ever taught how to grieve."

It was an odd concept, being taught to grieve. But Len supposed Fauna was right. Before Nadia, she'd been to exactly one funeral, and that was for Dad's hermit uncle, whom they barely knew.

"Maybe," Fauna said. "Would you like me to come visit? We could see Nonni together. I'd have to stay in a hotel, though, because, well—" Her body trembled.

Len leaned her head on Fauna's shoulder, because the fact that she'd even offer, that she'd spend money she didn't have to help the rest of them deal with pain when she had so much of her own, it was almost too much for her. "Only when you're ready," she whispered. Fauna stroked her cheek, like Mom would.

"Do you believe in a Life Force?" Len asked.

Fauna sucked in a deep breath. "I believe Nadia's soul is part of something larger now, something that connects all of us." She rubbed her necklace again. "Something we can all feel and tap into. I don't know exactly how to conceptualize it." She met Len's eyes. "It's okay if you don't understand things the same as Mom and Dad. You'll find your own path."

Len's vision was blurry, her nose stinging. "What about signs?"

Fauna smiled wearily. "Your blue jay?"

Len nodded.

"I think things like that can be helpful to a point, if they help you process. But if they control you, that's something else, you know?"

Yes, Len realized, she really did. "Tell me something about Nadia," Len said. "Something you really loved, that not many people know."

Fauna cried, and then laugh-cried. And then she began to speak.

CHAPTER FORTY-TWO

SAGE

FAUNA AND DIANE TRIED TO PERSUADE THEM TO STAY THE
night, but Sage's mom had only let her take the car on the condition that she was back for school on Monday. That, and the promise that she'd start therapy at the first available session with the counselor they'd selected together. So after a delicious lunch of fried green tomato orzo salad and lavender crème brulee, Sage and Len found themselves back in the Subaru.

"They seem pretty awesome," Sage said, waving at Fauna and Diane as she reversed out of the parking space. A small smile crinkled Len's face. She hadn't said much during lunch, but Sage could tell something good had passed between her and Fauna while they'd been upstairs. Or maybe good wasn't the correct word. Something *needed*.

"You glad you came?" Sage prompted.

"I am." Instead of elaborating, Len turned on her camera, presumably reviewing the lunch photos she'd taken. Even Sage had noticed the artistic display of their food, and Len had pulled out her camera, arranging and rearranging their plates with the fresh cut sunflowers on the table, before she let anyone disturb a morsel.

Sage's phone map started spouting directions different from what Diane had told them. She flicked her eyes between the map and the road, trying to determine which lane she needed for the upcoming turn.

"The middle one," Len said, pointing. "But you won't turn till up there. It's weird. And a long light." Her gloved thumb tapped absently against one of the camera's dials. Sage had decided not to ask her to remove her gloves on the way home.

"Thank you," Len murmured.

Sage merged behind a spotless white pickup. "For what?"

"For making me come here and talk to Fauna." The cords of Len's neck went tight as she swallowed, clearly embarrassed. "Things had gotten bad with me. Really, really bad." She frowned. "And they still are, I know that. But it feels like maybe the bad isn't quite the same anymore? Like, everything that's happened, it can't be fixed, you know? But maybe, there might be a way through." She played with the camera's dials. "I'm not sure I'm making sense—"

Something shifted inside Sage, gears finally locking into place. "You are," she said. It was the same feeling, Sage realized, that had swept over her, unconscious until this exact moment when Len's words tipped it into the light.

Len must have noticed something, because her brow furrowed. "What is it?"

"I'm not gonna do physical therapy in college," Sage said. "I'm going to major in psychology." She swallowed. "I think . . . I think I might wanna be a therapist. Or maybe a researcher. Or both, I don't know." Speaking the possibilities thrilled her, ignited every cell in her body, something that hadn't happened with anything outside of volleyball.

Volleyball.

She'd kept herself so busy the last forty-eight hours that she hadn't let herself think too much about the truth: she really would never play volleyball again. Not competitively. She would never win a state title—not even in a rec league.

It was not okay.

It would never be okay or fair or anything short of a tragic ending to the path she'd busted her ass building her whole life. Volleyball had always been her lifeline. Her passion. Her way of making order and sense of the crazy, seriously messed up world. A way of mattering. And she would miss it forever. But maybe . . . Maybe people got more than one lifeline. Maybe she thought she only had one because she simply hadn't found another.

The psychology thrill wasn't as strong as her volleyball one, not yet. But it was made of the same stuff, the same embers, she could feel it. The thought of helping people like Len allevi-ate their suffering—that was a life worth living. It made those embers glow hot and bright.

Something touched her arm, and Sage looked over—shocked—to see Len's hand on her sleeve. It was gloved, of course, but still. The gesture from Len was like a bear hug from anyone else. Her eyes pricked, and Sage blinked, surprised to find herself crying.

No, she realized. More than crying. Letting go.

Len's hand gave her a small squeeze.

"It's strange," Sage said as she braked at a yellow light, "I'd never have realized how interested I am in this stuff—how much I care about it—without you."

Len's smile looked almost teasing. "So what you're saying is, me being crazy kind of saved your life?"

"You're *not crazy!*" Sage said. Her eyes slid to meet Len's. "But also . . . yes."

Len's laugh sparked out of her like tiny fireworks. And maybe it was that broken-free sound, or how the music of it made Sage notice the beat-heavy song on the radio, one of her favorites. Maybe it was all of those way-too-good espresso drinks. Or per-haps it was something else entirely that made Sage throw back her head, her lips pursed in what Kayla teased as her "dance face." The moon roof was open and there were cars in the lanes on either side of hers. Pedestrians packed the crosswalk.

It didn't matter. The song lyrics burst from her mouth, definitely off key, definitely *so bad*, but whatever. She didn't even know all the words, but that didn't matter, either. She made them up, added a few "la da das" in the places she couldn't remember. Her hands twisted up and out and she let her body move, snaking to the beat.

The car beside her honked. She must look—and sound—ridiculous. She laughed, messing up more lyrics, and sang louder.

Chut. Chut. Chut-chut-chut.

It took Sage a moment to process the sound. She turned. Len held her camera pointed at Sage.

Chut-chut-chut.

"What are you doing?"

Len's grin widened beneath the lens. "I have it," she said. *Chut. Chut.* "Finally." *Chut.* "The theme for my series, for the Melford Scholarship." *Chut-chut-chut.* "The thing that ties it all together."

Sage's favorite line of the song burst from the speakers, and her body twisted to it without thinking, free and flowing. "What?" Her shoulders shrugged so exaggeratedly they set off Len's fireworks laugh again. "Bad car dancing?"

"No. Definitely no."

The light above them turned green. Sage reclaimed the wheel, her foot lifting off the brake.

Len lowered her camera. "Hope."

The End

AUTHOR'S NOTE

Years ago, I suffered a trauma that, unbeknownst to me, unlocked a severe form of OCD to which I was genetically predisposed. I thought I was losing touch with reality and, confused and mortified, tried to hide my symptoms and convince myself things were okay. I entered a darkness I hadn't known possible and could not have found my way through it without the love and support of incredible friends and family members.

Once I found my way through the hell of undiagnosed OCD, I discovered how many people around me also suffered from a form of the disease, or loved someone who did. I also realized, unfortunately, how many people still don't understand (or refuse to believe) that mental health conditions are as real as physical illnesses. I determined that one day, when enough time had passed for me to process and separate myself from the visceral pain of my experience, I wanted to write the book I wish I'd had during that dark time. Meanwhile, Sage's story was already percolating in my head. When I realized she and Len inhabited the same world, that they actually knew each other, *The Edge of Anything* started to materialize.

Symptoms of obsessive compulsive disorder, like those of many other mental health conditions, can vary greatly by individual. If you suspect that you or someone you love has OCD and/or depression, it is crucial to talk about it, tell your doctor, and seek help. You are not alone, and life *can* get brighter.

The following organizations and websites have fantastic information and treatment locating services:

International OCD Foundation. https://iocdf.org/ and https://kids.iocdf.org/for-kids/how-do-i-get-help/

The Behavioral Health Treatment Services Locator. https://findtreatment.samhsa.gov/ or call the Treatment Referral Helpline of the Substance Abuse and Mental Health Services Administration (SAMHSA) at 1-800-662-HELP (4357)

The National Alliance on Mental Illness. https://www.nami.org/

Anxiety and Depression Association of America. https://adaa.org/

Beyond OCD. http://beyondocd.org/

I also have these resources located on my website, noracarpenterwrites.com.

ACKNOWLEDGMENTS

I am indebted to so many wonderful people. To my incredible agent, Victoria Wells Arms: thank you for loving my words and championing me in every way. You always have wonderful suggestions for making my stories stronger, and I'm so grateful. Also, the pep talks. ☺ I am so glad the universe (and Sandra Nickel! You're the best, Sandra!) brought us together.

To the entire Running Press team, especially my wonderful editor, Julie Matysik: thank you for falling in love with Sage and Len, and for believing in me. Your insights helped me shape this book into exactly what I wanted it to be. Huge shout out to Val Howlett, too, for introducing me to Running Press and working so hard to get my books in front of readers. Thanks also to Fabio Consoli for your brilliant cover art, to Frances J. Soo Ping Chow for the design that ties everything together, and to Jennifer Hartmann for tidying up all my small changes.

To my VCFA family—from advisors and workshop leaders to students and fellow alumnx (shout out to my Secret Gardener classmates!): thank you for the innumerable ways you have supported me since I first stepped onto that magical campus. It blows my mind how many selfless, caring, and absurdly talented people make up the MFA WCYA program. A special thank-you to my semester advisors: Coe Booth, Tim Wynn-Jones, Shelley Tanaka, and Uma Krishnaswami. Thanks also to Amanda Jenkins for that take-out cafeteria dinner during which you asked the questions that led me to the heart of this story, let me cry about how painful it was to write, and then assured me it was important.

Thanks a ton to the brilliant Anna Drury Secino and Tirzah Price for being this book's first readers and offering insight, support, and laughter at every step. Our text chains keep me sane throughout the writing process, and I am eternally grateful. Thanks also to writing partners (current and those who've moved away) Miriam McNamara, Rachel Hylton, Meg Cook, and Kelly Anne Blount.

I could not have written this book if I didn't have amazing help with my littles. Huge thanks to our beloved friends Anna White, Katie Flow, Annie Bullock, Charlotte Bailes Garcia, and my momma for keeping my babies safe and loved while I teased out Sage and Len's story. To my children, thank you for the unabashed joy you have at even the tiniest bit of good writing-related news. ("Mom, you got a free parking spot at your conference? That is INCREDIBLE!") You make every part of my life incredible, and I'm so proud of each of you. I'm sorry I screamed when I learned about my book deal and accidentally made all of you cry.

To Dr. Brad Friedman, you are welcome for making your dreams of being in a book come true. I expect this novel to have a permanent display in your office. ☺ Seriously, though, huge thanks to you and your wonderful staff for allowing me to badger you with questions about hypertrophic cardiomyopathy, for putting me through Sage's tests, and for all the incredible work you do for your patients every day.

Thanks to my filmmaker and photographer sister, Emma Shalaway, for encouraging me throughout this journey and making sure I didn't botch my photography terminology. To Chip Bryan, thank you so much for my author photos. Thanks also to Jason Watkins for answering all my EMT-related questions and to Chad Pauley for schooling me on North Carolina high school counselor guidelines. Any errors are mine alone.

To my parents, Linda and Scott Shalaway, thank you for surrounding me with books, encouraging my writing from the very beginning, and giving me the tenacity and stubbornness without which I don't think many writers can survive. To all of you aspiring authors out there, keep telling your stories. Keep reading. And keep persisting. The world needs your voices.

As this book is about deep, life-changing friendship, I would be remiss not to thank the three women whose friendships first taught me that kind of bond existed. To Joanna Mulligan, Monique Buckley, and Sarah Dean, thank you for being the best kind of people and the best kind of friends.

Finally, to my very best friend and soul partner in everything, Josh Carpenter: thank you for being my biggest champion, for never doubting even when I doubted myself, and for the incredible love and example you provide our children every day.